JESSIE HARRELL

DESTINED

MAE DAY PUBLISHING

MAE DAY PUBLISHING
Jacksonville, FL

Cover designed by Joshua Longiaru
Cover photography (c) Perri Eriksen

Printed in the USA   Second Edition
10 9 8 7 6 5 4 3 2   ISBN 978-0-615-50095-9

DEDICATION

To Holt, my own personal Eros.

CHAPTER 1 — PSYCHE

My stomach churned as the smell of ground charcoal and nearly-rancid oil smeared across my eyelids. Whoever decided that greasy anything should be part of a daily beauty routine deserved permanent exile.

The stink never seemed to bother Maia though. She hummed quietly while layering on the goop -- and it was driving me nuts. My teeth ground into my cheek until I managed to shred another piece of skin.

"Will you stop fidgeting? I'm going to have eye paste all over your face if you don't hold still."

Servant or no, Maia was good at keeping me in my place. "Sorry." I stopped chomping my cheek in favor of twitching my foot.

Maia placed her weathered hand against my forehead; her eyes wrinkled around the edges with concern. "You don't seem yourself today. Are you sure you're well?"

My eyes darted to the bird sitting on my shelf. Maia followed my gaze and gasped.

"Good heavens, Psyche. How'd a pigeon get in here?"

She dropped the makeup onto my vanity and made as if to shoo the bird away. Instinctively, I snatched her wrist.

"No, don't. I let her in." I paused, debating whether it was worth correcting her that the bird was actually a dove, and not a pigeon. Or noting that the dove would turn into Aphrodite as soon as Maia left.

Better just to let it go.

"I like having her here. I'm just worried Father will make me get rid of her." I met Maia's eyes and plastered on my best smile -- the one Aphrodite helped me master when she wasn't a bird.

Maia's shoulders relaxed and she started in on phase II of my beautification regimen: crushed mulberry blush. But there was no relaxing for me.

Something was up. This was the fifth day in a row Aphrodite had come to visit. Sure, she'd shown up a couple of months ago, just after I started getting daily admirers at my window. She'd said she liked watching beauty get the attention it deserved. It was part of her domain, after all. And then she'd dropped in randomly after that, but not daily.

Even though I pretended like nothing was different, I knew she wanted something. Something *more*. Goddesses don't just hang out with mortals for the fun of it. But what?

Was she somehow soaking up the energy from the crowd outside? If so, would she want me to stand at this window every morning for the rest of my life? And then what would happen when I wasn't young enough, or pretty enough for her anymore?

I gulped when I was struck by an even worse thought: what if she was spying on me, watching how *I* reacted each morning. Would she call me out for Hubris after being the one who encouraged me to really pan to the crowd?

My chest constricted under the weight of my worry; my nerves felt frayed, like the end of rope that's been snapping in the Aegean breeze too long.

Maia has got to stop humming!

I started to turn my head so I could ask her to knock it off, but she just brushed at my tangle of curls harder when I moved. "Maia, please," I moaned, "can you quit with the humming right now?"

With Maia now silent, I was left with only the rhythmic brushing of my hair and the dove-made tapping. Her nails clicked against the wooden shelf where she paced. As honored as I was by her presence, I almost wished I could reverse the past few months. I wouldn't have sat for the portrait at the art academy. The artist wouldn't have gotten famous by drawing my face. My face wouldn't have ended up floating around Greece. And Greeks wouldn't have started showing up at my door to see if the real thing looked as good as the paintings.

Even the tokens of admiration they brought with them were inadequate to pay for all I'd lost. My parents' coffers were robust and juicy, but my life was sucked dry. I wanted shopping trips to the Agora with Mother, jaunts to the Baths with my sister, gallops through the fields on my horse -- all things I'd been denied in the name of safety.

As Maia finished looping my favorite silver headband into my hair, Aphrodite-the-bird fluttered down to the vanity for a closer inspection.

"Shoo." Maia flicked her hand at Aphrodite before I could stop her. "Get off, you dirty, old thing."

"Stop." Leaping to my feet, I scooped the bird goddess into my palms. The feathers around her neck stuck straight out and her head bobbed frantically as she gurgled up a strangled coo sound.

"There, there," I crooned as I stroked her with my fingertip. "Maia didn't mean that."

Maia huffed. "Don't know why I bother trying to help you sometimes."

"Maia," I said, dragging out her name and giving her my best pout. "You know I love you. Don't go away mad, okay?"

She sighed. "I know. Just go away." As she moved to the mahogany door, Maia gave a pointed look over her shoulder at my window. "Your admirers are waiting. Wouldn't want to disappoint *them*."

"What's that supposed to --" I started before the door clicked closed. "Mean?"

When I turned around, Aphrodite sat sprawled across my marble vanity, her legs crossed at the knee as she reclined.

"She," Aphrodite nodded her head at the door before flicking a golden tendril over her shoulder, "is no fun."

I eased down onto the stool beside her, glad to see she didn't look as angry as I'd feared. "Maia's not that bad. I just don't think she likes all the people hanging around outside. It's gotten a lot worse lately."

Aphrodite raised a narrow eyebrow. "Worse? You've got admirers flocking from every corner of Greece to lay gifts at your feet in exchange for one glimpse of your face. That's not a *bad* thing."

I nodded, but had no response. Goddesses might enjoy collecting tributes, but for me, it felt wrong.

Aphrodite plucked a bottle of lily-scented almond oil off my vanity and rubbed it into her arms. "You heard what she said, didn't you?" Aphrodite asked.

"About me disappointing the admirers?"

She shook her head. "Not that. She said I was *old*."

"Don't be... silly." I almost said 'ridiculous,' but then remembered who I was talking to. "You're the most beautiful goddess in Greece. And you're *not* old."

She set aside the oil and clasped my face in her palms. "No, she's right. I have a son your age. You're the new beauty in Greece, Psyche. It's you now."

Whoa. I was pretty sure accepting that compliment would earn me unending torture in Tartarus one day. While I was still stammering for something to say, Aphrodite nimbly hopped to her feet and circled the room. "I can feel it. Today's the day."

Her crystalline eyes were wide and wild and I didn't like the direction this conversation was headed.

With more drama than any actor, she flung her arms toward the wooden shutters still barring my window. "Go to your people. They're waiting."

"What?" It came out more a stammer than an actual question. They weren't *my* people. They were subjects of their own cities; devotees of the gods. But mine? Never.

When her eyes locked back on me, a radiant smile spread across her face. In a quick movement, she scooped up my hands. Her touch sank into me like a sun-warmed stone. "This is what I've been waiting for. This day. I learned from my mistakes with Helen. But you?" She shook her head and smiled. "Oh, Psyche, you're going to make me proud."

Maybe Maia'd been right and I was sick after all, because I was pretty sure I had a disease that made my tongue swell and my jaw lock closed. Was she really comparing me to Helen? The face that launched a thousand ships? The slut who started the Trojan war with her affair?

I couldn't compare to Helen. I didn't *want* to compare to Helen. That wasn't me.

Racking my brain, I tried to remember what role Aphrodite played in the war. What lessons she might have learned. But I drew a blank. My brain was a dog chasing its tail, never quite getting what it's after.

With a gentle turn, Aphrodite planted me in front of the window and then stood clear as she flung apart the shutters. Sunlight and deafening cheers drenched my room before the sky began to rain jewels. Pearls and gold, diamonds and coins. Anything to show the mob worshipped at the idol of beauty.

"Catch me," Aphrodite whispered before morphing back into her bird form. Her white feathers carried her in a wide arc outside my window and then back in again. Obediently, I held out my cupped hands for her to land.

If the mob was cheering before, now it was undergoing an eruption. I seemed to be the only one who didn't know what was going on. Sure, I knew doves were Aphrodite's sacred bird, but my dove had been coming and going for a solid week and this reaction was a first.

Maybe there was something special about them seeing us together?

Then one name cut through the voices, taking shape slowly, little by little, until all those below me were chanting the same thing: Aphrodite. I looked down at my feathered mentor and she winked back before fluttering away.

Too many thoughts raced through my brain for any one to become clear. *Do they think I'm her? Does she want them to think I'm her? Or do they know the dove is her? Oh gods, what does this mean?*

"Come back," I screamed, desperate for answers and figuring no one would hear me over the deafening crowd.

Frantically I scanned for any trace of the dove -- raking over faces, casting aside flesh in my search for feathers. But I halted when a pair of eyes from the back of the group caught mine. The woman made her way forward and the mob parted to let her pass, like she was a magnet pushing away an opposing force. Almost hypnotically, the chanting died down and attention focused on her.

As she stood directly under my window, a sharp breeze rustled her robes, carrying up the unmistakable fragrance of lily-scented almond oil. Her crystalline eyes met mine and I knew it was her.

Aphrodite.

She just stood there, letting the glamour of her mystic's disguise settle over the crowd. If I didn't know better, I'd have thought she was one of the fortune-telling gypsies myself.

"Finally, she makes her daughter known to us." Aphrodite reached up a now-wrinkled hand and pushed back the hood of her burgundy robe. Silver hair tumbled down her back in a thick braid. "Our attentions have not been in vain. Aphrodite has finally sent us a child to spread mortal beauty through the world!"

I'd never heard such roars in all my life. The crowd around her jumped and surged, yet she remained rooted in an island of calm. In the din, Aphrodite mouthed three words to me before vanishing unnoticed.

I'll explain later.

CHAPTER 2 — PSYCHE

Before I could fully process what was happening outside my window, my name erupted from down the hall like a Santorini volcano. "PsyCHE!" Father always emphasized the "K" part of my name when he was angry or excited, and I wasn't sure which way this was going.

After a quick goodbye wave to the crowd, I slammed my shutters closed and pressed my back against them. Sucking in a deep breath, I put on my best serious face and marched from my room and into the scroll-lined walls of the library. As always, my parents were there, waiting to count the treasures I received that morning. The cold sweat trickling down my spine evaporated when I saw their faces.

Ebullient.

Aphrodite'd taught me that word earlier this week. She thinks beauty is even more powerful when it's backed with knowledge. And she insisted that I "certainly ought to know a word that described a cheerful and energetic person like myself." Today, the word fit my parents' expressions. Their eyes shone like a thousand candles blazed inside their heads and their smiles threatened to permanently engrave laugh lines into their cheeks.

"Today. At the window..." Mother covered her mouth with her tiny hands.

JESSIE HARRELL

"Well, you know what this means?" Father cut in. "Aphrodite has spoken." He crushed me against his chest in a spine-crunching hug. He released me when my bones actually popped.

"Sorry, baby," he said. "It's just -- we've waited so long for this news. All the signs were there, the crowds, the tokens. Still, we were starting to think you weren't going to be chosen."

Mother reached out her hand. Taking it, I sunk down next to her on the couch. "Of course," she said, "we never doubted *you*. But it's only been two generations since Helen, so we thought perhaps she was still biding her time before picking another daughter."

"What do you mean -- daughter? I'm not her daughter," I stammered.

Tears leaked from the corner of Mother's eyes. She rubbed them away while trying to smile. "It's a figure of speech. More symbolic than anything. Aphrodite has a history of picking a mortal girl to serve as her daughter. Kind of like how Apollo has the Pythia in Delphi." Her gaze settled on my face as she studied my features, so like hers.

"I'm surprised she didn't explain this to you already." As her emerald eyes shifted to Father, she bit her lip. "Is it a bad sign that she didn't come to Psyche before the announcement?"

Here we go -- signs, omens, superstitions. Mother was about to get on an unstoppable tangent unless I stepped in.

Father stroked his beard. "I'm not sure I'd call it a --"

"It's *not* a sign," I interrupted. "She's visited me

before. She just made me promise not to tell anyone, and well..." I threw up my hands at their incredulous looks. "What'd you want me to do? She's a freaking goddess."

I'd read enough to know that crossing the gods was bad news. Do something they tell you not to? Game over. No way would I blab Aphrodite's secret, even if her visits were the coolest and most terrifying things I'd ever experienced.

Father smiled at Mom. "Well, I guess we didn't need to worry about the decision, now did we?"

Releasing my hands, Mother smoothed out the folds of her tunic before slowly rising and pacing over to the window. I thought she'd be relieved to hear there were no evil omens descending on our palace.

"Phoebe? Are you alright?" Father asked.

She sniffed as she waved him off. "I'm just...I'm worried. There'll be a lot expected of Psyche now. The mortal daughter of Aphrodite. It's a big responsibility."

Father gave her shoulder a gentle squeeze. "And the first pure mortal too." His gaze, so full of pride -- the same expression he wore whenever he returned from a successful duel or a neighboring king came to pay homage -- washed over his face. "Helen was so beautiful because she was half-immortal."

And I'm not.

I wondered if that made me more or less special.

"Wow." I tucked my legs in close to my chest and gave them a squeeze. "You guys should've told me. I had no idea. I don't even know what to say or do when she comes back." I looked up and met Mother's eyes. She was the one who always had answers for me. "Am I supposed to act like I'm part of the Olympian family now or something?"

Flinching, Mother spun into Father's arms and sobbed. Shudders wracked her tiny frame; all he could do was smooth her hair and whisper to her.

"What'd I say?"

Father looked over at me. "She's just upset because you'll be getting married so soon now. I'm sure she thought she had more time with you girls."

Wait. What? I'd just been adopted by a goddess today - wasn't that enough of a status change to last for awhile?

I rubbed at the bridge of my nose as the tinges of a headache started to bloom behind my forehead. "How does me being Aphrodite's adopted daughter require that I get a husband?"

"Honey, your Mother and I already talked about this. We decided that if Aphrodite did pick you, then both of you girls should be eligible for marriage immediately. She *is* the goddess of love, so naturally she'll want our family to represent that for her."

"So what? I have my whole life to do that. But I know Aphrodite didn't match Helen up with Paris of Troy until long after she'd already been married to Menelaus." And inadvertently starting the largest war in history. "So why do you guys think..."

Then something Aphrodite said that morning registered in the back of my mind. *I learned from my mistakes with Helen.* Maybe that meant she wasn't planning on waiting with me, letting me find my own course before she intervened. She was going to control it from the start, wasn't she?

Father was yammering on, probably answering

my question even, but I'd stopped listening. Chara was older than me, and she wasn't married yet -- didn't want to be. We loved living in Sikyon. We didn't want to leave behind the artists who painted portraits for an obol, or the tragic plays that flowed through our theaters with the changing seasons. This was my home, and though I always knew I'd someday have to leave, I wasn't ready to go yet.

"Psyche, are you listening to me?"

Father's voice shook me out of my trance. "I said, go tell Chara we'll start accepting suitors tomorrow."

If there'd been any color left in my face before, it had to be gone. *Tomorrow?* I blinked, forcing back the edge of panic I felt rising in the pit of my stomach. "We don't need to rush into this. I mean, Aphrodite hasn't even dropped by to see her 'daughter' since the big announcement."

Father leaned forward and whispered, "You're obviously pretty good at keeping secrets, so I'll trust you not to share this with your sister. But in addition to honoring Aphrodite in her union, Chara's bride price will be a lot higher right now because of your news."

I'd have been less surprised if the roof of our palace collapsed on my head. Mother and Father wanted to sell us off now because we were at the peak of our bride price? Seriously?

Thankfully, Maia found me before I could start shrieking at my parents or tearing out my hair like a raving lunatic. "Psyche, child, I need your help for a minute. While I was making up your bed, your *pet* returned." She lowered her voice so only I could hear. "And it's brought a friend."

The constriction in my chest lightened even as my heart skipped erratically. Maybe Aphrodite would have some better answers. Surely she'd say my parents were insane and forcing the princesses of Sykion into early marriages hadn't been part of her grand plan.

"A pet?" Father mused. "Psyche doesn't have a --"

Mother broke away from her sobs long enough to figure out what Maia really meant. "Aphrodite's back in her bird form, isn't she?"

"Probably," I admitted, already hurrying to the door. "But I want to see her alone first. Have some mother-daughter bonding time."

And see who in Hades she brought with her.

Maybe it was one of my goddess aunts? Would Athena show up as a dove too, or did she only do the owl thing? What about Hera?

Brushing past Maia, I raced down the hall. Curiosity aside, my new mother and I had some issues to discuss about certain forthcoming wedding plans. After reminding myself that I needed to thank her for choosing me before unloading all my family drama, I pushed open my door and stepped inside.

CHAPTER 3 — PSYCHE

When the door was closed, I spun around, eager to see who Aphrodite had brought with her.

I was two steps into my room when they changed. Expecting a goddess, I couldn't have been more stunned by the additional visitor.

Or wrong.

Those soft blonde curls and piercing blue eyes didn't belong to any goddess. Only the most amazing guy - *god?* - I'd ever laid eyes on.

My heart took off at a sprint and the blood rushed to my cheeks. He shot me a coy smirk that made my stomach slush with uneasy delight. So when a pair of pristine white wings unfurled from his back, my knees almost buckled. And here I'd thought he couldn't be any more magnificent. No doubt about it, this guy was divine.

Aphrodite threw her arms wide, demanding I place my attention on her. "So, are you surprised?" she asked.

Although she'd never hugged me before, I knew it was what she wanted me to do. To sweep myself into her embrace and prove myself grateful of my new role as her mortal daughter.

"Surprised isn't the half of it," I mumbled, stepping into an awkward hug.

Her arms tightened around me as she rocked me

side to side. "This is so exciting for you. And for me." She pushed me back at arms-length and stared at my face, her eyes searching mine. "You're the one I've been waiting for. I can just tell."

Beside her, the boy's wings ruffled. "You've had your little mother-daughter reunion. Can we go now?"

Still keeping one arm draped over my shoulder, Aphrodite wrapped the boy up with her other arm. We were so close I could almost smell him, just a hint of rugged sunshine. "Don't be silly, Eros. We *all* have much to discuss."

Eros? Like the god-of-love, shoots-everyone-with-magic-arrows, son-of-Aphrodite Eros?

"Do we have to do it here?" His gaze swept my room and obvious distaste curled down the edges of his lips, wiping away that delicious smirk. "It's so... pedestrian."

What's that supposed to mean? My temptation to bite his head off was tempered only by my need to stay on topic.

"Aphrodite --" I started. "I'm not supposed to call you 'mom' now or anything, am I?"

That infamous smile of hers pulled her lips tight and a perfect dimple flared on her right cheek. "Not yet, sweetie. Soon," she shot a knowing look at Eros, "but not yet."

I felt like I needed to sit down. Was the room spinning?

Rubbing at my temples, I tried again. "Okay. I'm sure I don't understand most of what's going on today, but we really need to talk. Because what my parents are planning makes no sense either." Aphrodite perched on the edge of my vanity and cocked her head like she was waiting for me to continue. "See, here's the thing. My parents are really happy."

"They should be," Eros half-coughed into his fist.

I shot him a glare before continuing on my rambling speech. "But, they think you'll want me to get married right away. Which is just insane, right? I mean, you said I'd help you promote the worship of beauty, but we never talked about your other ... well, attributes. And so anyway, my parents are sending out requests for suitors, and my sister is going to get married off too, and this is all just ... wrong. Please tell me this is wrong."

"Completely wrong," Aphrodite confirmed with a wave of her hand. I didn't realize how tightly I'd been squeezing my fingers until I let them go and the blood rushed back.

"Well, maybe not the part about your sister, but definitely about marrying you off." She gave this throaty chuckle that erased all the insta-relief I'd had just a second ago. "Your parents don't get to pick your husband. I do."

Eros snorted and dropped onto a tripod stool on the other side of my room. "Yeah, and we all know how well that turned out last time."

Aphrodite rose and paced toward her son. "What do you know about Helen?" Her voice fell an octave as she whisper-hissed. "You weren't even born yet, you ungrateful little twit."

Eros flicked his eyes to his mother. When he finally responded, his voice was level. "I know you started the worst war in the history of Greece and it all revolved around a pretty face." He turned his stare on me and nodded. "So now you've found another one. Bravo, mother. What'll it be this time. Can you use her to start a ten-year plague? Famine maybe?"

Aphrodite raised her hand like she was going to slap him, but then stopped. Her fist clenched, she lowered her arm and slowly turned to me. Her permagrin could've frozen lava in the summer.

"I'm sorry, Psyche. Had I known my son would be so... ill-mannered, I might've told you this news privately."

My eyes darted from Aphrodite to Eros and back. She cleared her throat as she reached out and clasped my hand between hers. "Psyche, darling, you knew there'd be a time when I would need something from you? A small service?"

I nodded. *Here it comes.*

She raised my hand up near her heart. "I would consider it a personal favor if you would do me the honor of marrying my son."

My jaw fell slack and I tried to back away, but Aphrodite had a death grip on my hand. Eros, on the other hand, had no such restraint. His sudden jump to his feet upended the tripod.

"Are you kidding me?" His wings spread wide behind him as he puffed himself up like a giant peacock and stormed his mother. "You think *I'm* going to marry *her*?"

"Yes, actually, I do." Aphrodite twisted her mouth into a smiling snarl. "Or the next time Zeus wants to strip you of your arrows, I won't stop him." She finally released my hand to pat Eros on the cheek.

His lips pressed together so tightly they looked in danger of disappearing altogether. "A mortal or my arrows? That's my choice?"

Aphrodite sighed, long and heavy. "I know she looks like the last one, but Psyche's far prettier, don't you think?" She turned to me and drenched me in a motherly smile. "And this one won't break your heart."

A muscle in Eros' cheek twitched and I had the sudden feeling he was about to give in. Not that I felt the least bit sorry for him, but I had less than no interest in spending the rest of my life with the biggest jerk I'd ever met. Considering some of the Senators who'd come through our palace, that was saying something.

Before I could stop myself, the words tumbled out of my mouth. "Maybe we can figure something out." Both of their blue-eyed stares nailed me to the ground.

"I mean, I'm not ready to get married yet. And really, Eros and I just met, and well, I'm not sure we're the best match -- no offense." *Crap. That came out totally wrong. Did I just tell the goddess of match making that she sucked it up on this one?* "I'm sure we'd *look* really good together and everything, but maybe our personalities don't exactly mesh." I was trying to smile but it felt way more like a grimace.

"Speak for yourself. No god looks good toting around mortal baggage."

Had he really just said that to me?

Aphrodite's tongue was quicker than mine to respond. "And I suppose that's why you use your arrows to make Zeus fawn all over those mortal girls.

Or why you fell in love with one yourself. Because they're baggage?" She reached out and clenched my upper arm before thrusting me at her son. "I found you the most beautiful girl in all of Greece and this is how you thank me?"

Eros threw up his hands. "You want me to *thank* you?" He looked me up and down, his eyes slowly raking over my body from head to toe. "Thanks, but no thanks."

Snatching my arm free from Aphrodite, I bore down on Eros. Instinctively, my finger poked him in the chest like I was reprimanding a child. "Now you listen to me. I don't give a crap who you are. Your mother has been nothing but good to me and you can *not* talk to her that way in my house."

Eros's fingers clasped around my wrist, sending a tiny charge racing through my body. When his eyes briefly widened, I was sure he felt it too. Our stares locked, only inches apart. I could even feel his breath tickle across my lips as he worked to slow his breathing.

As quickly as the moment came, it was gone. Eros threw down my arm and shot a glare at his mother. "Really? You think I'm going to marry *this*?"

Ugh. I had so had it with him. My palms hit his chest hard enough to rock him back a step. "I would never, ever, marry you. So don't even think you can reject me, you pompous, arrogant... creep. Because I reject you. You hear me? Get out of my room."

The initial look of shock on Eros' face was washed away by pure delight. His eyes sparkled and danced like embers soaring over a bonfire. "With pleasure." He took a sweeping bow, then turned to his mother. "I think that about settles things here, don't you?"

Before she could answer, he morphed into a dove and fluttered through the cracked opening in the shutters.

I'd thought all the tension would've left the room on those wings, but I found myself working solo with a goddess whose usually-porcelain face was now visibly red. Sure, she'd come to me before, huffing about slights or infractions. Like the time some farmer referred to her in a prayer as ox-eyed, when everyone knows that's Hera's moniker. But right now, she could put a steamed lobster to shame and I had a really bad feeling I was about to take the brunt of her anger.

"One thing. All I ask of you is one, little thing and you won't do it?"

"He started it." *Way to be mature*. I gave myself a mental eye roll and forged ahead. "Besides, you were supposed to ask me to do something related to beauty, not love or sex or those other things."

"What made you think that? My terms were always left open. You accepted my advice, rose in fame, filled your family's coffers." She gestured wildly at my window, shaking her whole body enough to rattle the golden seashell necklaces draped around her neck. "It's not like I've asked you to be a whore in my temple. You'd be married to a god."

When she said it like that, she had a point. Still... I needed to think and her glare was halting my brain. Slowly, I took a step back toward my bedroom door. Maybe I could ease my way out. I was pretty sure she wouldn't follow me in her actual body and she clearly needed some cooling off time. "I'm sorr--" I began.

"I made you my daughter." Her voice echoed like thunder off the mosaic walls of my room. "And then you refuse my son? A child of my actual blood?"

I continued my backpedal and tried to think of a way to stall. "Just, give me a little time, okay? I said I was sorry." Behind me, my hand found the door knob and turned it. "He can't say those things to you. It's not okay."

"It was not your place." Her screech followed me down the hall as I tore out of my room for the second time that day.

Chapter 4 — Psyche

A note to self: when attempting to hide from a goddess, think broader than outside your bedroom. My scrambled brain led me down the well-worn hall to my sister's suite and that's as far as I got.

"Oh my gods!" Chara squealed when I barged into her room. Her blonde curls swirled around her shoulders like a golden whirlpool as she bounced. Apparently she didn't notice I was freaking out as she danced and clapped.

Running past her, I dove into her bed and pulled the silk blankets over my head. Almost instantly, Chara tackled me and the bed shook under her continued jumping.

"What are you doing, silly? Come out." Chara's voice sounded light and airy enough to fly.

When I didn't answer, she finally stopped her incessant bouncing.

"Psyche?" She shook my shoulder. "Is everything alright?"

No. It's not alright. Not for me. Not for you. Nothing's even close to alright.

"Not really," I croaked.

The covers yanked away and I peeked up to see Chara standing over me. "Spill it. What's up?"

I recovered my face with my hands. "You don't even want to know. Seriously. It's that bad."

She tugged my hands free. "Come on. It can't be that bad. You *are* Aphrodite's daughter now."

I nearly puked on the bed.

"Fine." I sat up and took a deep breath. "Here's the short version. Everyone wants me to get married. Like yesterday. Aphrodite demanded I marry Eros, but that didn't work out--"

"Whoa. Wait," Chara cut in. "*The* Eros? She wants you to marry her son?"

"The correct word is *wanted*. Past tense. He pretty much hated me, was a jerk and I kicked him out of my room."

My sister's silence confirmed that yes, it did sound as bad as I thought. I forged ahead, determined to get to the part affecting her too. "So, that was her and now she's pretty ticked and all, which is one thing. But Mom and Dad are still on a rampage, planning a double wedding or something and sending out announcements for both of us."

Chara dropped my hands in favor of slapping them over her soundless scream. Or maybe she was about to puke too.

When she finally spoke, her words tumbled out fast and reckless as rapids. "That's imposs--. Are you sure? I was supposed to have another year."

All I could do was huddle with her as we formed our own pulsing pile of tears, sobs and runny makeup. "I'm so sorry," I moaned. "I knew she'd want something, but I didn't know it'd be this. I should've asked."

Chara looked up at me, her gaze telling me I'd slipped up before the accusation even came out. "What do you mean, 'should've asked?' You knew Aphrodite before today?"

Swallowing hard, I realized Chara had gone from sharing in my agony to looking ready to toss me to the lions. "It's not what you think."

Liar, liar.

"She's just been visiting. Mostly as a bird. Sometimes helping me with the window." I rubbed at my nose with the back of my hand. "It wasn't that easy, you know?"

"How long?" she demanded.

"I don't know." I shrugged. "Two months. Maybe three."

"Three months!" Her shriek almost frightened me more than Aphrodite. "You've been having visits with a goddess for three months? What'd you think was going on? You *had* to have known."

"I didn't. I swear. She just told me it added to her power when beauty was important and that I was helping her. That's all I knew."

Chara thrashed off the bed, jerking the covers with her. "Unbelievable."

"I know," I pleaded, "help me. What am I going to do?"

"You?" Chara's look was incredulous. "Help *you?* I'm supposed to be at least a year out from having to play nursemaid to some ancient king. I like it here, thank you very much. But now what? Now I have to suffer because you were too dumb to see the obvious?"

As I searched for the words that could possibly explain myself, Chara tore out of the room. "I can't be here right now."

The door slammed behind her like the crack of an axe.

CHAPTER 5 — EROS

Eros whipped through the cool night air, still struggling to control his temper. His mother's audacity had hit a new low.

He couldn't believe she'd told him to marry a mortal. She knew how he felt about them since --. He couldn't bring himself to even think *her* name. That scar had finally healed and he wasn't about to tear it open again. Especially not over Psyche, a girl who apparently detested him on sight.

What he needed was a distraction. Something to keep his mind from circling back to the arc of attraction he'd felt when he touched Psyche that morning. Or the way just seeing someone as beautiful as her made him want to seal his heart up in a metal box. He wouldn't let himself be hurt again. Ever.

Trimming his wings, Eros landed just outside a throbbing mass of people. Bacchus' all-night party would certainly do as a distraction. In the midst of half-naked women who actually wanted him, he figured he'd drink himself stupid. And find someone who'd make him forget Psyche's green eyes and how much they reminded him of ... *her*.

Pushing through a crowd of gossiping nymphs, Eros sidled up to Bacchus. As Eros hoped to be by the end of the night, Bacchus was draped in girls. He held a goblet of wine, sloshing its crimson contents to the ground.

"Bacchus, old friend," Eros said, clapping the beefy immortal on the back, "looks like you started the party without me."

Bacchus swung his wobbly head toward the voice and worked to squint Eros into focus. "Zou made it..." he slurred. "Have some wine!" Bacchus raised his glass and wine splashed onto the chest of the woman sitting to his right.

While Bacchus made a mess of helping the lady dry her toga, a reveler whisked over and placed a goblet in Eros's hand. He downed the wine in one long drink.

"Here, let me get that for you." Eros turned to find a nymph he'd known for years refilling his glass.

"Kalliste!" Eros threw an arm around the nymph. "Good to see you again."

"You too, Eros." Her auburn hair sparkling in the torchlight was almost as captivating as her smile.

Eros leaned closer to Kalliste and lowered his voice. "Since when did you become one of Bacchus's followers? I didn't think you liked this sort of thing." He nodded his head in the direction of a group of swirling women.

"A girl has a right to change." Kalliste brushed her bangs off her forehead. "Probably a lot has changed about me since I saw you last."

"Do tell," Eros replied, finishing off his wine and raising his cup for another refill.

"Maybe. First I want to know about Eros. Have *you* changed any?" Kalliste asked as she poured.

Eros raised an eyebrow. "Me? Why should I change?" He bumped her shoulder with his. "I'm pretty prefect as is, don't ya think?"

"Mmmm..." Kalliste ran her hand up to his shoulder. "You are a treat for the eyes, but you're murder on the heart."

Eros laughed and threw back another gulp of wine. "Me? You don't know the half of it." He'd seen murder on the heart, but it wasn't his doing.

Kalliste narrowed her eyes as she leaned in to hiss in his ear. "You've got to stop with the arrows, okay? I know you've been laying low for a few weeks, but Zeus sent me to confirm that you're done. He's serious this time. No more mortals for him."

No more mortals for anyone, if Eros had any say in the matter.

"And you need to make things up to Hera," Kalliste continued. "You've been quite the homewrecker."

Eros let his head fall forward. He wished he weren't having this conversation tonight. Or ever.

"What does she want?" he groaned.

Kalliste laid her arm over Eros's shoulder. "Just let some nice goddess make an honest man out of you. You know how she is about family. Settle down, stop sending her husband chasing after mortal girls, and all will be forgiven."

Talk about a joke. Zeus has been chasing women since long before Eros was born. But what could he say to the little messenger-nymph that wouldn't make it back to the Olympian rulers? Nothing.

Eros snatched the jug of wine and refilled his glass. "You know, Kalliste? You're the second person today who's tried to set me up."

Kalliste's lips twisted into a pout. "Oh. Did

someone else already talk to you about Iris then?"

Eros about spat out his wine. "Iris? That multi-colored freak show? Gods, that's almost worse than a mortal."

Kalliste bumped her knuckles into his shoulder. "Don't be an ass. It was Hera's idea." When Eros didn't respond, she added, "She'd *really* like to see you settled down."

"Yeah, well, so would my mom." He threw back another gulp of wine. "People are going to have to learn to deal with disappointment."

Kalliste's face paled as her gaze locked on something behind Eros.

"What?" he asked, turning.

Aphrodite was so close, he had to stumble back so he didn't step on her. "Disappointment is a bit of an understatement, don't you think?"

"Not here," he said. "I'm not talking about this tonight. With either of you," he added, glaring back at Kalliste.

Aphrodite's eyes cut to the nymph as she spun her son in the opposite direction. "You'll excuse us."

"I said not now." Eros jerked his arm loose from her grip and stopped. "I don't care what you say, I'm not marrying a mortal, okay?"

Aphrodite leveled her intense blue eyes at him. "Okay."

Um, what? Eros rolled his shoulders and tucked his wings back into place. "So why're you here?"

"It's painfully obvious that there's not much I can do to *you* for refusing my arrangement. *She*, on the other hand, is a different story."

"And you came here to tell me that?"

Aphrodite snatched the goblet from Eros' hand and threw it to the ground. "No, I came here to tell you to take care of her punishment. She rejects my son? Fine. Make her fall in love with some despicable and hideous mortal. I don't care who, frankly. Just make sure he's as awful to the women in his life as you are."

***

A doorman peeked into the dining room as Eros was finishing breakfast. "My Lord, Aphrodite sends word that she's gone to holiday at sea. She said to make sure you do your job quickly so she won't have to be bothered with the details."

Eros's fork clattered onto his plate. He slammed his eyes shut as the noise echoed inside his brain like symbols. Damn. After three days' worth of festivities, he'd forgotten his mother had made him her do-boy again. What was it she wanted?

His brain felt like pulp. Something about Psyche, he remembered that much. And *not* having to marry her. That news alone justified his three-day bender. His stomach settled as the memories pushed their way forward.

"Will there be anything else, Sire?"

Eros wiped at his mouth with a napkin. "See that no one comes in. Apparently I have work to do."

As the man scurried away, Eros took a last gulp of ambrosia and headed for the courtyard. But his mutinous feet didn't want to make the trip. Psyche's emerald eyes flashed in his brain -- so full of fire and life. Granted, he wanted nothing to do with her and the inevitable heartbreak she'd bring. But he sort of hated thinking he'd be the one who'd drown out her spark.

When had using his arrows gotten so messed up? He longed for those early, innocent years, when his arrows did only one thing: make people who were supposed to be in love stay that way. Still, what choice did he have? If he didn't give his mother what she wanted, no telling what retribution she'd plan.

Convincing his body to finally budge, Eros made his way into the courtyard and reclined against a golden bench. He leaned back and focused on an empty patch of wall. The Greek landscape flickered behind his eyes, his second sight honing in.

The spinning visions made him nauseous. *How much wine did I drink?* He took deep breaths to keep his breakfast down and tried to think about who he ought to be looking for. Random searching when he felt like a weak-kneed sailor was clearly not in his best interests.

Maybe a Cyclops? No, he'd probably crunch her bones into tiny pieces. As cruel as he knew her beauty could be if he ever got close, death wasn't a sentence he wanted to impose. And fortunately wasn't what he'd been tasked with.

How about Argus? Eros bet she couldn't find a way to break his heart with 100 eyes staring back at her. Not that he really liked the idea of her being perpetually creeped out, but she'd get used to it. Argus wasn't a bad option really. Not mean, just gross. Aphrodite would probably be satisfied with that.

But that option was out too. The eyeball-endowed man was serving as a watchman for Hera. Good call on that one, actually. But that meant he was too close to the gods to be wretched enough for his mother's purposes.

Groaning, Eros let his head fall back against the bench. He'd use the arrows like he'd been ordered. But didn't his mother realize that just thinking about her was starting to peel back the wound? Why'd he have to find the target too? Oh yeah, because Aphrodite clearly didn't want to be bothered with the details. As long as she was on "holiday at sea," as his doorman had announced, she wouldn't be able to use her second sight even if she wanted to.

How convenient for her.

Eros ran his fingers through his tangled hair. Something sticky caught in them and the nausea resurfaced. He didn't even want to know. Thank the gods there were no mirrors in the courtyard. He probably looked scraggly enough to be the groom himself.

Now there's an idea, he thought. Someone who looks (and feels) as bad as he did right now.

He knew exactly what he was looking for then. There'd been a rumor spreading about it during the parties, and sure enough. The uproar projected into his brain, leading his vision easily to the target.

His eyebrows furrowed as he stared at the blank wall, not seeing the stone at all. The scene unfurled just as he'd hoped. A mob was chanting. "We must end the drought! Cast the *Pharmakos* out!" Faces were twisted in angry snarls; the victim was jostled forward on the arms of his captors.

Swallowing back the lump in his throat, he told himself this was the right call. Aphrodite asked for hideous and the *Pharmakos* qualified. But after delving into the man for a moment, Eros picked up on a few positive traits too. He wasn't harsh; he didn't have a sharp tongue; and Eros was pretty sure he'd worship the ground Psyche walked on.

He didn't know why, maybe just the lingering affection he felt for *her*, but Eros really didn't wish Psyche ill. He knew his mother was overreacting, as she'd done a hundred times before. But she always got her way. If he didn't impose the sentence, Aphrodite would find a way to make it even worse.

For both of them.

Realizing he was out of options, Eros settled on his choice. He could condemn Psyche to life as a vagabond if the person holding her hand would be her partner through it all. Deep down, it's what his nature drew him to do - make good matches - not call on his talents in revenge.

Here's hoping the pairing is something everyone could live with.

CHAPTER 6 — PSYCHE

For the next few days, there were no birds. No visits from my sister. I was alone with my crowd. Their constant, muted rumble played like the song of my heart. An endless rise and fall with no definition. Like a shape without sides. And though the sound pulsed and writhed to its own rhythm, the dullness made it feel unreal.

I wanted it all to be unreal.

The crowd, I snubbed. My sister, I craved. Each day that passed without her made my soul bleed. I could feel the walls building between us. The knocks on her door that went unanswered. How she left a room whenever I walked in.

Some things can be forgiven. But this?

Not that I'd known or meant any of it. Still. Maybe I deserved her impaling hatred. And I wished I could go back in time. Back to when that milk-white bird had first fluttered through my window. I'd tell her everything. Even though Aphrodite made me promise not to breathe a word. I'd tell Chara, and she'd keep my secret, and neither of us would be where we were now.

Those were the dreams of my tears. They gave me solace in the hours between sleep.

Until the knock on my door finally came.

Flinging myself out of bed, I raced for the door, absolutely sure I'd find Chara on the other side. I didn't dare hope she'd forgiven me, just cooled enough to talk. To hear my side. To help me on a solution for us all.

I couldn't even stop myself from blooming into a smile, I was so giddy she'd finally come.

The reality of my visitor slammed me like colliding with a slab of marble. My father's messenger waited, column-strait, when I threw open my door. His eyes were fixed on a spot above my head. No eye contact.

"My Lady, your father sends word that you are to be ready by sundown. The first suitor has arrived. You are not to leave your room until that time."

As if.

He bowed, averting his eyes, and left with his toga flaring behind him in his flight to escape my presence.

Once I closed my door, I sank into a pile on the floor. It was here. Already.

I'd been thinking through this moment, making sure I was ready to do the right thing for my sister. And the only thing that could possibly save myself.

There'd been so many dead-end thoughts; paths down a Minotaur's labyrinth that had no end. Only one idea seemed even plausible. I'd make sure the first suitor who came married me. My stomach clenched as I went over my reasoning for the millionth time.

If I was married first, maybe Chara's bride price would drop. And then it wouldn't matter *when* she were married and Mom and Dad could let her wait. Like they'd always planned.

Plus, if Aphrodite really meant what she'd said about learning from her mistakes with Helen, then she'd have to give up the matchmaker role once I had a husband. No more wars over women, right? I'd simply have to stay her hand the only way I could.

In all time I'd spent alone in my room the past few days, I hadn't come up with a better solution.

So why was pushing myself up off the floor to get ready the hardest movement I'd ever had to make?

***

As the sun began to set, I made my way down the long marble stairs from my room. I'd selected an olive-colored dress that brought out the green of my eyes. Maia had wrapped my hair up in a loose bun and made my skin sing with the heady perfume of sage and lilies.

The admirers had made me painfully aware that I was pretty enough without the added effort, but I asked Maia to really give it her all tonight. If I was going to marry this stranger to save myself and Chara, I needed him to see only me. I suspected my bride price was way higher than my sister's. Plus, since he arrived so quickly, it meant his City had to be nearby. The selfish part of me loved the idea of not moving too far from home.

I found my parents and sister entertaining our guest in the courtyard. He looked about father's age, but was far leaner. Although bald, his long, angular face was grounded by richly dark eyebrows and a well-trimmed beard. The effect made him look distinguished, in a harsh, old-person sort of way.

When I crossed the threshold into the courtyard, everyone stopped talking and fixed their eyes on me. Attention being nothing new, I did what was expected of me: I radiated a smile and curtsied.

My father cleared his throat. "Psyche, I'd like you

to meet King Andreas of Corinth."

Lowering my eye lashes, I nodded my head in greeting. "It gives me great pleasure to welcome you. Thank you for coming all this way." Of course, Corinth wasn't far at all (*I'd been right!*), but that wasn't the point. My intent was to charm and flatter him.

He looked me over from head to toe. His gaze passed like a winter chill over my body. After several seconds, he turned back to my father.

"Darion, she's every bit as lovely as the rumors made her out to be. How much are you asking for her?"

That's it? That's as much as he needs to know about me before trying to purchase me for his wife? Andreas hadn't even bothered to speak to me.

"Sire," I cut in, stepping between him and Father. "Forgive me for interrupting, but I thought you might like to get to know me first before proposing marriage."

His calculating eyes bore through me. "There is nothing more I need to know other than the price. Either I can afford you or I cannot."

I staggered back a step, feeling suddenly queasy and mortified. Embarrassment burned my cheeks like I'd been slapped. My sister had been right to be afraid. This was worse than anything I'd ever imagined. They were discussing my purchase price right in front of me.

My pulse felt like it could stampede its way free from my veins. I'd learned my lesson about shoving important-but-insulting guys, but my blood pressure responded to Andreas with the same hostility I'd felt standing before Eros. Leaving before I did something equally as stupid seemed like a good idea.

"I assume someone will tell me if you win the

auction, Sire. Happy bidding." Giving a quick bow, I turned and fled into the courtyard.

The rush of humid spring air didn't provide the relief I was looking for. And entering the dark of dusk from the brightly lit foyer made my eyes strain, like the sinking sun was bleeding all the colors from the sky.

As I passed through the gardens, totally absorbed in my own thoughts, my hip collided with a man bent over a bush. He jumped and whipped around to face me as I staggered back a step.

Through the dim light, I noted that the stranger's face was lean, his teeth just a bit too large, and his hair flopped into his eyes. Between that and the whole nose-in-a-bush thing, he struck me as out-of-place here.

"I'm sorry," I said. "I didn't mean to crash into you like that."

"Not at all," he answered. "I was just studying this unusual flower. I've never seen another like it."

"Do you often look at flowers?" I asked, trying not to smirk.

"Actually, yes. I've been studying them at Athens." He brushed the hair from his eyes, revealing invitingly dark brown eyes.

"Oh." I laughed nervously, suddenly glad I hadn't assumed he was Andreas' servant. Servants do not study in Athens.

"I know it's sort of a strange interest," he continued, "but I get bored only thinking about war or sports. History never changes and I never get better at sports. Flowers are different though. They're pure and fragile, like life I guess."

Was this guy a second suitor? I was pretty sure

Father's servant had only said one suitor was here, but what else could this guy be? He was well-educated, well-rounded and obviously a pretty good catch. Would it be selfish to want him for myself? Maybe letting Chara have him would be a better peace offering.

"Sorry, I have a tendency to ramble. Probably spending too much time studying philosophy. That's the rage in Athens and all. I'm Rasmus by the way. Rasmus of Mycenae." He extended his hand and I offered mine.

He was a suitor then -- had to be. Silence hung between us as my brain tied to work through my options. What could I possibly say that would interest him? How would I appeal to him with more than looks? And did I want to appeal to him or should I let Chara have him? Then I realized, I hadn't even introduced myself. And I was still holding his hand!

I dropped his hand too quickly to be subtle. "Oh, I should have introduc... I mean... I'm Psyche." I mentally kicked myself for not being able to spit out a coherent sentence. Then I added, "I'm sorry you were out here all alone. It was rude of us not to be more hospitable."

"That's alright. I've been enjoying myself." His tone told me he meant it. Some other nobles would've been put off by not being doted on, but he wasn't. If I was being truly selfless, I knew that Chara deserved this man. Still, my mind wasn't quite made up.

After looking over my shoulder to ensure my family hadn't decided to chase me down, I turned my attention back on Rasmus. "I can show you around the gardens if you like. There's an area a little ways off that I've always loved. Perhaps you'll see some more new flowers before the sun fully sets."

"I'd like that," Rasmus said. "But I'm not sure the flowers will be the loveliest things in the garden."

Wow. Maybe they teach the art of giving compliments in Athens too. I could really get to like this guy.

I led Rasmus down a limestone pathway and under a canopy of olive trees. As we walked, Rasmus told me about his family. He had two younger sisters, but his mother had died several years ago. When he wasn't studying in Athens, he helped his father by traveling for him so the old king wouldn't have to leave home.

As he talked, I felt how relaxed and at ease he seemed with me. As my fame had grown these past few months, only my family seemed comfortable in my presence anymore. What was even more of a gift though was that we were having a conversation. Rasmus was talking with me like an old friend. And it wasn't about eye paste or the latest silks. I hadn't realized how much I needed this.

We reached the end of the path and stood before a tall iron gate, flanked on either side by hedges higher than our heads. "I don't know about you," I said, "but the Trojan War has always fascinated me. Who knows," I added, shrugging my shoulders, "maybe I've just glamorized it because of this place."

Rasmus's eyebrows knit together. "I'm not sure how you can glamorize war."

I tipped my head toward the gardens and pushed open the gate, inviting him into the small courtyard. The floor was tiled in a colorful mosaic picturing a battle scene. In the center of the courtyard was a fountain sculpted in the likeness of the Trojan horse. Elaborate stone benches sat around the fountain, carved with images of our heroes: Achilles and Agamemnon, Ajax and Odysseus.

"This is my family's tribute to the battle of Troy. My great grandfather traveled with King Menelaus to win Helen back from Paris."

"It's ... impressive." Rasmus drifted, as if pulled by the nectarine-hued flowers smiling at us from the hedges.

"Our gardeners claim those flowers come from the shores of Troy." When he didn't answer, I added, "But they could be wrong. I don't really know about flowers like you do."

Rasmus took in the flowers, and the rest of the courtyard, in silence. Finally he said, "Thank you for bringing me here. I can see why this is one of your favorite places." His eyes continued to roam the courtyard. "Still, I can't agree that there's anything glamorous about war." He leaning over to give my shoulder a playful nudge with his. "You maybe, but not war."

That was flirting, right?

I had to bite my lip to keep the smile from bursting off my face. "I'm glad you like it. I haven't had anyone to share it with in a long time." *'Cause I sure didn't bring Aphrodite out here.* I looked down at my feet, kicking at a little pebble. "Maybe you can come back again. With me."

When I peeked up from under my eyelashes, Rasmus was looking at the purple sky. A sad smile played on his lips. Then he looked back at me, holding my gaze with his darkly intense eyes. "Psyche, there's nothing in all the world I would like more. But I'm afraid that's just not meant to be."

My mind reeled. How could that be? He liked me. I knew he liked me. He had practically just said he liked me, didn't he? My jaw fell open. I could only form the word, "But..." It came out as barely more than a whisper.

Rasmus took my hands in his and guided me to one of the benches.

"I don't know where to start," he said. He gestured to the Trojan horse.

"The beauty of a single woman started a ten-year war." He huffed. "My father decided it's not in the best interest of our City to marry the most beautiful woman in the world. Troy is still too fresh in his mind. He won't make the same mistake as Menelaus."

"Your father?" I asked. "What about you? I ... I don't understand."

"Psyche, I'm not here for me. I'm here on behalf of my father. He sent me to bring your sister back to be his new wife. I've already arranged for Chara to return with me."

Tears welt up in my eyes and I struggled to hold them back. I didn't want Rasmus to see me cry, but I'd just lost my hope for saving Chara. I'd failed her.

I'm a failure.

As I sat there in stupid silence, a thought came to me so quickly that my mouth started forming words before my brain was done processing.

"But if Chara ... your father ... then you could still ...."

Rasmus looked down at his hands as he shifted on the bench. "My father has already arranged for my marriage to someone else. It's what's in the best interest of our City." He looked up at me. "I have no doubt my bride will pale in comparison to you."

Rasmus leaned forward and wiped away the tear that finally spilled down my cheek. "Please don't cry. Tears do a disservice to such a beautiful face."

Sniffing, I managed a half-smile and swallowed the lump in my throat. "I'll be okay."

Deep lines etched into Rasmus's forehead. Apparently he wasn't convinced.

"What?" I asked, wiping at another tear with my finger. "You think I can't get a husband or something?"

At least that drew somewhat of a smile from him. I'd had enough guilt to last me a lifetime, I didn't need to worry about whether I'd made him feel bad too. "Seriously," I told him, "I'll be fine. I just want to be alone for a little while."

Rasmus stood and looked down on me. "Of course. Thank you again for sharing your garden with me." His lips pressed together like he was holding something back. "I'll always remember ... it."

CHAPTER 7 — EROS

Eros might have mentally made his decision, but his body refused to execute on it. Instead, he watched the *Pharmakos's* exile unfold like a sick tragedy. The sheer stupidity of it was almost mind boggling.

How long had the Greeks believed they could rid their cities of the major problems --famine, disease, plague, drought -- by casting out a *Pharmakos*? It was ludicrous. Like just because some cripple left the city, everything else bad would follow?

As Eros looked on, four men wrestled the *Pharmakos* forward, driving him toward the gates. The surrounding mob readied their stones. Dragging his right foot behind him, the scapegoat struggled to keep up with his captors.

With a final, unforgiving surge, the horde jostled the man forward past the gates. He tried to run, but his crippled leg slowed him down. Two stones caught him in the middle of his back, nearly causing him to fall, before he managed to scramble outside of their range.

Deciding he needed to get a move on before he lost track of the wretch, Eros hopped to his feet. He suddenly wished he could impose his mother's sentence on the woman who'd basically chewed up his heart and spit it out. But, he reminded himself, there were certainly more painful choices he could've made.

And at least this way, Psyche would never have

the chance to destroy a man's pride.

When Eros arrived in Sikyon, he hid amongst the long shadows in a forest of evergreens. There, he disguised himself as a traveler, donning a pock-marked face, greasy dark hair, and covering his wings and quiver with a heavy cloak. As he looked in on Psyche with his second sight, he saw she was alone in an isolated part of her family's garden. The time had come. Eros's palms began to sweat as he silently crept forward.

Eros told himself just to think of *her* -- the one who'd shattered his soul. He would not let his facade crack. He'd accomplish his mission and move on with life. Once the task was complete, he'd never have to think about it, or Psyche, or *her*, ever again.

When Eros approached the garden alcove, he saw Psyche sprawled face-down across a bench. Her shoulders visibly shook from sobs. Soft ringlets obscured her face, tucking her hypnotic green eyes away from sight.

Soundlessly, Eros slid his bow off his shoulder. Pulling an arrow from under his cloak, he brought it to his lips and whispered, "*Pharmakos*." Then, he repeated the familiar process of placing the arrow in the string of his bow and drawing back the missile. Eros took aim and prepared to release the arrow.

But then he faltered.

Something in the back of his mind - or perhaps the back of his heart - prevented him from actually following through. He'd been sent to destroy the second mortal who'd rejected him, but right then she already seemed ruined. He wondered why Psyche was sobbing. Had someone hurt her the same way his own heart had been crushed?

In the seconds that he paused, Psyche raised her head. Wiping her tear-stained face with the back of her hand, she rose from the bench like smoke wafting from a fire.

"I don't know who you are, but if you think a guy with an arrow is my biggest concern right now, you're wrong." She squared her shoulders and tossed her hair behind her shoulders. "Get out."

If he'd been listening, he'd have heard Psyche kick him out of her home a second time. But her words weren't registering. How had he missed it? She wasn't like the first girl at all. On the surface, they were so similar, but underneath -- their cores were completely different. He'd dropped his guard long enough to really feel her, *know* her, the way he could any mortal if he payed attention long enough. Even with tear trails still fresh on her cheeks, Psyche glowed from the inside out.

As a soft breeze carried her heady scent to him, Eros vaguely heard her repeat her command to leave. The words didn't carry her intended message, but instead bore her soul. Her emotions doused him; poured over him in soothing waves. Her anger and fear pulsed on the surface, but underneath those rhythms was the chorus of her spirit -- love, tenderness, good intentions -- a package that made Psyche far and away different.

Without realizing he was doing it, Eros lowered his bow. "Psyche," he muttered just before the arrow grazed his knee. The tip left only the tiniest of scratches, but it was enough.

Eros rushed forward on instinct, grabbing Psyche's arm and dragging her in close to his chest. Her lips froze in an "O" while her eyes went wide with fear.

What was he doing? Eros shook his head as if the sudden feelings that had just overwhelmed him could be cast aside as easily as shaking off a few drops of rain.

Dropping Psyche's arm, he backed away. This wasn't him. He didn't fall for mortals. *Wouldn't* fall for mortals. And certainly not his mother's little minion….

Aphrodite. Could she have set this up somehow? Was she forcing him to love Psyche so he'd change his mind about marrying the girl? His chest labored under ragged breaths as his anger rose. He would not allow her to manipulate him like this. He'd made his choice. Psyche had made her choice.

This couldn't be happening.

And yet there it was: an need in his core that made it impossible for him to do anything but stare into the loveliest green eyes he'd ever seen. His breathing slowed as a calm washed over him; knowledge that he could find peace again in someone's embrace. It was terrifying and exhilarating all at once.

His eyes tore from hers and traveled down her arms until he found her hands. Psyche's hands could give him the comfort he'd been denied the last time he'd tried to love. Why did she have them balled into fists at her side when all he wanted was her to stroke his cheek? How could she not be feeling their connection?

Suddenly Psyche lunged, making a move for something just behind him. The arrow. He stomped on the tip before she could reach it, making it dissolve into a pool of light. Psyche sprawled forward, grasping for the missing weapon. Unable to leave her prone on the ground, Eros leaned down and gently lifted her to feet.

Even as Psyche trembled under his grasp, touching her again set off a concussive burst in his nerves. Before, with *her,* he hadn't felt this strongly. This was something new entirely, almost like he was under a spell.

The realization made a shudder roll down his spine. Had he done this to himself? His mind cycled backward. He'd whispered Psyche's name, that could've changed the target. Had he poked himself? It couldn't be, the arrow hadn't dissolved. He'd had to crush it into oblivion. But then again, he'd never shot anyone gently before either. Was it the impact and not the use that made the arrows vanish?

Psyche tore herself free, skittering back to her bench as if the stone would shield her. His heart nearly cramped as he felt her exposed fear. He yearned to sit beside her, pull her into his lap, soothe away her worries. He wanted nothing more than for them to be in love.

What did it matter whether these feelings were self-inflicted? He was on a high he never wanted to come down from. And he wanted Psyche. Wanted her love. Wanted her at his side. Wanted everything.

But he needed time to think. His mother's curse had set certain events in motion. Taking Psyche now would have consequences. Maybe even ones *he* didn't want to face. He had to get out of there before he did something even more colossally stupid than shooting himself.

"Go inside, Psyche. Someone will come for you soon."

Whether Eros came back himself or he led the *Phramakos* to her door, one way or another, someone would be coming.

Pausing only long enough to catch the rising moonlight reflecting in her eyes, Eros turned and ran back to the forest.

CHAPTER 8 — PSYCHE

I walked to where I thought the stranger with the arrow had been standing, but I couldn't see any footprints. There was no sign that the clay pathway leading to the forest had been disturbed. A lone pine needle twisting in the grass was the only sign of movement.

That settled it; I must've fallen asleep on the bench and dreamt the whole thing. It had all seemed so real, but then again, dreams often do -- especially omens.

An omen? Could it be? If the stranger in my dream had said that a "someone" would be coming for me, maybe he meant a husband. Maybe it wasn't too late to save myself from Aphrodite after all. Would that be any more bizarre than nearly being impaled by an arrow only for the hunter to turn around and run away?

Gathering up the lengths of my dress, I rushed back to the palace. The foyer and dining rooms were empty, so I rushed to my sister's suite. Chara was finishing her packing. Wooden trunks were strewn about her room, overflowing with her various worldly possessions. She sang softly to herself and her movements were like a candle-lit dance as she glided one way to tuck away a nightgown and back across her room to retrieve a forgotten hand mirror.

Chara's normally a bubbly person, but this felt wrong. Was this the same girl who'd banished me from her room for putting her in the position of having to marry an old king? I didn't know how old Rasmus's dad was, but he couldn't be young.

When Chara saw me standing in her doorway, she rushed over and pulled me into her arms, giving me a quick but crushing hug. "Psyche, I don't want us to say goodbye on bad terms, okay? I forgive you."

I tried to smile but was too confused. What was I missing?

Chara apparently mistook my confusion for jealousy and laughed. "I'm sure you wanted him for yourself. But seriously, let me enjoy having *something* special for once."

Before I could ask what in Hades she was blabbering about, Rasmus came to my side in the doorway. "Psyche, I don't mean to interrupt, but if you're done with your sister, I have a bride to take home with me."

"You're heading out tonight?" I stammered. "Can't it wait till morning?"

"The sooner we get started, the better. Mycenae is eagerly awaiting your sister's arrival."

Chara let a trunk lid slam closed. "If you'll call the servant boy back up here for the last of the luggage, I'll be ready." When Rasmus walked off to do her bidding, she mock-whispered, "I'm going to be a princess of Mycenae. And he's so young." Returning to her normal voice, she added, "This is so much better than I could've ever hoped. I'm sorry I was mad at you all week. Can we be friends again? Please?"

Before I could answer, Rasmus returned and took Chara's hand. "Shall we?" he asked.

Chara gave me a hopeful smile and slid out of her suite. I wanted to scream at Rasmus that he was a big, fat liar for everything he'd told me in the garden, but then he looked back at me. The look in his eyes was both pleading and stern, begging and warning me not to tell Chara what I knew.

My eyes grew wide as I broke gaze with Rasmus. Of course Chara was acting like a love-struck fool. She thought she was going to marry Rasmus. He must not have told her that although she would be *a* bride, she wasn't going to be *his* bride. I wondered if that'd been his father's idea or my parents' inspiration. I was sure the Rasmus I'd just met wouldn't willingly deceive anyone. But here he was, leading my painfully oblivious sister away.

What would happen if I did warn her? Could I save her from what was already done by telling her? Or would I just be prematurely stripping away her joy?

In the second I paused to decide, Father moved in beside me and wrapped an arm around my shoulder. His dark eyes pierced mine, making me feel small and helpless. "This is a good allegiance for our City, don't you think?"

What could I do but nod my agreement? Chara was headed off to be a queen. Not a princess even, but the queen of a powerful City. Of course it was good for Sikyon – the more friends we had, the better. But the feeling of wanting to be sick was too powerful to stay there. I couldn't see her off. Not like this.

Trudging back to my room, I climbed into bed with one of my favorite tragedies, *Oedipus Rex*. Maybe I could convince myself that his life was more screwed up than mine. Not that it should make me feel better, but I liked the idea of not being alone in having a messed up family. And if I didn't find solace in the scrolls, at least I could count on my bed to wrap me in comfort until the soggy emptiness of the past couple days subsided.

I hadn't been reading for long when I heard a soft knock. Mother nudged the door open, but waited in the threshold to see if I'd invite her in. I did.

"Andreas?" I asked.

"Gone," she answered. "Apparently Corinth isn't willing to pay through the nose for a sharp-tongued princess."

Thank gods. At least one thing I'd done this week had worked out in my favor.

Mother sat on the edge of my bed and patted my knee. "How you holding up?" she asked.

"Do you care?"

Yeah, it was rude, but the last time she'd really spoken to me, she was hysterical with the news that her daughter had been adopted by Aphrodite. Then she'd shunned me just as much as Chara these past few days. She wasn't getting back on my good side just by showing up.

"Psyche, don't be like that." The lines around her eyes creased. "You've always been the understanding one. Try to see things from our perspective."

"What perspective is that?" I tossed the scroll down to the foot of the bed and began waving my arms at her as my voice perched on the edge of a yell. "The perspective that you decided to sell off your daughters because we're at the peak of our bride price, even though you promised Chara she had at least another year? Or the perspective that you just let Chara dance off to a wedding without even knowing who her husband is going to be?"

Mother didn't answer, so I scooted off my bed, unable to stand sitting next to her any longer. "How am I supposed to trust you?"

She sighed, long and heavy, as if weighing the possible responses. Finally, she said, "You knew about Chara, huh? Why didn't you tell her?"

Now it was me who didn't have an answer. I didn't want to admit I'd been too afraid to act. That the looks from Rasmus and Father had frozen me. That I'd convinced myself Chara's temporary happiness would be better for her than the truth.

"I know, Psyche," she said. "Things aren't always as straightforward as they seem."

Keeping my back to her, I rearranged the perfume and lotion bottles on my vanity. The sudden sense of losing everyone I cared about, even Aphrodite, nearly overwhelmed me. She hadn't been back since our fight and I missed her sprawling herself across my room, playing with my hair, letting me try out every new fragrance I got on her first. Did our girl chats not mean anything to her? Was she missing me at all?

When the lily scent of the last lotion I'd used on Aphrodite hit me, I had to swallow back a sob that threatened to choke me. *How had my life gone so completely wrong in just four days?*

To keep from crying, I jerked my hair into a tight braid, pulling harder every time I thought I felt tears forming. And I focused my attention back on Mother.

"Whose idea was it to let Chara go like that? Tell me it wasn't yours."

In the mirror, I saw her looking down at her clasped hands. "Not mine, no; but I'm as much to blame as anyone. I didn't stop it."

I spun around to face her head-on. "Why? What possible reason could you have for tricking her like that?"

Mother's eyes snapped up at my accusing tone. "Have you seen her the past few days? She's been sullen and withdrawn. There was no way she was going to pull it together unless she thought she was headed off with someone like Rasmus."

"I still don't get *why* though. Why not wait for another suitor? It didn't have to be the first one that came along."

Mother sat up, arrow straight. "The role of a royal daughter is to solidify alliances with her marriage. Do you know how powerful Mycenae is? We weren't willing to turn them away because Chara was weepy-eyed."

I was too shocked to answer. It was one of the coldest things I'd ever heard her say. But as she stared at my shuttered window, the flame from my bedside lamps amplified the moisture pooling in her eyes. "Do you think your father rode in on some white horse and I got to choose him from among other suitors? Our marriage was arranged before I was barely old enough to understand what the word meant." Her words dropped to barely more than a whisper. "It's through time and a shared vision for this City that we've grown to love each other."

My shock fell away as I realized she'd been through this exact same thing. Maybe it was awful that she was willing to sell off her daughters; or maybe it was just the way things worked and no one could change that. Either way, I felt like I saw my mom from a slightly different angle now. Like her scars had been made visible under different lighting. Did she have other wounds too hidden for me to know about? I didn't want to hold grudges against her that weren't hers to bear.

She must've seen me soften. When she patted the bed beside her, I obediently sat. "So, how'd *you* know about Chara?"

I told her about finding Rasmus alone and the talk we had in the alcove, but left out the details that'd suggest we'd been flirting. Better she not think I'd ventured too far down Aphrodite's path already. Then I told her about my odd dream and suspicion there could be more to it.

As I described it, Mother pinched her lips closed in thought. "I don't know if I've ever told you, but our family has a history of receiving prophetic dreams."

I rolled my eyes. She might have mentioned it once or twice.

Slowly, she repeated the words of my dream. "Go inside, Psyche. Someone will come for you soon." She shook her head. "I don't know. Prophecies can be very double-sided."

I flopped back against my bed and let my arms sprawl out to the side. "Typical. I finally get some hope and..." I paused, blinking back fresh tears. "I don't think I can handle any more bad news today, Mom."

She blew out my lamp and smoothed the few strands of hair around my face that I hadn't forced into a braid. "Just sleep, baby. Tomorrow's a new day and I have a feeling the prophecy will reveal itself soon."

CHAPTER 9 — EROS

As soon as Eros launched toward home, he began plotting. Of course, Aphrodite couldn't know about this since she apparently *hated* her new daughter. And she'd demanded Psyche fall in love with someone wretched.

So if Aphrodite couldn't know about his plans, it meant he had to keep Psyche in the dark to some extent too.

Talk about "hating" something.

The idea of never showing himself to Psyche again hit harder than a kick to the kidneys. She deserved better than never knowing the name of the man who loved her, never seeing his face looking down upon her when she first opened her eyes in the morning.

But how long could a mortal keep his identity a secret? It was a risk he couldn't afford to take. No, he knew the only way to ensure Aphrodite didn't figure things out was to ensure Psyche herself never knew.

But then what did that mean - keeping himself a secret? How do you spend the rest of your life with someone and not know their real name? How do you avoid ever seeing their face?

He could blind Psyche, but that'd be torture for them both. Without her sight, she couldn't possibly be happy. She's never be able to read, or watch a play, or enjoy blooming flowers again. He wouldn't sacrifice so much of what she loved out of life for his own happiness.

That alone had to be a sure sign he was really in love -- Psyche's happiness mattered far more to him than his own. Eros almost smacked himself for being such a sap. But he couldn't be angry with himself when he thought of Psyche.

Retreating to the courtyard of his palace, he trained his second sight on Psyche. For the time, watching her was all he needed. The pulse of her lips as she spoke filled him; the flutter of her eyes restored him.

As the hours slipped by, servants scrambled to bring the god something to rouse him from his trance, but Eros couldn't be moved. All he wanted was to gaze at Psyche until he thought of a way to hold her without risking both their lives.

Life.

That's what he wanted with her. But how? How, when his mother had forbidden it? How, when Psyche despised him? How, when the way to get what he wanted involved tricking the only two women who mattered in his life?

As Eros looked on, a caravan of suitors approached the gates of Sikyon; nobles with their horses and wagons paraded up the hill from the port. A cold sheen of sweat coated Eros's brow. The threat of losing Psyche to someone else, *and* failing to carry out his mother's sentence, slapped his googly-eyed brain into motion. Finally, Eros knew what he had to do.

His first stop was Aphrodite's palace. Praise Zeus she was on vacation. She never let anyone *look* at the natural antidote to her powers, let alone *take* some if it. There'd be no way to explain what he was doing if she caught him helping himself to the potent waters. He filled two flasks from the Spring of Abstinence, surprisingly delighted by the thought that the suitors would enjoy a full month of absolutely no sense of love or lust. Usually he prided himself on inflicting such sweet torture, but perhaps a lack of passion was something even worse.

With his flasks filled, Eros disguised himself as an old servant and sped to the gates of Sikyon just as the suitors approached.

"Hail good Lords!" Eros called to the men. "My master, King Darion, awaits your arrival at his palace, but he knows you still have some distance to travel before you arrive. Please accept some water on behalf of the King to make the rest of your journey more comfortable."

"Now this is hospitality," one of the men said, brusquely snatching a flask from Eros's hand. After taking a long drink, he threw the flask to another of the nobles. "Krios, I don't remember you sending out water bearers when I came to visit you."

"Heh! You're lucky I even let you in my City."

"Lucky you let me in? You're the one who should be thanking me for gracing that rat hole with my presence."

"Oh yeah, I almost forgot," Krios replied. "Your great grandfather's second cousin's uncle was related by marriage to a god. Why, you're practically a god yourself."

While the barbs flew, the suitors passed the flasks

between themselves, laughing and drinking.

When they'd emptied the flasks, the suitors continued on their way to the palace, never looking back at the aged servant who'd already disappeared.

CHAPTER 10 — PSYCHE

The afternoon following my dream, I snatched a glimpse out my window to see a line of suitors marching toward us. For once, Mother's skepticism was misplaced. My dream was a good prophecy that was coming true already.

I watched as no less than a dozen kings and princes bore through the mob and were welcomed into our home. After a while, Maia came and told me the men had caravanned together from the port of Corinth. She also told me -- in no uncertain terms -- that my parents wanted me to stay in my room until they sent for me. They were planning a banquet and Maia was under strict orders to keep me hidden until then.

As if waiting to lay eyes on me would somehow add to my allure or something.

I rolled my eyes and thought of trying to slip past her out of sheer defiance, but that wouldn't get me anywhere. No doubt Mother had elaborate plans for tonight and I didn't want to be the one to ruin them.

But the waiting made me anxious. By the time the sun was low in the sky, I'd tried on nearly every dress in my wardrobe and had Maia redo my hair three different times before she finally had to leave to help Mother prepare. I wasn't sure why I even cared what I looked like. My sister was gone and I hadn't heard from Aphrodite in days. If getting myself married first was a game, I'd already lost. What was the point in continuing to play? Other than, as Mother said, to solidify an alliance for our City?

Someone stop me from fainting; the sheer romance of it all might overwhelm me.

When darkness finally arrived, Maia came back to my room.

"Everything is ready, child," she told me. "But if I may be so bold as to add one thing." Maia pulled a golden laurel wreath from behind her back. The crown sparkled even in the dimness of the oil lamps. Each leaf was different, with veins laid in silver, and tiny diamonds resting on some of the leaves like dew. I knew the crown even before she spoke. It was the one my mother had worn when she married my father.

"She wants you to wear this tonight." Without saying another word, Maia expertly wound my upswept curls around the crown. She stepped back to study her handiwork and smiled. "It doesn't do you justice, but it'll do just the same."

I threw my arms around her neck. "You're too good to me, Maia. What would we do without you?"

"I suppose you'll learn how to manage if you go running off marrying one of these oafs." She studied me with as much pride as if I were her own daughter. "You shouldn't be so hard on yourself, you know?"

The smile she'd encouraged out of me wilted. She was wrong. I'd been a horrible friend to my sister, kept secrets from my family. If anything, I wasn't being hard enough on myself. The crown suddenly felt too heavy, the leaves poking at my scalp like javelins as I shook my head "no."

"She'll never forgive me, Maia."

She lifted my chin with a crooked finger, leaving me no choice but to meet her eyes. "You're sisters. Nothing's more important than family and Chara will realize that soon."

I pushed at the crown, which felt like it was constricting my head. Thinking hurt my brain; but *feeling* was worse. I couldn't bear the feeling that my sister would never speak to me again. My mind was spinning through a mantra of "I can't do this anymore" when Maia squeezed my hand and led me to the door.

"Now get out of here. There's nothing worse than showing up late for your own party."

As she shooed me from my room, I saw that our courtyard had been transformed into a glowing celebration. Oil lamps cast their dancing light over the guests. Servants were pouring wine into onyx goblets and some of the suitors were already swaying. The courtyard was full of talk and laughter and life.

After the emptiness of my room, it all felt surreal.

When I reached the threshold, Father came to my side and linked elbows with me. What probably looked like a friendly escort to everyone else felt like an iron clamp. "You see how hard your mother worked to prepare your party?" he said in his deepest whisper. It wasn't a question so much as a threat -- *don't you dare ruin this night for her.*

I nodded and he patted my hand. "Glad we understand each other, then." He led me to the musicians and ordered them to stop playing.

The abrupt end to the music got everyone's attention. "Excuse me, gentlemen," my father said. "I first would like to thank you for making such a long journey to be with us tonight. While you, my friends, are always welcome in my home, I know it's not me you've come to see. I would like you to meet my daughter, and now Aphrodite's daughter," (that got a round of knowing chuckles) "Psyche. She'll come around to meet each of you in person and I'm sure you will find her as engaging as she is beautiful. In the meantime, enjoy your wine and the food will be ready shortly."

Only because I'd spent months bowing to crowds was I able to function. The unfamiliar eyes on me, so close, so prodding, left me stripped and raw. The feeling of wanting to puke was becoming way too familiar.

But as the music started up again, I plastered a permanent smile on my face and met each of the suitors one by one. As I made my rounds, I tried to add to whatever discussion I happened to join. If the men were talking politics, I added in the latest news from our own Senate. If they were talking war, I analogized their battles to ones I'd read about in my scrolls.

There was a balance between acting like a know-it-all and letting them know I could discuss any subject that interested them. Actually, I enjoyed the challenge of finding something insightful or humorous to say about so many different topics. Despite the obvious implications of the evening, it turned out to be a better distraction from my worries than I'd hoped.

After I'd chatted with everyone, I knew only one of the men had really caught my attention: a young king, Krios of Tegea. He struck me as good-natured and more interested in me than himself. I lingered when we first met, and after my rounds were done, I returned to him so I could sit beside his couch during dinner.

The banquet may have been in my honor, but women didn't dine on couches in my home.

Pulling up a soft, leather tripod, I sat as close as I dared, hoping the other suitors would take the hint that I'd made my pick. Of course, the choice wasn't exactly mine to make.

As we ate, he told me about his city; the lush green mountains, the endless rows of olive trees, the twin rivers that always carried fresh, cool water, and the bountiful harvests that the hard-working farmers produced. The way he described it, I could already imagine myself at home there. I'd never needed a large city to keep me happy. In fact, separation from crowds would probably be a welcome delight. I wasn't sure his little City was exactly the "alliance" my parents were hoping for, but I was already dreaming of fading back into anonymity.

"It sounds perfect," I told him.

"Ah, Psyche. Perfect is sitting here beside me. But Tegea is a close second."

I looked down as a warm blush crept up into my cheeks.

"Tell me I haven't made you blush, Psyche," Krios teased, leaning closer. "Certainly you've received greater compliments than that before."

"Not from someone whose opinion actually matters."

Now it was Krios's turn to blush.

The banquet room was full of deafening chatter and the sounds of eating, but all I heard was the silence that hung between us. After a few moments, Krios finally said, "You might as well know this." I felt my cheeks fall slack as I braced for his attempt at a gentle let down. *Seriously, why was every man I was remotely interested in turning me away?*

Krios's eyes panned the crowd. "All of us rode out to meet you and your sister. I had hoped maybe I'd have a chance with Chara, but I never dreamed of marrying the great Psyche."

"I'm not *the great* Psyche," I cut in, grabbing Krios's hand.

"No, Psyche, listen. This is important. You deserve to know this. None of these men, including myself, came here to marry you." Krios paused to correct himself, his mouth twitching in a slight grimace. "Well, maybe at first we did, but something changed along the way. By the time we reached your palace, we agreed that none of us could take on the obligation of protecting you."

"Protecting me from what? My father hasn't had any problem looking out for me," I said, dropping Krios's hand.

Krios closed his eyes and exhaled. "I simply don't have the armies, Psyche. I can't afford a war for you." He added in an apologetic whisper, "None of us can."

Although I knew what he was talking about, I couldn't believe all of Greece was so consumed by fear of another Trojan War.

"I'm not Helen!" I stood up and shouted at Krios.

Conversation and eating came to a halt as all eyes turned to me. I felt the stares boring into my back as I loomed over Krios, gritting my teeth to keep from spitting out my accusations.

"You don't even know me, but you assume I'm the sort of person who'd run off with another man. Why? Because I have a pretty face? Because I'm Aphrodite's new daughter?" I balled my hands into fists to keep them from trembling at my side. "You have misjudged me. I'm as fiercely loyal as any woman you'll ever meet."

My father rushed to my side. "Psyche, no one is questioning your loyalty, or even Helen's. Helen was powerless to resist the will of Aphrodite."

"She's a goddess, not a puppet master," I shrieked, turning my outrage on my father. "I turned down her marriage choice once and I'll do it again if I have to."

Father's teeth audibly crunched when he clamped his jaws back together. Guess I'd forgotten to mention the whole Aphrodite-proposed-on-behalf-of-Eros thing. More damn secrets. I was over it.

Pushing past my father, I stormed to the center of the room. "My sister is gone and you don't want to marry me, so I assume you're just here to eat our food. Maybe hear a good story. Well how's this for gossip? Aphrodite asked me to marry her son, and I said no." I met each of their silent stares and patted my heart. "Yes, I refused an arrogant, pompous god because I knew, deep down, that one of you would be better. But apparently I was wrong." *Let that sink in for a minute.* "Can it really be that none of you are brave enough to take on a pretty wife?"

No one answered.

I faltered. The challenge hadn't worked and my father was bearing down on me now.

"Psyche, that's enough." My father spun me away from the men before handing me off to Maia, who'd rushed over as if on cue.

Speaking loud enough so that the entire room could hear, Father told Maia, "Psyche is obviously feeling ill. See that she gets the rest she needs."

As Maia led me away, I could hear my father apologizing for my outburst and explaining that I was overwhelmed by my sister departing so recently. Under normal circumstances, he promised, I would never be so bold and would be an obedient wife, very respectful, et cetera, et cetera.

But I knew he was wasting his words. Krios hadn't been lying to me. Why would he? He had nothing to gain from a lie. As I slowly climbed the steps to my room, I knew none of these men would be taking me home.

Which is a thought that should've brought relief. After all, I didn't want to be married yet. As I thought back on it, I didn't even know why I'd challenged those men to marry me. I already recognized it as a stupid burst of pride getting the better of me. So why was I so upset by the whole thing?

As I crossed into my room, it hit me. What if never finding a husband was Aphrodite's punishment for turning Eros away? I didn't necessarily want to get married now, I wanted it some day. A princess without a husband is nothing once her parents die. I'd probably have to rely on Chara just to survive. And how likely would she be to help?

70

Slumping on my bed, I studied my reflection in a hand mirror. Although the room was only lit by oil lamps, I could make out all of my features. I inspected every inch of my face, as if it was to blame for my long string of failures. But there was no flaw in the reflection. The flaw was inside me.

Shrieking in frustration, I threw the mirror into the stone wall at the far side of my room. The mirror shattered into tiny, jagged pieces that spewed across my floor.

Maia scurried to clean up the mess, but Mother stopped her. "You can leave us. She'll clean it up herself." I hadn't even heard Mother come in.

Maia lowered her head and fled the room, muttering apologies to my mother as she went. I turned and glared.

"So now I've gone from being the second-coming of Aphrodite to a servant girl?"

"You're lucky you don't end up homeless after that stunt you just pulled." She shook her head. "I never thought the distant attention would make you so brazen. Or maybe it's Aphrodite. Do you think you actually *are* her daughter now?"

"Of course not." I flopped back against my bed. "She hates me after refusing her son. I haven't seen her since the day of the announcement."

She paced the length of my room, muttering almost to herself. "Well that explains the lack of a proposal, at least. You angered the goddess of love and she's denying you a husband. It's pretty obvious."

I'm glad she thought so, because it'd taken me awhile to figure it out.

When she halted, her dark emerald eyes bore into me, full of anger and disappointment. "I used to think I knew you so well. But I don't get you at all anymore. It's like you've considered every reasonable action and then done exactly the opposite."

"Eros was a jerk and he talked to Aphrodite like she was a dish rag. If any of those men down there talked to you like that, I'd refuse to marry them too." I felt hot tears welling up in my eyes again.

"And if you mean tonight, I'm scared, okay? I'm pretty sure Aphrodite hates me after..." I pressed my fingertips against my eyes as I thought. "When Krios said none of the men would marry me, I panicked."

"Oh, Psyche," Mother sighed as she sank down next to me on the bed and wrapped me in her arms. "I know what it's like to be young and impulsive." She gave me an extra squeeze. "Trust me, I do. But at the end of the day, discretion is the better part of valor."

I cracked one eye open to peer at her and make it very clear I had no idea what she was talking about.

"Keep your mouth shut," she answered. "If you make a mistake, move on. Don't go spreading the news across Greece. It incites gossip and eventually hurts those you love the most."

My muddled brain knew enough to register that she was speaking from experience, but I didn't have the energy to pry. Instead, all I could think was how her advice was to continue keeping secrets when all I wanted to do was bare my soul.

"So tell me what to do now. I'm lost." I blinked and a warm, salty tear escaped. "I wrecked your party. I'm sure the whole Aphrodite thing is going to erupt soon. I just don't know what to do any more."

She pushed my hair back from my forehead and placed a kiss on my temple. "Sit patiently and wait for your father to return from Delphi. He's decided to consult the Oracle. We won't make any decisions until he gets back, deal?"

I nodded, not sure I could speak and hold back a flood of tears at the same time.

My father was going to Delphi to learn my fate. Not knowing what was going to happen to me was scary enough. Finding out I was going to know what fate lay in store for me brought sheer terror.

CHAPTER 11 — EROS

Eros stretched in satisfaction as he flew. Making sure the suitors couldn't be as captivated by Psyche as he'd been brought him an unexpected peace. Now, he just needed to find Hermes and finalize his plan.

But even for an experienced tracker like Eros, Hermes was too speedy to easily spot using just second sight. When he was unable to instantly track down his friend, Eros swooped in to Hermes's temple-of-choice. The imposing shrine overflowed with gold and marble statutes cast in the young god's likeness. Eros trotted up the stairs and toward the main chamber. In the far corner of the temple, one of the priests was removing the remnants of a meal and carting away a half-drunk pitcher of wine.

"You!" Eros barked. The priest dropped the ceramic pitcher. The crack as it exploded against the marble floor was tampered only by the dull splash of undrunk wine. "Where's your master?"

"He ju--ju--just left," the priest stammered.

"Where?" Eros growled. His newly-found tranquility was now as shattered as the pitcher. He had a deadline after all. Not that King Darion would reach Delphi for a few days, but if his plan wasn't set before then, it'd be too late.

"I don't know, my Lord. He got called away to escort an important shade to the Underworld, but I don't know who it is that died, or where."

"Damn!" Eros kicked at a chunk of pitcher, sending more wine spraying.

"If I may be so bold, you might try waiting at the Alcyonian Lake. Hermes will have to bring the shade there to catch a ferry to the Underworld."

Eros clenched his jaw and spoke through gritted teeth. "I don't have time to wait."

Dropping his head, the priest mumbled, "Of course, my Lord."

"You're excused now." Eros exhaled. It was true: he didn't have time to wait. But since his second sight wasn't working, he didn't have other options either.

When he arrived, the shores of the lake were empty. Eros couldn't tell whether Hermes had come and gone, or if he still had yet to arrive. For the remainder of the day, Eros paced along the bank, still scanning unsuccessfully for Hermes. The descending sun pulled a misty blanket in its wake, covering the lake in a thick, hazy shroud of fog.

In the comfort of the night, Eros kneeled on the shore and cupped the cool water in his hand. The liquid slipped back through his long fingers as he moved them slowly apart. He absentmindedly dipped his hand and strained the water several more times, deciding whether it would be safe to take a drink.

The Alcyonian Lake fed the rivers flowing into Hades, but did the waters flow back out? Sure, he'd heard rumors that once you drank from the lake, you'd be condemned to the Underworld, but Eros was immortal. The water couldn't possibly hurt him. Besides, the late spring afternoon had been hot.

Unseasonably hot.

Eros dipped his cupped hands into the pool. He pursed his lips together to sip, when a cracked voice called out from the misty darkness.

"I wouldn't do that if I were you." Eros dropped the water back into the lake reflexively. "Of course, I'm not you, so drink up." The voice cackled out a series of gruff laughs that gave way to a fit of coughing.

Eros squinted into the haze, wishing his eyesight were better at night. He wasn't afraid, but his skin still crawled with an eerie prickle.

As Eros stared into the fog, he began to make out the skeletal figure of a ferryman coming closer. The ancient man's skin stretched across his bones, unsupported by muscle or meat. His long nose protruded from his face like a hooked beak, while his eyes sunk into their sockets. A mess of grayish hair, caked with sweat and grime, clung to the sides of his bony scalp. With great effort, the man plunged his staff into the water ahead, sinking into the soft bottom of the lake, and lurching the ferry forward.

Eros had never met Charon before, but this had to be him. The ferryman of Hades, who moved souls from the shores of life into the depths of the Underworld. For a small fee of course. Nothing in life -- or death -- was free.

"Where's your coin, boy?" Charon called out.

Boy? Had Charon just called him boy? Eros rose up to his full height and spread his wings behind him. The show of bravado only made Charon laugh again.

"You'd better take care who you mock, old man."

"Or what? There's nothing you can do to me.

You gods *need* me."

"Fool. The gods don't need you." Eros took a step closer, daring the old man not to back down. "*I* don't need you."

"Ha! If I didn't ferry the dead down to Hades, your precious earth would be overrun with shades. What would become of your playground then? I'd like to see you try to woo a woman with all of her dead family standing around watching."

Charon cackled again, and then his thin, pale lips curled into a smile. "Besides, boy, you do need something from me. Some information, perhaps?"

Eros glared at Charon. He kept his gaze icy while trying to assess whether he could ask about Hermes. Charon held his stare, refusing to look away.

"Go on, boy, ask me. Ask me what you want to know."

"What will it cost me?"

"So you are clever. Never mind my fee this time. Your mother will be paying my toll soon enough."

Eros lunged at the old ferryman. "How dare you threaten my mother's life."

Charon pulled away, faster than Eros had given him credit for, and Eros splashed into the lake, soaking the ends of his tunic.

"It's no threat, boy. There's no force on Earth or Olympus that could kill that woman. But I expect she'll be sending someone my way soon enough, and that will be all the fee I require."

"You collect gold, not souls," Eros accused. He didn't trust Charon or his promise to answer a question for free.

"I could build a staircase to Olympus with all the coins I've collected. What can they buy me? Can they buy me freedom from this unending toil? Can they buy me repose in a magnificent palace? Can they buy me the love of a beautiful woman?"

Eros suddenly saw the human frailty of Charon. A weakness he could exploit. Of course, like everyone else, Charon wanted love, didn't he?

"Is it love you want? You needn't wait for my mother. Just ask me."

Charon broke out into his coughing laugh again, practically choking himself. His full weight bore down on the staff as he struggled to keep from falling over. Charon finally coughed out, "Love? Love is for fools, boy. I've just tired of seeing the shades of the old, decrepit and diseased. I want a face to light up the gloom. *The* face..."

The weight of Charon's words crushed into Eros's chest. "You will not have Psyche."

"You can't stop your mother, boy. She'll send Psyche to the Underworld one way or another. You mark my words."

"I'll make you pay for those words," Eros snarled from behind clenched teeth.

"Your mother already has paid for them," Charon replied. "And so now I'll answer your question. Hermes isn't here. He hasn't come this way yet. Of course, I do expect him in the next two, three, maybe even four days."

Eros stared at Charon in steely silence, his fists clenched into tight balls at his side. He struggled to keep his breathing at an even pace while fighting the urge to tear Charon's head off of its puny neck.

"I see you've grown tired of my visit," Charon said. "Perhaps I better take my leave."

With a few swift strokes of his staff, Charon dissolved into the mist.

CHAPTER 12 — EROS

Eros barely slept that night. He crawled up into the branches of a tree nearest the gates to Hades and wrapped his thick, white wings around himself. The spring night wasn't cold, but an uncomfortable chill seeped into his bones.

Every noise broke his fragile slumber. He didn't dare sleep through any sound for fear he'd miss catching Hermes before he handed the shade over to Charon and left again. But Hermes didn't come -- that night or the next. Eros's time was ticking away and there was nothing he could do but wait.

He obsessively looked in on King Darion and his progress toward Delphi. If Eros was right, the king would reach Delphi in less than a day. The seas had been gentle and the winds swift. *Of course they had. Aphrodite was out dancing on the waves. Sailors were always in luck when she played in the ocean.* But even still, Darion made faster time than Eros predicted.

If he couldn't get Hermes's help with his plan in time, Darion would receive a true prophecy from the Oracle. When Eros agreed to make Psyche fall in love with a wretch, her fate had been written in the stars. And if the Oracle foretold that destiny, Eros would be powerless to change it.

He'd have to make her love another.

With mere hours before time would run out,

Eros had worked himself into a frenzied state of panic. He felt his hold on reality slipping, thinking he heard sounds that were never made and saw visions that never existed. Which is why when Eros heard two men fighting in the distance, he questioned whether his ears were tricking him again. But the men moved closer and the sounds of their skirmish grew louder.

"You don't know who you're talking to. Get your hands off of me."

"I don't care who you *were*, you're dead now. D-E-A-D; dead! The sooner you accept that you're a shade now, the better."

Eros could hear one of the men grunt and strain.

"Senator, let go of that tree. You're going into Hades if I have to drag you all the way there myself." Eros knew that had to be Hermes, arriving with the important shade at last.

Then Eros heard a light clang, like a coin being tossed against a rock, and then a plink as it plopped into the lake.

"Oh, now why'd you go and do that? You need that coin to give to Charon."

The shade sounded exuberant. "Exactly! No coin, no ferry ride. I'm not going anywhere."

"Yes ... you ... are." Hermes dragged the shade by his elbow toward the bank of the lake.

This is it, Eros thought. *He's here.* Eros launched toward his friend, "Hermes! Hermes, I need a favor from you."

Hermes shoved the shade at Eros. "Hold this senile old fool while I get his coin back." Hermes plodded into the water, peering below the ripples for the coin.

"Hermes, didn't you hear me? My life is at stake here."

"Just a minute," Hermes murmured, still searching.

"I don't have a minute," Eros snapped. He looked over the water for a moment, then reached down and plucked out the coin. He slapped the coin into the shade's hand. "You will hold on to your coin."

"Thanks," Hermes said. "This guy's been nothing but trouble. I can't convince him he's dead. You wouldn't believe what he pulled on the way here ..."

"Hermes," Eros cut in. "I'm sorry this guy's been a problem, but I need your help. Now."

Hermes studied his friend and wagged his thick eyebrows. "Have you played another trick on Zeus again? If you want me to hide your arrows from him until he calms down, I'm not sure even I can fly fast enough."

"No, no. It's not Zeus who's after me. It'll be my mother if I'm not careful, and I'd rather have a hundred Zeuses mad at me than one Aphrodite."

"How'd you manage to cross your mother?"

"It's sort of a long story. I'll tell you while we take this guy to Charon." As they walked, the shade in tow, Eros explained.

"I'm not even sure what happened really," Eros said. "One minute I was standing there, about to shoot Psyche and the next minute ... I just couldn't do it." He rubbed his temples with the tips of his fingers. "Being near her was intoxicating or something."

"Tell me this doesn't end how I think it ends."

82

Hermes stopped walking and glared incredulously at his friend.

Eros looked down at his dusty sandals. "When I lowered my arrow, I nicked my knee."

Hermes shrugged his shoulders and looked at Eros like he was an idiot. "What, did you miss the how-not-to-impale-yourself-with-your-own-arrow lesson? How on Earth did you shoot yourself?"

Eros huffed. "I just told you. She bewitched me or something."

"You expect me to believe a mortal made you lose your hand-eye coordination? I think something else is going on here." Hermes studied him. "Are you just trying to get back at Aphrodite for being a harpy your whole life? Because I don't need to be on the wrong side of her either."

Eros took a step back and his shoulders slumped. "Fine, you want the truth? Yes. Yes, a mortal made me love her." He closed his eyes, remembering. "Psyche's soul sang to me like a siren. Somehow I knew I needed to choose her and I did."

Hermes turned and started walking again. "Then un-choose her. Just get your mommy to undo the magic. You don't need me for that."

"You don't understand," Eros called, rushing back to Hermes's side. "I need her now. I don't want this undone. I want her."

Hermes stopped short. "Listen to me. Let it go. She's just a girl."

"No way," Eros shook his head. "She's more than that. She's everything."

"You're serious?" Hermes asked, his arched

eyebrow implying he was more than skeptical.

Eros nodded. Hermes only looked away, shaking his head.

"Please, Hermes, I need this."

"Fine, what'd you want me to do?"

"I need your help with the last part of my plan. I was able to divert Psyche's suitors by having them drink from the Spring of Abstinence before they could reach her palace, but --"

Hermes interrupted. "Psyche's suitors? You gave chastity water to Psyche's suitors?"

Eros's brow wrinkled. "Yeah. So?"

"Those men made offerings and prayed to me to keep them safe on their journey to Sikyon. How am I supposed to help you now?"

"What's your problem? I gave them a little water. They'll never know the difference."

Hermes shook his head. "Negative. You ruined the whole point of their trip."

"Come on. Lighten up a little, buddy."

"I'm serious, Eros. Travelers are some of my most devoted followers. If you betrayed them, I can't help you."

Eros buckled. He'd come so far; waited so long. For what? This couldn't end like this. He had to have Psyche.

Dropping down to his knees, Eros grasped Hermes's cloak and looked up at him. "Hermes, I am begging you. No, I'm praying to you, as a traveler who's journeyed to the gates of the Underworld to find you. You can't turn your back on me. I will be your most devoted servant. I'll --"

"He's asking so nicely, you really ought to help him," the shade cut in. "I always used my position on the Senate to help people."

Hermes shot him an icy look that said "shut up and mind your own business."

Then he sighed loudly as his head fell back. "This is pitiful. Get up, you love-struck idiot." Hermes wrenched his cloak free from Eros's hands. "Besides, I don't want a fool for a servant. Psyche can have you."

Eros clambered back to his feet. "You'll help me then?"

Hermes smiled. "I'm tempted not to just because I like seeing you squirm with love instead of it being the other way around."

Eros's mouth tightened into a line as his usually full lips pressed together. "I suppose I deserve that," he said as he folded his arms across his chest.

Hermes sucked his teeth with a smack. "Oh, stop being such a girl. What is it you want?"

Eros pulled a folded piece of parchment from under his tunic and pressed it into Hermes's hand. "I need you to carry this message to Apollo. But you can't tell him it's from me. He'd never agree to help me himself."

Hermes snorted. "That's the truth. I don't think he'll ever get over the time you used your arrows on him."

"But he'll help you. You're his brother."

"Half-brother," Hermes corrected.

"You're changing the subject. Are you going to help me or not?"

"I already told you I would," Hermes said. "What

exactly do you want me to tell my half-brother?"

Eros rolled his eyes. "Just give him the note. Tell him you had a vision of Psyche's future and you want the Oracle to give Darion your prophecy."

Hermes just blinked at Eros. Even the shade shifted uncomfortably.

"Come on," Eros said. "It's not much different from what Apollo would foretell himself. He'll believe you had this vision."

"So let me get this straight. You want me to tell my brother, Mr. Overlord of the Future, that I had a random prediction about some princess and he should let me use his precious Oracle to try my hand at the whole fortunetelling thing. Really?"

Eros gritted his teeth. "You're not exactly selling it when you say it like that."

Hermes clapped his hand to his forehead and closed his eyes. "I'm just giving you a reality check, man. There's no way Apollo's going to go for this."

Eros turned his gaze away from Hermes for a moment and let his eyes glaze over as he used his vision to look in on King Darion. As quickly as he had looked away, Eros's eyes snapped back to his friend.

"If you don't hurry, we'll never know whether Apollo will go for it or not. Darion's ships have landed at Delphi."

Shaking his head, Hermes eyed his friend. "You're crazy. You know that, right?"

"Please, Hermes. Please."

"Fine. I'm leaving," Hermes said. "You're in charge of the shade. Don't leave here until he gets onto the ferry."

CHAPTER 13 — PSYCHE

The waiting was excruciating. I wished my parents had let me sail along with my father to Delphi. I could've consulted Apollo's Oracle myself. Why should I have to stay home when it was my future hanging in the balance? Besides, sailing the Gulf of Corinth and visiting Delphi would've been a much-needed diversion.

Anything was better than waiting.

My mind ran endlessly over different scenarios that might play out when Father returned. I knew there was a good chance he'd come home with bad news. He might learn I was destined never to have a husband as I'd feared.

Or the Oracle might just tell my father to start planning my funeral. Aphrodite was known to have torn men to shreds for lesser crimes than personal insults.

At this point, I wasn't sure which would be worse.

To settle my swirling mind, I read everything I could about the Oracle. About the girls who became the oracle, trading their lives for a chance to know the divine.

As I read, I could almost picture her. She would be a noble girl. Not a princess, of course, but still pretty high up. After spending all of her young life in service to Apollo, she'd be selected to become Apollo's highest priestess, the Pythia, when the Pythia before her died. She wouldn't have had to wait very long. Serving Apollo at such a high level took its toll on all of them. No one selected as Pythia lived for very long after her service started.

And yet these girls did it anyway. Going willingly into service for the god. Delivering Apollo's predictions to the Greeks who came to have their fortunes told. Once named Pythia, the girl wasn't allowed to have any more connection to her family, her friends or her former life. Whatever her name had been, she would be known only as Pythia until her death.

How completely opposite was that girl from me? She had no contact with family but met with the world. I had only contact with family while keeping the world at bay. She was loved by a god and I was now hated by a goddess.

I guessed we had one thing in common though: I was eerily afraid neither one of us would live much longer.

CHAPTER 14 — EROS

Eros could do nothing but watch as he sat with the shade, waiting for Charon to show up and lug the old man down to Hades. He saw Hermes deliver the message to Apollo, but Apollo hadn't said anything. He'd just scowled a lot.

Damn it.

Eros would have to wait for the prophecy to find out if Apollo had gone for his plan. Now that he knew his message had been delivered, Eros willed Darion to hurry up.

As if obeying Eros's silent command, Darion sought out Apollo's priests as soon as he made landfall and presented his offering. He'd brought an ornately jeweled lyre in tribute to the god. Eros shook his head as he looked on. Mortals were so predictable. Bring Apollo a lyre -- no one's ever done that before.

Still, the priests were impressed by the show of wealth, and Darion moved to the front of the line instead of having to draw lots to determine his place. Darion approached the temple with measured steps, carrying the lyre on outstretched arms before him. He looked as if he expected the god to reach down and personally accept the gift. But as he stood in the shadow of the massive temple, Darion's fleshy arms began to weaken. He was forced to present his tribute at the base of the temple. Like everyone else.

After leading a procession of supplicants to a side entrance of the temple, Darion descended into the Sanctuary of the Oracle. The room was dark and damp, the flickering lanterns barely illuminating the cavern. Its silence was punctuated only by trickles from the stream running through channels in the floor.

Darion approached the screen separating him from the Pythia and placed his hand against the coarse fabric. Eros shared Darion's anguish. The girl on the other side of that screen held both their worlds in her hands. Darion's forehead dipped until it too pressed against the screen. Eros held his breath.

A priest cleared his throat nearby. "Sire, the Pythia is waiting. You need to ask your question."

Darion raised his head, but didn't back away from the screen. His voice cracked when he spoke. "Pythia, sacred maiden of Apollo, I come to learn the fate of my daughter, Psyche. What lies in store for her?"

The Pythia sat silently on her tripod, pinching laurel leaves between her soft fingers and gazing into a cauldron of still water. Slowly, deeply, she inhaled the vapors rising from a crevice in the earth. Her low-ceilinged chamber filled with the intoxicating scent of the god, swirling around her, inviting her to taste immortality. The light, tinkling sound of the sacred stream filled the cavern as she waited to receive Apollo's message.

The Pythia began to sway as she balanced on her tripod. Her arms stretched out to the sides, palms up, letting the leaves fall away. Seconds ticked by and Eros felt his heart thud its every beat in his chest. Suddenly, the Pythia erupted in a peal of laughter, throwing her head back with such abandon she would've tumbled from her stool if an alert priest hadn't caught her.

"Get ready," the priest whispered to Darion. "It's coming."

Eyes rolled back in her head and panting, the Pythia breathed out her prophecy. Foretold Psyche's future.

Darion dropped to his knees as the Pythia collapsed into the priest's waiting arms.

CHAPTER 15 — PSYCHE

More than two weeks after my father departed for Delphi, the sounds of marching woke me from a restless sleep. It didn't take long for the haze to fade. Marching could only mean one thing. I ran to my window and saw Father's troops escorting their king to the palace door.

I didn't bother to dress before tearing out of my room and flying down the stairs to greet him. He was just coming through the door when I flung my arms around him.

"Father, you're home! You made it. What did she say?"

I felt like a child again, clinging to my dad and begging for a treat. Only when I paused to breathe did I finally notice his expression.

He didn't answer me. Instead, he wrapped his arms around me and pulled me into his chest. His chin rested on the top of my head as he slowly stroked my hair. I drew back a little and looked up into his eyes. Father's amber eyes usually sparkled with life, but today they were dull, empty. He tilted his head back and blinked, an obvious effort to keep the tears pooling in the corners of his eyes from spilling. I'd never seen my father even come close to tears before. The sight of him like that made me tremble.

"What is it? Tell me what she said." My pleas

were barely more than a whisper.

After a long pause, he said, "We should get your mother first."

"I'm here." Her voice cracked as she called out from a shadow in the foyer. Neither of us had noticed her silently enter. I could tell by her expression that she too already knew the news was bad.

Father extended an arm and she rushed to join our embrace. We stood that way, the three of us together, for what seemed like hours. It was like we believed that as long as we were together, the Oracle couldn't touch us. That we'd be immune from the destiny already laid out before us.

I was the first to pull away. "Knowing nothing is worse than knowing the truth. Just tell me." Father didn't answer me still. My voice exploded with desperation and panic. "Father, please!"

He closed his eyes and sucked in a deep breath. Slowly, he recited the message he'd received from the Pythia.

> *Dress Psyche in her blackest mourning cloth,*
> *And leave her on the craggy mountain top.*
> *Her lover is not born of human blood,*
> *But is as dire and fierce a serpent as may be sought.*
> *He flies with wings above in starry skies,*
> *Conquering even gods who seem so wise.*
> *On his whim all creatures fall in pain,*
> *With him always Psyche shall remain.*

The blood drained from my face so quickly that my cheeks turned numb. I'd been right to suspect that Aphrodite hated me. But this I hadn't seen coming.

Love and passion were her tools; her blessing or

her curse. The one possibility I'd never considered was clearly the worst fate imaginable. I'd have traded death for life in the arms of a monster. Or maybe certain death was what awaited me in those arms -- the prophecy did say to dress me in funeral garb.

My head reeled as I tried to wrap my mind around the Pythia's words. I pictured a massive serpent, coiling its scaly body around my ankles and folding me into an embrace in its oily, jet black wings. I saw its face rising slowly to look at me with slitted, yellow eyes before darting out a slithery, forked tongue toward my lips.

The last thing I remember before the room went dark was hearing myself scream.

***

I don't know how long I was out, but I felt strangely calm when I woke. When I opened my eyes, I was looking up into my mother's tear-stained face. She was cradling my head in her lap and stroking the long coils of my hair.

"Psyche," she whispered. "I ... it shouldn't be you having to go. I wish it were me."

"It's okay, Mom." I sat up and turned to face her, but she couldn't meet my gaze. I watched helplessly as she began to shake and sobs overcame her. Then she fell forward into my lap and wept. I couldn't do anything except stroke her hair as she had done mine.

When she was cried out and finally stopped shaking, she sniffed and looked at me. Her eyes were red-rimmed, and for the first time, those eyes gave away her age. She looked older and less alive to me. My heart broke as I looked into her eyes and understood that she was already mourning me as if I were dead.

"Don't, please. I'm not gone yet."

"You're right." She grasped my hand in hers. "We'll fix this. There's got to be something we can do."

I simply shook my head, unwilling to crush her hopes with my words.

"No," she protested, wringing my fingers harder. "We'll call in the army to guard the palace. The beast will never make it past. You won't have to go. We can stop this, Psyche. We can stop this." Her words were so rushed. I'd never seen her this frantic before.

"Shhh," I hushed, pulling her into my arms. "You're going to make yourself sick. I hate seeing you like this."

"We've got to try." Her broken voice nearly choked on another sob.

"No," I whispered. "You're the one who always told me: *You cannot escape what is destined.*"

Chapter 16 — Psyche

I never thought I'd see my own funeral. But less than two days after my father returned from Delphi, that's exactly where I found myself.

The wheels of the wagon cart jostled me over the rough stone roads as we made our way south to the top of the craggy hills that lay beyond the City gates. We left the palace before dawn, surrounded in blackness. I tasted blood as I chewed and shredded the inside of my cheek.

With every bounce of the cart I could feel the rough black shroud I wore scrape against my skin. The predawn air was too cool for such a thin dressing, causing an involuntary shudder to crawl up my spine like a spider. The golden hoops in my ears and around my neck felt too heavy. As I locked my grasp on the edges of the cart for balance, the weathered wood splintered and ground into my hands.

At the front of the procession, the hired mourners played shrill and sorrowful music on their flutes. Of course I knew the music. I'd been to funerals before. But something about the songs this time were even more grating. A painful reminder of the death-like fate that awaited me at the top of the hill.

Mixed with the flutes were the mournful wails of my family. Walking just behind the cart, my mother moaned and wailed; pitiful sounds that didn't even form words.

My father and male cousins marched ahead of the cart. They too lamented, uttering low moans over and over. With them, they led a massive black bull that would be sacrificed as part of the funeral ritual. His hooves, combined with the footsteps of the two mules that pulled my cart, created a rhythmic drum beat tying all of the other horrific sounds together.

I could smell the livestock ahead of me, a rancid mixture of old hay and manure. The thick, dank odor of the oil lamps leading the procession wafted back, stinging my nose with every breath. Second to these pungent aromas, but present nonetheless, was the slightly sweet smell drifting up from the honey cake that sat precariously on my lap.

Because the Pythia's prophecy was so vague, we weren't sure if I was actually facing death, or if my fate would simply be as dire as death. In any case, my father had insisted I carry the cake in case I did find death at the top of the hill. I would need the honey cake to feed Cerberus, the three-headed dog who guarded the Underworld. No shade passed him by unless they distracted him with food. I also had a coin to pay Charon -- just in case.

As my procession neared the top of the hill, the sun began to rise. It glowed so brilliantly it was almost white, surrounded by an aura of red and orange. Outside of the brilliant glow, the remainder of the sky was a milky purple, like no color I'd ever seen in the heavens before. As I stared at the sky in awe, a massive eagle soared across the horizon, drifting from left to right. I knew both the eagle and its course foretold good luck, but I didn't dare place my hope on the wings of a bird.

My cart came to a sudden stop at the top of the bluff. I looked down from where I sat to see my mother racing up from behind the procession. She groped for my hand until she held it tight, but she was trembling. Her face was matted with dust and dirt that had caked on her tear-soaked face.

I looked back to the beautiful morning sky to steel my courage and then climbed down from the cart, careful not to drop my honey cake or coin. Mother wrapped me in her arms and began sobbing on my shoulder. I wanted to cry with her, but I was too numb for the tears to come.

Eventually I pushed her away and passed her off to Maia. I knew she would hold Mother until the world ended if that's what she needed.

I'm not sure I even knew where I was going, but I pressed forward through the crowd of mourners until I reached the head of the procession.

Father had just sacrificed the black bull. Its blood surged from the slit in its throat and spilled over the rocky ground, eventually pooling around my sandals. Reaching down, I stroked the dead animal's massive head. I was sorry it had to give its life so that I could be properly buried -- or whatever was about to happen.

Father handed off his knife to one of the other mourners and turned to me. He cupped my face in both his hands. The tears he had worked so hard to hold back two days ago spilled freely down his face.

His pain broke my numbness and hot tears of my own bubbled up and slipped down my cheeks.

"Goodbye, Father," I whispered.

"I'll stay with you until it comes," he answered. The pain in his voice was obvious.

"No, please go. You don't need to see this."

My father dropped his head and shook it side to side in protest.

"Please," I insisted. "I want you to have happier memories of me."

Father looked into my eyes for the longest time. It was as if he were searching my soul to see if I could do this alone. At last, he pulled me into a tight embrace and covered my forehead and cheeks with kisses.

"You'll never know how sorry I am, Psyche. I wish I'd paid more attention; counseled you better. You don't deserve to die for your mistakes."

"Don't. Please don't do this." I shook his shoulders gently and squeezed. "You can't blame yourself for my choices. And Mom needs you to be strong for her right now, okay?" Giving him a pep talk actually made me feel better somehow.

His eyes scrunched closed and his forehead was wrinkled in anguish. "I love you," he whispered.

I stood up on my toes and kissed his cheek. "I love you too, Daddy. Now go. I need to meet my fate alone."

Slowly, he released my hands and backed away. When our fingertips fell apart, I knew that was the last time I would ever feel him again.

I watched him and the procession depart for only a moment before I turned my back on them all and looked out over the horizon.

The sun had climbed higher in the sky and the

red-orange hue was nearly faded away. In its place was a steely bluish-gray. Then the wind picked up, swirling my shroud around my legs. My hair whipped, slapping my face and sticking to my wet lashes.

As I pulled a strand of hair from my mouth, I saw what looked like a wet cloud descending on me. The cloud swooped behind me and caught me like a cushion as a gust of wind blew me backward. Suddenly, I was in the air and flying out over the edge of the hill. I hadn't even had time to scoop up my coin or honey cake before being launched into the sky. I looked down as we flew and knew that if I fell, I'd be dead.

I really wished I'd held on tighter to that coin and cake.

The cloud swooped into the valley below. When we neared the ground, the cloud dropped me so quickly that I didn't have time to get my feet planted. I fell face forward into the dirt and scrambled to roll over. Pushing myself up onto my elbows, my heart thundered as I readied myself for the monster's attack.

I even thought I might be ready to fight.

But no fight came and no attacker appeared. Instead, I heard a low, booming voice that seemed to come from all around me.

"It has been my pleasure to escort you to your new home. Your palace awaits."

Looking back over my shoulder, I saw a palace so magnificent it made me gasp. The alabaster walls were blindingly white. Even without the sun's rays, they sparkled as if encrusted with a million diamonds. And the roof was the purest gold, glistening like no drop of rain had ever fallen on its eaves.

Each of the massive columns supporting the roof was an intricately carved figure. Some were beautiful women, with their dresses billowing around them. Others were athletic young men displaying their muscled torsos. The two center columns, leading to the massive entrance doors, each had two figures. On one, a man and a woman were locked in an embrace, staring deeply into each others' eyes. On the other, the couple was kissing in a gentle and soulful way.

It took me awhile to process the sheer enormity and beauty of what I was seeing. I can't even say how long it was that I sat there staring awe-struck at the palace.

When I finally came back to my senses, I told the invisible voice, "Are you who I'm supposed to be meeting here?" I thought that sounded considerably better than are you the one holding me prisoner?

The voice laughed as loud as thunder. "No, my lady. I am but your humble servant. You may call me Zephyrus, or simply the West Wind."

I should've been shocked at having a discussion with air particles. Instead, I asked, "My servant? Does that mean you can carry me back home?"

"No," he answered. "I serve you only because I serve him. He would not appreciate my stealing you away."

I'd known even before asking that the answer would be "no." Still, I twitched my nose to hold back the fresh tears I felt coming on.

"Do not despair, Psyche," he said, and then was gone. As Zephyrus left, the haze that had filled the valley lifted as quickly as if it was being pulled away on the tail of a comet. The sun now radiated all around me and the magnificent palace that lay before me glittered invitingly.

Which reminded me of another one of Mother's sayings: if something appears too good to be true, it probably is.

CHAPTER 17 — PSYCHE

I looked around the valley for escape, but there was nowhere to run. Up behind me was the impossibly sheer cliff I'd just been standing on. Ahead of me lay the palace. And all around was thick, dark forest. The trees looked so tightly woven together that I wasn't even sure I could pass through them, much less run away.

Besides, why run now? I'd accepted my fate. I told myself there was no more cause for alarm walking toward this palace than there was looking out over the hilltop and waiting for death. If the palace was some sort of opulent trap, so be it. There had to be worse places to die.

Moving to the entrance, I paused in front of the palace doors. Solid gold and tall as trees, they were decorated with a gem-encrusted garden scene. Flowers of rubies and sapphires bloomed amidst beds of emeralds. If nothing else, I couldn't complain about the exterior of the place.

I lifted my fist to rap on the door, but then pulled it back. Was I supposed to knock? If this was going to be my home, then knocking wasn't really necessary. Still, I couldn't imagine just barging into this palace like I owned it. I lifted my hand again, but the door swung open before I could touch it.

"Greetings, my lady. We've been expecting you."

I peered inside the door and all around the palace

hall, but no one was there. At least, no one I could see.

Then a strong hand took hold of my forearm and steered me inside. "Don't be frightened. Come in." Whoever it was, he was apparently invisible.

The massive door pushed shut behind me and the sound of it closing echoed through the seemingly endless hall. My chest constricted with the painful thought that I'd just been sealed inside the world's most elaborate tomb.

"I'm Mathias," the voice told me. "You may call on me for anything you need." His hand was still wrapped around my arm and he guided me further inside.

Too dumbstruck by everything that was happening, I couldn't even respond. The deeper into the palace we walked, the more elaborate it became. The walls were covered in impossibly detailed tapestries of gods and creatures romping through forests and swimming in rivers. The mosaics on the floors were made of tiles barely bigger than a pearl.

We stopped walking when we reached a sitting room. Awash in the morning light, the space glowed with warmth. Couches overflowed with silky pillows and wool blankets dyed in creamy yellows and soft oranges and juicy limes. It was if summer had arrived early and was welcoming me into the folds of its cozy arms. In a million years I couldn't have dreamt up a room that suited me more perfectly.

I slid onto a couch and sank into the pillows, drawn to the enticing oblivion of comfort. And sleep. I didn't think I'd slept since Father had returned with the prophecy.

"Forgive my intrusion," Mathias said, "but perhaps you might enjoy a warm bath before napping in your room."

I looked down at myself and immediately wrinkled my nose. I was still wearing the horrible black shroud and my skin was covered in dust and dirt from the wagon ride.

"Sorry," I said, clambering back to my feet, "I didn't mean to get the couch dirty."

No sooner had I spoken the words than a beautiful female voice spoke up. "No worries. All you need is a nice soak in the tub. I have everything ready."

The invisible person behind the pretty little voice eagerly grabbed my hand and began leading me away. The palace was a maze of hallways, alcoves and rooms.

"I can't tell you how excited I am to have you here. We're *all* excited, of course. But I'm really excited. It'll be so much more fun now that you're here. And trust me, you're going to love this place."

This invisible girl talked *way* too fast for my bewildered brain. I just nodded and let her lead me into the maze. "I can already tell you'll fit in wonderfully here," she chattered on. "It'll be like this palace was made for you. And I'm sure you and I will be great friends."

A friend? Now that would be something.

"Oh, I shouldn't be talking so much. Like I said, I'm just so excited. Anyway, here it is," she said as she pushed open an ornate golden door.

Inside was a massive marble tub. Thick, brocade curtains covered the windows, blocking out most of the sunlight. Hundreds of white candles surrounded the tub, casting dancing light everywhere. Steam rose invitingly from the bath water.

"Do you need help getting undressed?" she asked.

"No," I blurted before I realized I'd just snapped at the girl who wanted to be my friend. "Thank you, but no."

After untying my sandals, I gingerly stuck a toe into the tub to make sure it wasn't too hot, but it was perfect.

"I won't look," the girl said. "Go ahead and get in."

Ditching the shroud, I sank below the surface, closing my eyes. The scent of lavender enveloped me and I felt the stress of the past several days slowly releasing my muscles from its painful grasp.

"I'll leave you in peace for a little bit. If you need anything, just call me."

"How?" I asked. My eyes barely managed to stay half-open. "I don't even know your name."

"Oh gods! I'm such a goof sometimes. I'm Alexa. Just call for me whenever you need anything. If you're in the palace, I'll hear you."

"Thanks, Alexa," I mumbled as the door clicked closed.

I soaked in the tub for what felt like hours. I'd expected the water to cool, but it stayed warm the entire time. I relaxed as best I could, but my head started swimming with questions.

Why were the servants invisible?

How could Alexa hear me from anywhere in this huge palace?

How much information would Alexa give me? And could I trust it?

When would I meet the beast who may or may not eat me?

Did my parents know I was okay?

Was I okay?

Would I ever see them again?

I couldn't sit still anymore. Rising from the tub, I looked around, but there were no towels in sight. I sighed.

"Alexa," I called softly, feeling self-conscious talking to an empty room. "Could you please bring me a towel?"

The words were hardly out of my mouth when the door swung open again. Luxuriously thick, white towels floated into the room.

"Here you are," she said. She wrapped one towel around my shoulders and gently rubbed the water from my pruny skin. Then she carefully wrapped my dripping hair in another towel. "Feel better now?"

"A little," I said. And it was true. As many questions as I had, I still felt better than when I'd arrived.

"Let's get you dressed then," Alexa said and grabbed me by the wrist again to lead me to an adjacent room. "This is your room," she said as she swung back the heavy wooden door.

My jaw dropped when I looked inside. The banquet hall at my parents' palace wasn't even as large. To the right, and against the wall, was a bed layered with plush silk blankets. The massive headboard was a deep, rich mahogany and rose half the height of the wall.

Above the windows, gossamer-like fabric hung from golden rods. A breeze coming through from the gardens blew back the curtains in a way that looked almost ethereal.

Opposite the bed was a fireplace so large that my bed at home easily could have fit inside. The hearth was already prepared, with the grate holding mature trees for fire logs.

I didn't have time to take in any more of the room before I saw Alexa coming toward me. Well, I didn't see her of course, I saw what she was carrying: the most beautiful red gown I'd ever seen. I could only stare.

"He had it made special for you," Alexa told me, and I heard the smile in her voice. "It'll fit you perfectly."

I gasped. In a flash, Alexa had snatched away my towels and was passing the soft gown over my head. I wasn't sure I would ever get used to having invisible servants since I couldn't tell what they were about to do. But Alexa worked quickly, and I was fully dressed before I could even complain.

Then I felt her hands softly pushing my shoulders in the direction of a golden vanity. Before I could see myself in the mirror there, she flipped it around. Like so many other things I'd seen in the past few hours, the back of the mirror contained an intricately-detailed scene forged in gold.

"No peeking," she teased.

I was starting to be put off by the unabashed opulence. I'd never liked any of the people I knew who were so flashy with their wealth. Every last one was egotistical, rude and self-absorbed. Maybe he was planning on making me choke to death on my own disgust.

"Is *everything* in this place made of gold?" I asked.

"Well, no. Of course not." Alexa answered quickly. She must have heard the edge to my voice. "It's just.. well... you're a *princess* after all. Don't you like gold?"

"Sure, who doesn't? But this is a bit much. Is he really that full of himself?"

"None of this is for him," she said, and I heard her smile had returned. "This room exists only for you. If you don't like it, we'll have it changed."

"For me?" I gasped and spun around. "What do you mean this is for me? How long has he known I've been coming? A room like this doesn't just spring up overnight."

She laughed, but I was angry. How long had this monster been lying in wait for me? Was my whole life just some cruel joke? Had I been led to think I could live a normal life but really been destined for this beast since birth?

My nostrils flared as I took deep breaths trying to control my temper. The only sound in the room now was my huffing. If it weren't for the fact that a golden hairbrush was floating in front of me, I would've thought Alexa had bolted.

"Tell me how long he's known," I repeated through gritted teeth.

"If I tell you the truth, you'll think I'm lying. If I lie, you'll be angry. I'm sorry, Psyche. I don't know what do."

"I'll believe you," I said cooly. "I've been driven to my own funeral, flown down a hillside by the West Wind, greeted as the mistress of an ornate palace, and am being attended to by invisible servants. All in one day. Try me."

"Fine," she sighed. "Two weeks."

I looked around again at the room. The fireplace would've taken longer than two months to construct. "Two weeks?"

"If you really want to know the truth..." she added hesitantly.

"Yeah."

"Actually, well ... the whole palace was built for you about two weeks ago -- three tops." She sped through the words as if I might not focus on them if they passed me by in a blur.

"That's not..." My voice trailed away as I stared down at the floor. I was going to say possible, but none of this was possible. Everything that had happened was so unbelievably impossible, I had no choice but to believe.

After moments of silence, Alexa started working on my hair. I think she might've even warned me that she was going to start brushing, but I was too numb to hear her. I felt her tug and pull at the strands of my hair, but I barely noticed. Then she dusted my face and eyelids and cheeks with make-up and glossed my lips. When she was finished, she spun me around and flipped the mirror back over.

"There!" she said proudly.

I looked into the mirror and saw the reflection of

a person I barely recognized. Alexa's talent for primping others was breathtaking. She'd expertly twisted my hair up on top of my head and nested it around a silver crown. In place of the heavy golden jewelry I'd been forced to wear for my funeral, delicate silver twists dangled exotically from my ears. I no longer wore a necklace at all, but the dress didn't need one.

The silk draped over my right shoulder and cut down under my left arm, so that my left shoulder was bare. The fabric was ridiculously soft, and although there was enough of it to create delicate ripples, it clung to my body, revealing every curve. I'd been laced into the gown with silver cord, crossing back and forth around my waist, to where it finally ended in a bow in the small of my back, the tails hanging down almost to the floor. The tail of the gown flared into a tiny train.

I had grown up a spoiled princess, but never in all my life had I had a dress like this.

"Thank you, Alexa," I finally said. "Not for this, I mean," and I gestured to my face and body with a circling motion. "But for being so nice. Today was supposed to be the worst imaginable day of my life... granted, it could still end that way, but ... What I mean is, you've made a bad day better. *Really* better. And I might not be here tomorrow to thank you, so ... thanks."

"What do you mean you might not be here tomorrow?" she gasped. "You're not going to run away are you?"

I let out a nervous laugh. "I hadn't figured I'd live long enough to have a chance to run," I said, as I picked at the skin around my fingernails.

Alexa sighed in a way that I knew would've been accompanied by an eye roll if I could've seen her. Then she wrapped her soft, invisible arms around me.

"Psyche," she said, "you believed me when I told you this palace was just built for you, right?"

I thought for a moment before answering. "Yes."

"Then please, *please*, believe me when I tell you that you worry too much. The truest thing I could ever tell you is that he loves you with all his heart -- all his being. No harm will ever come to you here. Not from him."

Nervous laughter played from my lips as I wrung my hands together. He didn't even know me yet - how could he love me? As badly as I wanted to trust Alexa, the idea was absurd.

I stared out the window and saw the sun beginning to set below the tree line. Closing my eyes, I took in a long, deep breath. Then I slowly exhaled. Alexa was waiting for me to answer.

"I believe you," I whispered, finishing in my mind "that he won't hurt me." Not in a million years did I think a monster could love.

She hugged me again, tighter this time. "You're just as wonderful as he said you would be."

Now I was the one who rolled my eyes. She grabbed my hand and tugged at me to follow her out of the room.

"Wait. Where are we going now?"

"To get dinner, of course," she answered. "You can't meet him on an empty stomach."

CHAPTER 18 — EROS

Eros paced deep in the forest near his new palace. The sun had already dipped below the horizon, leaving little light amongst the trees.

"Will you calm down, man?" Hermes said between bites of apple as he sprawled underneath an oak tree. "It worked, didn't it? Apollo gave Darion your prophecy and Psyche is here." He gestured with the half-eaten apple in the direction of the palace. "All you have left to do is go in there and meet her. Again."

"That's what I'm worried about," Eros snapped. "She doesn't want to meet *me*."

"Seriously? How can you be worried about something like that?" Hermes asked. "You can change that in a second with your arrows."

"I won't do that to her." Eros paused his pacing to run his hands through his hair. "You don't understand what it's like. Being obsessed by love like this makes your soul feel like it's -- I don't know, being crushed out of your body. I can't think of anything but her." Eros punched the oak. "I won't make her suffer from this much love."

"You're a piece of work," Hermes said, tossing the apple core to the ground as he hopped to his feet. "You're so close to having everything you want and you're not willing to seal the deal."

"I will not use my arrows on her. End of discussion."

113

Hermes slapped Eros's shoulder. "Good luck dealing with a girl who thinks you're a monster then. If it were me though, I'd use the gifts I was born with. Think about it."

Hermes winked at Eros as he launched into the air.

"Where are you going? It's not time yet. You can't leave me here to wait by myself," Eros called after him.

"You'll be fine," Hermes yelled back. "I have too much work to do to listen to you whine anymore. No one stopped dying just because Eros fell in love."

Eros turned and kicked Hermes's apple core, launching it deep into the trees. Then he sat under the oak to wait until it was time to meet Psyche.

Hopefully they wouldn't have a replay of the last time he'd been her bedroom. He wasn't sure he could handle it if she kicked him out now.

Chapter 19 — Psyche

The banquet hall would've been large enough to hold forty tables and couches, but only one grouping stood in the center. Chandeliers of hammered brass dangled from the ceiling and their thousands of candles danced light across every inch of the room. I paused before crossing the threshold, as if the enormity of it all might suck me in. Alexa nudged me forward to the dining couch.

Even though I couldn't see anybody, the room pulsed with life. Tentatively, I reclined across the pillows. I wasn't used to eating on a couch, since at my home they were reserved for men. But that's where Alexa guided me, so that's where I sat.

As I settled in, musicians began playing lyres and flutes. The songs were so much happier than the ones that'd been played during my procession up the hill that morning. *Had that really only been a few hours ago?*

Plates of food and a goblet of wine floated down and landed on the square table in front of me. I recognized some traditional foods of welcome: slices of pomegranate, baskets of bread, honey and sesame seeds. But there was so much more. My invisible servants brought plate after plate of delicacies. As I ate, invisible tumblers swirled ribbons around the room in a hypnotic dance of color. I let the music and motion carry my tired brain away to place where I didn't have to worry, or think, or pretend to be anyone but myself.

Was this what relief felt like?

When I was already stuffed to the gills, a miniature cake danced toward me.

"Oh, I can't eat another bite," I protested.

"You've got to try this," Alexa piped up right behind me. I'd been so engrossed in the food, music and dancing, I'd forgotten Alexa was still with me. "This cake is truly divine."

Who was I to refuse dessert? "If you insist," I sighed, forking up a huge bite. The cake melted in my mouth. It was sweeter than honeysuckle and dripped with liquid caramel. I rolled my eyes as I indulged.

When only one bite of the tiny cake was left, I pushed it away. "I can't eat anymore. I'm about to burst out of this dress," I said, patting my full belly.

As I set the fork back on the plate, Alexa said, "There now. How's that for an easy first night?"

"I suppose," I agreed, "but it's not over yet. *He* isn't even here, or..." I lowered my voice, "is he invisible too?"

"No, he's not invisible," she assured me. "You'll be able to tell when he arrives."

I thought about her words for a minute. "That's not the same thing as saying I'll *see* him. You're hiding something."

"There you go, worrying again." Alexa was dismissive, so I knew I was right.

"Don't speak to me in riddles, Alexa. I need --"

She cut me off in a light voice, as if she hadn't been listening to me at all. "So, I figure in the morning, I can give you a proper tour. You haven't seen anything except your own suite, and I'm sure you'll just love the gardens. Plus, I want to show you the library and --"

"Just stop." My voice was so low and trembling, I barely heard it myself. "I can't think about tomorrow. Not when I question whether the sun will even rise for me."

"This again? I thought we settled this already."

"Yeah well, maybe my mind can't get past the bone-numbing fear quite so easily. All this food makes me feel like a sacrificial lamb, just being fattened up for slaughter or something."

"Your mind is too poisoned against him," Alexa told me softly. I felt her kneel in front of me and take my hands in hers. "Look around you. No girl in the history of Greece has ever been so well cared for. Can't you see the love he put into creating this palace for you?"

Her words pleaded with me to open my mind. And I wanted to, but I was still so filled with doubt.

"But what if all this beauty is just a cover for monstrosity?"

"It's not. Psyche, it's not. Please gods, what will it take to convince you? Would you feel better knowing I'd take your "monster" in an instant if it were me he wanted? Because I would."

I looked away from the spot I knew she occupied. Alexa had finally gotten through to me - a bit - but I still didn't feel certain. How could I? We'd never even met before today. Was I just supposed to trust her now because she was the best hair and makeup artist in all of Greece?

Still, I wouldn't reject something she so obviously wanted to her face. No point in being cruel.

"You're right," I finally said. "When will he be here?"

Alexa sighed with relief. "Soon, soon." She pulled me off the couch and hurried me down the hall. "We've got to get you touched up before he comes."

We wound back through the maze of halls and crossed into my room. The fireplace had been lit while I was at dinner, filling the room with the intoxicating aroma of cedar. Alexa pulled me back to the vanity for my final touch-ups. She reapplied my lipstick and dusted my cheeks again with blush. "Better?" she asked, spinning me around.

Instead if being gold, the vanity and mirror were now silver. I turned back with wide-eyed astonishment. "How is this possible?" I asked Alexa, pointing at the changed table.

"Anything is possible here."

She pulled me toward the edge of the bed and squeezed my hand to indicate I should sit. The bed bounced a little as she obviously sat down beside me. Alexa waited with me for him to arrive and I squeezed her hand so tightly I'm sure her fingers must've ached.

As he approached, I heard the flapping of wings, like an overgrown eagle. The sound dissolved as he landed at the edge of the open window. A rush of wind flew past me and extinguished the flames in the fireplace. Stars glowed behind him but his figure was encircled in black.

As he came in, Alexa released my hand. *How can she leave me now?* Behind me, I heard her close the door as she slipped out of the room.

Although I couldn't see him, I was too scared to

look away. I wanted to peek behind the darkened cloud surrounding his body so badly. I peered at him, trying to focus on any features I could define. I needed to see his face, however hideous. What was he hiding? Was he really as repulsive as the Pythia had warned?

Panic swelled through me as I stood to face my captor. I'm not sure how I kept my legs from following Alexa out the door. When I looked back over my shoulder to see how far it would be if I decided to make a run for it, he slipped in front of me and pulled my hands into his.

I choked back a startled gasp, horrified by the creature holding my hands as softly as if I could crumble.

"Look at me, Psyche." His voice was hypnotic, almost familiar. I stared into the blackness surrounding his form and found a pair of lovely blue eyes gazing out at me. "I know you fear me, but I beg you, believe that I will never hurt you."

"Why won't you show yourself then? If there's nothing to fear?"

His voice came back to me compassionate, but firm. "I didn't say there's nothing to fear. I said *I'd* never hurt you. Don't confuse the two."

That good old I'm-about-to-puke feeling made me wish I hadn't eaten every bite of food on my plate tonight. I reached back for the bed, easing myself down as I tried to figure out what could possibly be scarier than the invisible beast in my new bedroom. Or who else wanted to hurt me now that I'd already been condemned to a fate worse than death.

He reached a satiny, smooth hand to my face and

let his finger trail from my cheek down my jaw line. "Psyche, I am no monster. I love you, and I will love you always."

"You don't even know me," I shrieked, swatting away his hand. "How could you possibly love me?" Hurt registered in those soft blue eyes and he blinked them closed for what felt like an eternity. "Who are you?" I finally whispered.

His eyes popped back open with a glimmer of hope. Like I'd just thrown a life line to a drowning man. "Aristeo, but please, call me Aris."

That wasn't exactly what I'd meant, but I couldn't hold the literal answer against him. "Okay, Aris," I paused, sucking in a deep, jagged breath and steeling myself to ask the real question, "*what* are you?"

"You cut right to the chase." His darkened shape retreated a few steps until it looked like he must be sitting on the stool in front of my silver vanity. I welcomed the extra space between us, but the weight of those eyes I knew were watching me from across the room still felt intensely heavy.

"I'm the son of a harpy. Hence the wings." The night air rustled with the sound of feathers beating once and then refolding into place.

Well, that's new. Didn't know harpies even had kids - not that I'd ever considered it - or thought that harpies were anything more than a scary bedtime story to make kids shut up and go to sleep. But son-of-a-harpy sounded pretty foreboding. I mean, harpies were the ones who supposedly tortured souls on their way to Tartarus. And soul torturing gave me a clue as to why even the gods might fear him. I just hoped his supposed love for me was enough to keep his torturous side in check.

I swallowed. Hard. "So, um," I looked around the pitch black room, grasping for some way to save our floundering conversation before he got bored and decided to entertain himself with a little sadism. "Tell me something else about you."

He rose and moved closer. When he was right in front of me, he dropped down to his knees, leveling his gaze with mine. "I know you don't believe this yet, but the only interesting thing about me is how much I feel for you."

Seriously? The guy tells me he's a mythological creature and his feelings are the most interesting thing about him? The darkness must not have been enough to hide the rampant disbelief splashed across my face.

With an effortless move, he swept me up into his arms and laid me gently across the bed. "I know you're tired. And stressed. I can feel it coming off you in waves." His lips brushed across my forehead and I felt the soft wisp of a curl follow in their wake.

"Sleep, my love," he whispered. "You've had a long day. But know this one thing." I focused my eyes on his, now only a few inches away from my face, dreading the words that were coming. "I will earn your love."

As creeped out as that idea made me, my muscles relaxed. A great warmth coursed through my body, starting from where he'd placed the kiss on my forehead and moving down. I felt peaceful. And sleepy. The alarm pulsing through my veins faded, even as I tried to pull it back and keep myself awake. As sleep overtook me, I somehow knew I'd at least make it through this one night intact.

CHAPTER 20 — EROS

From back across the room, Eros watched Psyche as she slept, taking in the sweet scent of her hair and enjoying the soft rise and fall of her chest as she breathed deeply. He loved how at peace she looked. And he yearned for her to be as relaxed with him while she was awake.

Finally daring to ease onto the bed next to her, Eros unwound Psyche's hair from on top of her head and let it spill across the pillows. He stroked her long, chestnut strands, carefully keeping them away from her face. When the words threatened to rip open his chest if he didn't speak them, Eros whispered in her ear, "I will never hurt you, Psyche. I love you more than my own life. Love me, please," he begged. "Love me."

Psyche barely stirred as Eros pled softly in her ear. Perhaps he had hoped she would open her eyes and pledge her undying love for him too.

But that's not how his magic worked.

Slowly he rose, being careful not to wake her. He took a deep breath to assure himself he was about to do the right thing. Eros wanted Psyche to love him on her own, but he couldn't wait.

When he'd landed on the windowsill that night, he'd slipped off his quiver and hidden it behind the curtains. He reached into his hiding place and pulled out one of the long, powerful arrows. Hermes's words from earlier that evening played back in his head. "You

123

can change all that in a second with one of your arrows..."

Hermes was right. All he had to do was nick Psyche's skin with an arrow and she would be as hopelessly in love with him as he was with her. Granted, being with Psyche is what he'd actually wanted, at least subconsciously. He was pretty sure she didn't yet share the same sentiment. Eros slowly twirled the arrow in his hand and looked over at Psyche.

She was so soundly asleep, she'd never notice the sting as the arrow grazed her skin. And this time he wouldn't have to shoot her. He'd simply nick her with a caress. Not like the impersonal release of a bow. He wouldn't be hunting her if he marked her with his own hand.

He reached out to touch her, the arrow poised, but pulled away. His jaw clenched and his eyes scrunched closed. Something akin to physical pain kept him from hurting her. Eros knew all too well that the arrows would make Psyche suffer. During the daylight hours when he couldn't be in the palace, she would need him so badly that her heart would ache.

Eros didn't want her days to be unhappy. He simply wanted her love.

Sitting on the bed, Eros let the arrow fall from his fingertips, dissipating as its unused magic released into the floor. He'd have to do as he'd promised her.

He'd have to earn her love.

Chapter 21 — Psyche

As I slowly opened my eyes and took in the room, I realized I was alone. Sitting up, I studied myself. I was whole. Definitely still alive. And my dress was intact, though rumpled from sleep. Whatever bad things harpy kids might be, at least he hadn't harmed me while I slept.

As quietly as I could, I slipped out of bed and down the hall. Maybe I could catch a glimpse of him in the light. The tension of not knowing what he looked like seemed almost worse than just seeing what I was dealing with and moving on.

My toes barely touched the mosaic tiles as I crept along the corridor. When I reached the end of the first hall, I placed my back against the wall, took a deep breath, and peeked as little of my head around the corner as possible.

Since I couldn't see any floating towels or serving trays headed my way, I figured it was clear. As I prepared to bolt down the next hall, a voice rang in my ear.

"You're up. Did you sleep well?"

I jumped with a startled screech.

"Oh, sorry. I didn't mean to scare you." It was Alexa, of course.

"If you're invisible and don't want to scare someone, you ought to give some notice before you go talking in their ear," I snapped, more embarrassed than angry.

Alexa didn't seem to notice. "So..." she dragged out the word like we were in some conspiracy together, "tell me how it went last night."

Gross. Did she think I'd actually *do* anything with him? Or tell her about it if I did? I shrugged my shoulders. "Fine, I guess."

"Fine? That's it?" Alexa asked, squeezing my hand. "He's wonderful, isn't he? I told you you had nothing to worry about."

"Is he still here?"

"Oh no. He'll always leave before dawn."

"Why?" I asked. "Why can't I see him?"

"That's just the way it has to be. It's safer that way," she explained.

I leaned against the wall and sighed. "You too? What's safe for me about not knowing *anything* about him?"

"Stop exaggerating. Just because you can't see him doesn't mean you can't know him. What if you were blind? Does that mean you'd never know anyone around you?"

My head dropped back against the cool marble wall. She was right. Again. If she kept that up, it was going to get really annoying.

"Tell me what you're thinking," Alexa asked.

"I can trust you right?" I realized as soon as I said it, it was a dumb question. Like anyone would say no to that. "I mean, you'll tell me the truth if I ask you something, right?"

"Of course." She grabbed my hands in hers. "I'm here to serve you, but I want to be your friend too. I'd never lie to you. Promise."

I was afraid to ask the question on my mind, but I had to know.

"What does he look like? He told me he was a harpy's child, but I don't know what that means. Good or bad, I just think I'd feel better knowing."

"I can't tell you that." Her voice was an apology, barely more than a whisper.

"You just promised you'd tell me the truth."

"I am telling you the truth. I can't tell you that. It's forbidden."

"Is it really that bad?" I moaned.

"Are we going to go through this every day? Not everything you don't understand is bad." She wrapped me in a warm hug. "Please, Psyche. He loves you. Didn't you feel that last night?"

I swallowed back the lump in my throat and tried to calm my pounding heart. This was my life -- all around me in this palace. My future was in these walls. Invisible servants, mostly-invisible suitor? boyfriend? I didn't even know what we were supposed to be to each other. Whatever repulsion I felt to the idea though, I had to admit it was better than what I'd feared after hearing the Pythia's prophecy. And if every day was basically a repeat of yesterday, I could handle it. I'd have a friend in Alexa and eventually I'd get past not being able to see Aris. Not that I planned on loving him or anything, but how hard could it be just to talk?

***

While I ate breakfast, Alexa peppered me with questions. Mostly I answered absentmindedly. Alexa was just trying to make polite conversation but none of her questions interested me. I looked out over the palace gardens and sucked the honeydew juice from my fingers.

"Psyche?" she asked tentatively.

Here it comes, I thought. *Now she's going to ask me something more personal.*

"What was it like being famous?"

How to answer that question? I laid my head against the back of the couch and thought. I liked my visits with Aphrodite -- now that was fun -- while it lasted. But the rest of it ...

"It was okay, I guess. I didn't love it or anything."

"Why?" Alexa asked with a note of disbelief. "Wasn't it amazing to get all those gifts and have people want to meet you -- want to *be* you?"

"Maybe at first. But I ended up getting tired of it. I just wanted to be normal again after awhile."

"Is that why your mom wanted you to get married? So you could get back to a normal life?"

I grabbed a pillow from the couch and hugged it to my chest. Thinking about my mother, and never seeing her again, cut a little deep. "Can we talk about something else?"

"Sure," Alexa answered. "Want to tell me about your sister?"

"No. Something else." Not only would I never see Chara again, she'd probably hate me forever too. Might as well just cue the waterworks now.

"At least you only have one sister," Alexa said. "I have a bunch and most of them don't even know my name."

"What?" I hadn't given much thought to what

Alexa was, other than invisible, and I certainly hadn't pictured her with sisters. But how could your own sisters not know your name? "Why not?"

"Because there's fifty of us. And I'm third from the youngest, which means I'm as good as invisible at home too."

"Fifty? No one has fifty sisters." The pillow fell away from my chest as I sat up in surprise.

"Not for a nymph. Nymphs have that many kids all the time. I mean, my great grandmother was one of three thousand."

"Ah!" I gasped. "You're an Oceanid." The Oceanids were the only sisters I'd ever heard of who numbered three thousand.

"Not me, no," Alexa said. "My great grandmother was one of the Oceanids though. I'm just a descendant."

"So you're a nymph..." I pondered that knowledge for a minute, trying to draw on what little I knew about them. "What else can you do besides stay invisible?"

She sighed. "Nothing. I'm pretty much as boring a nymph as you'll ever meet."

"Well, I don't think you're boring," I told Alexa. "But if you don't have any special powers, then why can't I see you?"

"Because you're human. Powers or not, humans can only see us if we want them to."

"Really? Show yourself to me. Please!"

"I wish I could, Psyche, but I can't."

"Why? Is that another one of *his* rules?"

"Not hardly," she answered.

"Well, why then?" I looked as imploringly as I could in the direction of my invisible friend.

"Have you ever heard of anything good happening to a human who sees a nymph?"

I had to think about it. I didn't know much about nymphs actually. I'd heard of the Oceanids, of course, and I knew that most nymphs protected some sort of natural element, like a river or flower or something. Some gods also kept company with nymphs since they were a step above humans, but that's pretty much where my memory bank ended.

"I don't know," I finally answered. "The way you asked the question though, I'm guessing not."

"It's just the natural order of things. Something bad might not happen right away, but it would. I'm just supposed to be invisible to you. If I let you see me, the bad luck would find you."
She laid her hand on top of mine. "And I think you've had enough bad luck for one lifetime."

I put my other hand on top of hers, wishing I could see it. But after my run-in with Aphrodite, I'd had enough bad luck for five lifetimes. If seeing her meant I'd have more of the same, then she would just have to stay invisible.

"You want to take a walk?" I asked her. "I haven't seen the gardens yet."

"Yes!" she cried, tugging me to my feet. "He knows how you love gardens and this one is amazing."

With Alexa leading the way, we ran together down another long hallway and burst through a pair of wooden doors into the yard. Before us was an immaculate lawn, so expansive an entire race track could've easily been built in the space.

Beyond the lawn was a maze of hibiscus hedges blooming with flowers that ranged from yellow, to salmon, to garnet. Throughout the lawn and maze were bronze and marble statues. The one closest to me showed Helen and Paris of Troy. Paris had one arm wrapped around Helen's waist and his other hand held an apple. Helen had her body turned toward Paris, with her arms wrapped lovingly around his neck.

As I looked around at more of the statues, they all appeared to be couples locked in some sort of embrace. That was definitely not typical.

"What's with these statutes?" I asked. "I noticed the columns out front were couples too. That's *really* odd."

"What's odd about it? They're just couples."

"Most sculptures *aren't* couples, that's what's odd about it. And I've never seen a column carved like two people."

"I guess he's just been inspired by his love for you," she replied.

"Aris made these himself?"

"Sure. I told you last night, he made all of this for you."

I stopped in my tracks. "No, no, no. You told me that all of this had *been made* for me in the past two weeks. I mean, that right there is hard enough to believe. But you didn't tell me *who* made it. Now you're saying Aris did this all himself in under a month?"

"I'm sorry," Alexa apologized. "I keep telling you too much, too fast."

I took a calming breath so I wouldn't lose it. "It's

okay. I'll get used to it. Just, I don't know... tell me to sit down or something before you blurt out something like that."

Her light laugh danced through the gardens. "I'll try to remember that."

I rolled my eyes and sat down on a bench. We had walked to a circular portion of the garden maze. A towering fountain stood in the center of a pool. Like all the other displays in the garden, the fountain flowed from entwined figures. This particular couple was Perseus and Andromeda. They were standing on top of the now-crushed sea serpent that would've eaten her had Perseus not come along.

Just thinking of poor Andromeda made me shudder. "My mother never would've let me die for her. She would've taken my place up on that rock yesterday if she could've." Thinking of her again brought back the threat of tears.

"But thank the gods she couldn't." Alexa gave me a little jab in the ribs with her elbow. "You never would've met your own personal Perseus."

"I'm not sure you can compare harpy spawn to demi-gods, but okay."

Alexa's snicker tumbled out in rapid little spurts. "Harpy spawn is definitely one way of putting it."

Closing my eyes, I shook my head. "Are you intentionally trying to make me fret?"

"No." She rubbed my back in a few, quick strokes. "It's just his mom is such a, well, harpy, that harpy spawn seems dead-on accurate."

"Great," I mumbled. "Hope *she* doesn't show up next."

"You and me both," Alexa said, pulling me to my feet before leading me off down another path. We walked through roses and irises and a bunch of other flowers I couldn't name. As we strolled, I turned my face up to the glow of the warm sunshine, inhaling the sweet, earthy smell all around me. I suddenly felt more alive than I had in ages and the reverie stopped me in my tracks.

How could I feel so content when I was here?

Gravel crunched as Alexa came back to my side. "You can always be this happy if you choose."

Was she a mind reader too?

"I don't -- I don't know what you're talking about," I stammered, ashamed for basking in the peace of a spring morning when I should still be trembling under the covers.

"I want you to be happy here." She gave my fingers a light squeeze. "Happiness will always be your choice."

I looked around at the brilliance of the palace and gardens. And I thought about Aris, who'd seemed harmless enough under his cloak of darkness. Who was I to judge if he didn't want me to see whatever harpy features he'd inherited. I could live with all that -- for the simple reason that I was pretty sure I was actually going to live.

Just be happy.

It really didn't seem like too much to ask.

133

CHAPTER 22 — PSYCHE

By bath that evening, I'd decided Alexa owed me some more answers.

"How'd *you* end up in this place?" I asked. "Aren't you supposed to be guarding a flower or something?"

Alexa scrubbed my arms with a loofah. "I volunteered to come here. Nymphs who don't have anything in nature to guard often end up keeping watch over youth. You're young enough that you still qualify."

"Geesh, no natural object to care for *and* you got stuck babysitting me. I'm sorry."

"Trust me, I'm not missing anything. I spent a lot of time visiting my oldest sister who looks after daffodils. Her job is so boring."

"Ok. So why here? How'd you end up volunteering in this palace?"

Alexa was quiet as she lathered up a wash cloth and began polishing my back. "I didn't choose the place. I chose you," she finally said.

I looked up at the spot I knew she was at and felt my eyes start to mist over. "You chose me? That's the nicest thing--"

"Oh, don't get all sappy about it. It just means you're slightly more interesting than an inanimate object."

Alexa laughed. I beamed from ear to ear as I splashed water at her and hoped invisible nymphs could get wet.

"Kidding, kidding," she said until I stopped splashing. "Anyway, when Aris opened up the position, I jumped at the chance. In all seriousness, I just sort of knew what good friends we'd be."

I reached up and squeezed her arm. "Thank you," I said. "I don't deserve you."

"I think you do," she assured me. "And my job is to make sure you deserve me -- and everything else here. To make sure your future is as wonderful as it should be."

"But I'm here. My future's already written."

Alexa started in scrubbing my hair. "Nothing's as certain as you've been taught. Humans like to believe in fate so they don't have to take responsibility for their actions. But you still have some critical choices to make. I can help you with your decisions, offer my advice. But in the end, all decisions are yours alone. You hold the key to your own happiness. Never forget that."

Just be happy.

As I rose from the bath, a plain lilac sheet that was apparently my dress for the evening floated toward me. Something else new. I'd never seen a design like it. It had no straps to keep it in place. And there was no detail or embroidery trimming the edges. I cocked an eyebrow and scowled as Alexa brought it closer.

"You don't like it?"

"It's not that, really. I just don't, well... what is it?"

"It's a dress, silly. Strapless. It'll be the newest trend in Greece soon, and you get the designer's original."

"Who's the designer?"

135

"Me," she chirped. "It's one of my hobbies. Just wait till you see it on."

I followed the dress as we moved into my bedroom. She wrapped the gown around me, carefully tucking it under my arms and pulling it tight behind my back.

"How's it supposed to stay up?"

"This pin." Alexa produced an intricately knotted silver broach, almost the size of my hand.

"Wow. It's beautiful."

Using the pin, Alexa fastened the dress closed before sitting me down at the vanity to do my hair and makeup.

"This dress calls for something casually elegant. I don't want you to look too done up tonight," she informed me while she worked.

"I'm sure whatever you do will be perfect."

Before long, she flipped over the silver mirror for me to see my reflection. She'd hit her mark. My hair was loosely pulled back and little ringlets fell down around my face like a frame. She'd done my makeup so expertly that I didn't even look made up. I just glowed like the sun had come down from the sky and kissed me.

"You're amazing," I told her.

"I have an easy subject," she laughed, hugging my shoulders. "Come on, I want you to see the dress." She pulled me across the room to a full length mirror.

I hadn't had very high expectations. It seemed too strange and plain to be very pretty on. But when I saw it in the mirror, just the opposite was true. The dress showed off my shoulders with a look both new and stunning. I pivoted to look at the back. Where Alexa had gathered the material, it folded into a fan and cascaded down to the floor. The silver broach sat beautifully in the center of my shoulder blades. It was truly all the embellishment the dress needed.

"You're a genius," I told Alexa. "You should be designing gowns for the gods rather than babysitting me."

"I have to start somewhere, right?" I could hear the smile in her voice.

***

At first I sat on the edge of the bed to wait, staring at the open window. Doing this on my own was significantly harder than when I'd had Alexa with me last night. Unable to sit still, I went back to my vanity to add more lipstick and check my hair. But there was no detail in Alexa's handiwork I could improve on, so I returned to the edge of the bed.

As I waited, I picked at the skin around my nails. What was taking him so long? He hadn't taken so long to come last night. What if he'd decided he didn't want me? Not that I wanted him, but I wasn't sure how much more rejection I could handle in one lifetime. Having suitor after suitor want my sister instead of me had taken its toll on my ego.

Hopping up, I moved over to the fireplace to examine the mosaic surrounding it. The millions of tiny pieces of glass composing the picture amazed me and I got lost trying to figure out how an artist would even go about starting such a project. I was still studying the mosaic when the room went dark and I felt his strong arms wrap around my waist from behind. Spinning quickly, I looked back at him, but again, I saw only his eyes glinting at me from under a cloud of darkness.

"You're stunning," he told me as he pushed a lock of hair back from my temple and tucked it behind my ear. "I'll have to remember to thank Alexa for that dress."

His warm breath brushed my ear as he spoke, and he traced his soft fingers along my jaw line and down my throat, until they caressed my exposed collarbone.

I probably looked like a greased pig as I slid out of his embrace. "This hugging thing isn't working for me." The skin I felt beneath the cloud as I pushed him away was impossibly soft -- definitely not a lion's coat or feathers. That was a pleasant surprise. Still, it didn't mean he got to wrap his arms around me like we were a couple. Because prophecy or no prophecy, there was no way me and the harpy spawn were trading kisses.

"Please, Psyche," he begged, tugging gently at my hands to try to pull me back. "You know I love you, don't you?"

Pointing my finger at his chest and shaking my head, I told him, "No. No, no. I promised Alexa I'd try to be happy here. But you've got to stop saying you love me or I'm seriously going to freak out."

His body recoiled away from mine. "Everyone wants to be loved."

"I did. I mean, I do." I rubbed at the bridge of my nose as I tried to form a coherent sentence. "It's just, I don't love you - obviously - and we'd never even met until yesterday, so you can't possibly *love* me."

He sighed and let my hands fall away. "If only you knew."

Gods, that sounded ominous. I was pretty sure I didn't want to know, but what else could I do but ask. "Try me?"

I knew that look. It was the same thing I'd seen in my father when he'd returned from Delphi. He was being crushed from the inside out and his eyes played out every pain. "I've been in love before, but it wasn't anything like this. That's how I know I love you." He dropped my gaze and looked away. "If you want me to stop saying it, I will. But it doesn't change anything."

As I resumed picking at my nails, I stewed in silent guilt that his feelings were so one-sided. Of course, I'd always hoped to one day be with someone who loved me. He'd been right on that point. But I figured I'd feel something back. I didn't even know what love was or felt like. Was this the most I could hope for? And if it was, was I giving him a fair chance?

"Will you tell me about her?" I asked, giving his hand a little squeeze. "The girl you loved."

The desperation in his eyes was instantly replaced with a look of cold iron. "Why?"

I shrugged. "Maybe I can make some sense of this if I know you better. I mean, know more about who you are instead of what you are."

A faint glint returned to his eyes. He exhaled, long and slow, before answering. "Her name was Lelah. She took my breath away the first time I saw her."

Scooting onto the bed, I nested into a stack of pillows and made myself comfortable for his story. At the same time, I mentally slapped myself for feeling any tinge of jealousy. That was definitely not called for.

"I was in Media during a brief exile and she was

there." The bed sank as he sat next to me. "I'd dropped in on some sort of ceremony -- to see the differences from Greece, I guess -- and she was swaying by the fire. The flames rose almost to the roof of the temple, but she held her hands out to the blaze. Like she wanted to bring the heat closer. And I'll never forget when she turned those green eyes on me, peeking out from behind that thick, dark hair. I was lost before we even shared a word."

He looked at me and blinked, but his eyes weren't focused on me at all. "She was so kind at first, and truly caring. I felt how much she loved me. And when she finally kissed me, it was like lightening surging under my skin. We were almost perfect together."

And I thought I'd felt a tinge of jealously before? It was full-on blooming now.

"So what happened?"

He chuckled, low and sad. "Call it religious differences."

I sat up and peered at him. "You were totally in love with a girl and you left her because of her religion?"

"More like she left me." He must have closed his eyes, because the blue disappeared. "I don't know why I'm telling you this."

Carefully, I reached out and felt for his arm. I recoiled when my fingers first hit that baby-soft skin, but I quickly returned to him. Trying to soothe; to let him know I understood.

"I'm glad you told me," I whispered. "Really." I ran my hands down his arms until I clasped his fingers. "And I'm sorry if remembering her hurts."

He covered my hands in his. "It was worth it."

My shoulders slumped. Somehow we were back on me. How could I ever compare to his dream girl? Sure, we shared hair and eye color, but the way she'd made him feel -- that was something I hadn't, couldn't, give him. Was I just a religiously-aligned look alike?

"I want to know about the religion part. Why was that such a big deal?"

"Medians practice Zoroastrianism. Basically, they have one god who's the beginning and end of everything. When I told her who and what I was, she thought I was crazy. There was no room in her world for our gods."

"So when you told her you were descended from the gods, she sent you packing?"

"Pretty much." I heard him swallow. "But I know you believe. Given your relationship with Aphrodite and all."

A chill rolled through me, making the hairs on the ends of my arms stand on end. "How do you know so much about me? My family barely even knew about Aphrodite's visits."

"The same way I know I love you: I feel you." He tapped my chest just above my heart. "One of my gifts, I suppose."

My brow creased as I thought, but nothing made sense. "I don't understand."

His eyes burned like the blue in the center of a fire. "I'm not talking about physical touch. I'm talking about the feel of your heart, of your soul. Anyone can see you and think you're beautiful. But I know you're beautiful because I can feel what you do."

"So you know what I'm thinking? And feeling?" My whole body felt dirty, like I'd been stripped in front of a crowd. Without warning, my eyes welled with tears and I had to physically struggle to go a second night in a row without losing it in front of him. "I'm sorry," I said, waving my hands in front of my face like a fan. "That's just... it's creepy. I don't like thinking you can see right through me like that."

"But don't you get it?" he asked, leaning in close, "the more I see, the more I love you. How kind you've been to Alexa. How strong you've been with everything that's been thrown at you the past couple of days." He dropped his head into my lap, shaking it slightly from side to side. "You're amazing. I don't know what else to say."

When he put it like that, how could I complain? My hand fell to his head. A thick nest of curls threaded between my fingers. His hair was so invitingly soft, I couldn't help but play with it.

And the next thing I knew, he was asleep.

CHAPTER 23 — PSYCHE

My first thought when I woke up: it's my birthday and not a single person here is going to know.

Just as I'd thought, Alexa never brought it up, never wished me a happy birthday. Not that I knew when her birthday was or anything. But the void made me ache for my family all the more. This day never would've passed unnoticed back at home.

That evening, I sat on the bed and watched the sun set behind the gardens, casting a glow of brilliant oranges and reds across the landscape. Just as he had done the past two nights, Aris's darkened form flew in through the window. My breath caught in the back of my throat as I gazed at the obviously powerful creature now standing before me.

He didn't speak right away, then cleared his throat. "Sorry about passing out on you last night. Not exactly how I'd planned things to go."

I shrugged. "Don't worry about it. Seriously. You obviously needed the rest. I didn't mind."

"Yeah, well, I felt like I did all the talking last night and I want to know more about you. I already know *my* past."

"I thought you already knew everything about me." I couldn't help the playful barb; I probably even threw in an eyelash flutter for good measure.

He chuckled and I heard fabric shifting under his

personal cloud. "I don't know nearly enough. So I figured you could tell me everything -- over cake."

I took the package he held out to me. Once I'd untied the string and pulled away the cloth wrapping, I saw an amazing-looking cheesecake.

"Happy birthday to you," he sang in a low voice.

"How'd you know?" I asked.

"I figured it was something I ought to remember." He cleared his throat again. "I hope you like cheesecake."

"Who doesn't?" I slid onto the stool at my vanity, pulling the cake closer and breaking off a piece to pop into my mouth.

He stopped my hand before I could indulge. "Wait... this game has rules."

I looked at him with narrowed eyes. *Since when does eating cheesecake have rules?*

"I want one fact for every bite," he said. "Talk first, eat second."

Reluctantly, I backed the cake away from my already-parted lips. If he wanted to make a game out of this information exchange, who was I to complain?

"Fine. That's easy enough," I said. "What do you want to know?"

"Let's start with something easy. Tell me about your family."

I offered up my family's names and lineages -- the most basic of information really -- and popped a bite of cheesecake into my mouth. I smiled like an imp while I chewed.

"Hmmm..." he rumbled, but his eyes looked amused. "That's not exactly the information I was looking for. Tell me something about them that I don't know."

Swallowing the luscious bite, I pondered for a minute. I wanted to tell him something nice about my family, something that described how we were before the fame kicked in. But I was having a hard time seeing past our last week together.

"My mother and father were really worried about me when I left. The hardest thing I've ever done is watch my father cry when he said goodbye to me." I felt a sudden lump in my throat as I relived that painful memory. "Until he came home from Delphi, Father had always seemed so strong. I never even thought he could cry."

His hand caressed my arm, easing my guilt with the comfort of now as best he could. "They'll be okay, Psyche. You're a good daughter to worry about your parents more than you worry for yourself."

"You give me too much credit. I was worried sick about what was going to happen to me."

"But their pain hurts you," he said. "I can feel that."

"I guess that's just part of being human."

He turned my head and gazed into my eyes. "No, Psyche. That's part of being *you*. The depth of your heart is what drew me to you. Don't underestimate yourself."

Slowly, he guided my head to his shoulder and I didn't stop him. As I closed my eyes, the fresh smell of his skin, the gentle caress of his fingers against the back of my neck, played with my mind. *Could anything bad smell so inviting? Or feel so tender?* But more than anything,

I let him hold me like this because it was so nice to feel understood.

For months, I'd kept secrets from my family, pretended to be a diva for my fans, and done my best to impress Aphrodite with my every word. Now, Aris claimed he already knew me: my flaws and imperfections, my true self, and apparently he wanted me anyway. At least for tonight, I'd enjoy this feeling. No worries about tomorrow, or who Aris really was; no worries about anything.

I was just about to let myself consider falling asleep on him when he broke through our comfortable silence. "You want to get out of here?"

"We can do that?" My head snapped up and I was instantly more awake than I'd felt all day.

"You deserve a better present than cake that makes you sad. But," he paused and I bit my lip, waiting for him to continue, "you've got to trust me."

Trust Aris in exchange for temporary escape? A blink takes more time than I took to decide. What could he do to me outside the palace that he couldn't do here? The risk seemed more than worth it.

I smiled -- the winning one Aphrodite taught me -- and I hoped he melted just a little, if for no other reason than vanity made me want to be the green-eyed girl of his dreams. "Done. Now where to?"

"It's a surprise." Stepping in close, he wrapped his thick arms around my waist and I heard his wings unfold. "Hold on."

As I felt my feet lift off the ground, I had no choice but to cling to his neck. We passed easily through the window and over the garden. Peering over my shoulder, the hedges and fountains blurred into the oblivion of darkness and I clamped my eyes shut. At least when Zephyrus swept me off the cliff, we were headed down. The continuous upward spiral coupled with the steady beat of his wings made my head spin.

His arms squeezed tighter. "You hanging in there?" The warmth of his breath against my ear sent a delicious shiver down my spine.

"You could say that." I managed a half-laugh to prove I wasn't about to pass out or anything, but I don't think either of us was fooled.

Just then we passed through a cloud; white beams of moonlight reflected off its surface. Behind us, thousands of stars twinkled in the inky black night. For a second, I could almost believe I was floating, like in a dream, and the blackened form holding me in the sky was just my overactive imagination. But he broke the evening spell as quickly as it'd come over me.

"Get ready, this is the fun part." We tilted back toward Earth and careened forward. Wind gusted past us, tangling my hair and pushing against his wings with a force I thought might shred his feathers. An involuntary scream escaped before I could silence it and I gripped him even tighter. I swear he chuckled.

With a snap of wings, he slowed our descent. When we touched down, my toes brushed against smooth, warm rocks and I stumbled as I got my balance on the slick stones. Without the wind clogging my ears, a new sound took over. The crashing of waves hit me at the same time the warm, salty air curled through my lungs.

He'd brought me to the ocean. Did he know that

as close as it was, I hadn't seen it since I was a child? That I'd always dreamed of watching the white caps roll into the beach under a blinding moon?

His arms fell away and I made my way to the waves. The first lick of the water was almost icy and I shrieked -- a girlish, carefree laugh. I backed away from the next wave, but steeled myself by the third. As the water swirled around my ankles, the penetrating cold lessened and I walked out another step.

Looking back over my shoulder, I saw a void of darkness resting on the beach. "You coming?" I asked.

"I think I'll sit this one out. You go ahead."

Pulling up my dress around my knees, I trod deeper into the water. When the chill gripped the back of my knees, I turned and fled, running up the beach in a sprint. "Never mind," I panted, collapsing next to him. "That's way too cold."

"I'd warm it for you if I could." His eyes turned to mine and the space between us seemed impossibly narrow. Had I really sat down so close to him?

He might not have control of the waters, but the heat rolling off his body was strong enough to cross the space between us. As I met his eyes, his head dipped forward. My heart stuttered in my chest and my throat seemed to close tight. *Was this fear or desire?* His nose brushed mine as he leaned dangerously close and I felt his breath tease and tickle my lips.

When his hand slipped around my waist, pulling me a fraction of an inch closer, the spell was broken. It didn't matter that he'd carried me all the way out here, his touch chilled me. "Thank you for bringing me here," I said, turning my head and staring back out at the gently crashing waves. His hand slipped away and he sighed, long and low, as he leaned away.

"I'm just glad you trusted me enough to make the trip."

I tucked my legs into my chest and wrapped up in my own arms. Looking back over my shoulder at him, I could tell he was focused on the waves too. Anywhere but on me.

"Listen," I said, trying for a peace offering, "I still owe you some facts, right?"

His gaze snapped my direction. "A few."

"Name your topic," I offered.

Silence. His cloud stretched out and it was evidence he was laying back against the pebbles, staring at the moon-bleached clouds. "Me," he finally said.

"Excuse me?"

He cleared his throat. "I want to know what you think about me."

How do I answer that? "I'm not really sure what to think," I admitted.

"Why?"

"Do you really have to ask?" I ticked off the reasons on my fingers. "First, there's the prophecy. Second, there's the fact that you won't show yourself. Third, you create stuff out of thin air, which is just odd. And fourth --" I stalled, having run out of reasons to push him away.

"Yeah?"

"You fly way too fast."

His laugh bounced down the beach. "Would you be happier if I slowed down? With you anyway?"

I nodded. "That'd be a start."

He sat up and I heard him brush the pebbles off his palms. "Okay, done. What else? What else can I do?"

"Tell me why I can't see you. Really. Are you a nymph or something like Alexa and it'd be bad luck?"

"I told you, I'm not a nymph. But, bad luck? Yeah, you could put it that way."

"I don't want to put it any way," I protested. "I want you to tell me."

He leaned in close to my ear and whispered. "Don't ever repeat this out loud. It'd put us both in danger. You understand?" He pulled back to study me, making sure I understood how serious he was. Swallowing hard, I nodded.

His hushed story continued. "I made that prophecy up."

"You what?" I blurted.

"Shush. You want to get us both killed?"

"Sorry, sorry. Go on."

"When you made Aphrodite mad, she cursed you to fall for a creature too hideous for words. But I knew I could spare you from all that if I stepped in and worded the prophecy right. The only kicker was that you'd have to spend your days, or nights rather, with me. I figured it was better than the alternative."

I sucked in a startled breath. "You saved me? Why?"

"I thought you didn't want me to say I loved you any more." Coy. He was playing with me. And I wasn't actually minding so much.

Turning, I raised up on to my knees so I could whisper back to him more easily. "So why the darkness?

The whispering? If you saved me, why are we hiding?"

"What do you think would happen if Aphrodite found out her curse didn't come out quite the way she'd planned?"

That question made me sit back. *Nothing good*, was the only answer I could come up with.

"Yeah," he answered to my silence. "It wouldn't be pretty."

"Gotcha." I nibbled my lip, wondering if I dared to keep going. "So are you really the son of a harpy then?"

His shadow shifted as his head tossed side to side. "Yes and no. How 'bout we leave it at that for now?"

How could I say no? What more did he need to tell me now that I knew I'd fallen for a false prophecy? And he'd spared me from Aphrodite's wrath?

"Will it always be like this? Between us, I mean."

Softly, he placed a kiss on my shoulder. "If you let me stay, we can be everything you've ever wanted. And more."

Resting my head against his shoulder, I let my body relax into him. His arm wrapped around my waist again, but this time, I didn't pull away. As the waves danced across the beach stones, and his hand played slowly and endlessly through my hair, I let go of the day that had been my oddest birthday ever and surrendered to sleep.

CHAPTER 24 — PSYCHE

"Time to wake up, sleepyhead," Alexa called in a sing-song voice that would've made songbirds jealous. It just made me want to hit her.

"You are aware that I didn't go to sleep until really late at night, right?" I groaned as I pulled the covers over my head to block out the blaring sunlight.

"Um-hum," she answered, snapping the covers away, "which is why I let you sleep in. It's almost three in the afternoon."

Sitting up, I rubbed the sleep from my eye with a knuckle and winced. "I've been asleep for twelve hours?"

"Must be some evenings you're having."

"It's not like that," I blurted. "I mean, not that you care. Or that I should be talking about this. Or..." I flopped back onto my pillow. "I think I need more sleep."

"No you don't." Alexa grabbed my hand and hoisted me out of bed. "If you don't get up now, you'll never go back to sleep before dawn. Besides, you need to eat. You're having a late dinner."

Suddenly I was wide awake. "Why? He's not going to be late is he?" For some reason the thought of him not showing up right as darkness conquered light really bothered me.

"Aren't we paranoid today?" Alexa teased. "I'm sure he'll be right on time. But you'll have to wait to dine until he gets here."

"Dinner? He's coming to have dinner with me?" The warmth of excitement crept up my neck. First birthday cake and a trip to the ocean. Now dinner. *I could get used to these surprises.*

With sudden clarity, I realized I wasn't just getting used to his attention, I was craving it.

***

"So, exactly how late is dinner going to be?" I asked when my stomach growled a noisy protest. I hadn't eaten much lunch and was paying for it now.

Alexa combed my hair back and placed a silver headband around my curls. "Soon, Miss Impatient. Is it dark yet?"

"Close enough," I all-but-pouted. "I wish the days weren't getting longer. From now on, no getting me up early."

She laughed. "I wouldn't exactly call three early." She gave my curls one last tousle. "There, finished."

"Perfect, let's go." I grabbed her wrist and bolted with her in tow.

"You didn't even look," she complained.

I was now well-enough acquainted with Alexa's handiwork to know that anything she touched would come out with her mark of perfection. Looking wasn't necessary.

We rounded the corner into the dining room, but it was empty. No set plates or waiting goblets. No sounds of musicians tuning their instruments or the chatter of the servant's last-minute preparations. "If you'd bothered to slow down for a minute, I would've told you that you were going the wrong way."

My eyes snapped back in Alexa's direction. "What's going on? I'm starving."

Just then, all the candles and lanterns extinguished and the room was blanketed in dark. Alexa wiggled free of my grasp, but I didn't really try to stop her. He was here. His scent, a mixture of crisp spring air and subtle pine, announced his arrival as much as the darkness. *When had I memorized how he smelled?* My chest constricted like the time I dove too deeply into the river as a child; a pressure intense and crushing and exciting. Your body knowing it's more alive than ever from being on the cusp of something dangerous.

His voice rumbled at the same moment those hypnotic blue eyes emerged from the shadows. "I'm sorry to keep you waiting." Placing my hand into the crook of his elbow, he steered me toward the gardens. "I understand you're a little hungry."

"I'll survive, I guess," I said and smiled, hoping he got my sarcasm.

We sat together on a marble couch, reclining against the pillows to look at the stars. They twinkled and blinked, radiating a brilliant light.

"Which one's your favorite?" he asked as his fingers entwined in mine.

"A favorite star? How could you pick one out as different from any of the others?"

"You're not really looking." He pulled his fingers away. Laying his hand over mine, he guided my index to finger to point at the sky. "See these stars? They're the constellation Leo. See, there's his head." Our hands traced an invisible pattern in the air. "This is his body, and his tail curves like this to the right."

His touch sent rays of heat up my arm until I felt ready to singe. "Amazing," I whispered, and he released my hand. "Oh no, show me some more."

"Gladly, but I thought you were hungry."

I rolled onto my side to face him. "Food can wait, I guess."

His eyes cut behind me and I swore I saw a chuckle in them. "Perhaps," he said, "but I doubt Mathias cares to stand idly by while we look at the stars."

Feeling suddenly embarrassed for practically snuggling, I hopped to my feet and straightened my silk gown.

"No need to get up, my Lady," Mathias said. "I'll just set your food on the tripod here. Call if you need anything."

"Yes, of course," I blurted, still feeling awkward. My hands needed something to do, so I set about uncovering the plates of delicacies. "Umm... grape leaves, calamari." I lifted another lid. "Looks like lamb kabobs here. Where shall we start?"

"You pick," he answered. "But this game has rules too."

My hands flopped to my sides. "What is it with you and rules? Can't I just eat?"

"Come here." He held out a darkened hand and I obeyed, bringing the plate of lamb. As I sank into the couch, he took the plate and guided me back until I was reclining again. "Only one rule, this time. You have to let me feed you."

"What?" I asked, trying to sit up. His hand caught my shoulder, pressing me softly back into the pillows.

"I learned something new last night: I love watching you eat. It's beautiful, the way you lick little crumbs away from the corner of your lip. The way your eyes roll back in pleasure when you bite into something you enjoy. Please," he asked, "let me give you that."

He plucked one of the lamb bites from the kabob. My lips parted and my teeth sank into the juicy meat. A dribble ran down my chin, but he wiped it away with a long caress of his finger. I couldn't get over the feeling of being watched while I chewed. Covering my mouth so I could talk with my mouth full, I asked, "Aren't you going to eat."

"Sure," he said. Plucking another lamb chunk from the kabob, he tossed it into the air and caught it with his mouth when it fell.

I gulped. "Show off."

"I'm just getting started," he answered. "I have better tricks than that." His eyes smoldered into mine and I couldn't look away. Leaning in, I could feel his warm breath as my own breathing hitched in my chest. His lips were nearly on mine when my stomach rumbled again. Loudly.

"Apparently one piece of lamb wasn't enough," I said, giving myself an embarrassed pat on the belly.

"Hmm..." he grumbled as he backed away. "I guess I'm not doing such a good job feeding you then." He leaned over and pulled the tripod nearer. "Trust me?"

A smirk pulled at my lips. "Didn't we establish that last night?"

"Then close your eyes. It's better if it's a surprise." Obediently, I squeezed my eyes shut. "Okay, open up." A string of crunchy fried calamari wound into my mouth, the hint of seafood mixed with a smooth tomato puree.

"That's amazing," I said, looking up at him.

"Eyes closed, please." He pivoted away to block my view of the next plate.

"Sorry," I said with a swallow. Eyes closed, I asked, "Next?"

A burst of melon juice shot into my mouth as my teeth sank into the fresh fruit. Following the tangy calamari, the melon was all the more sweet. My tongue shot out to lick the juice from the corner of my lips. *That's what he thinks is cute? I'd never even noticed I was doing it before.*

"Now the grand finale," he promised. My mouth hinged open as I waited. His smooth fingers found my chin, pulling my mouth open wider. A mouthful of moist chocolate cake melted on my tongue. "Mmmm," I murmured, even as I felt my eyes rolling back into my head. *I guess I really do that too.* "You've got to try this," I said.

"I was just waiting for you to ask." His lips fell to mine. Food, even chocolate, was forgotten as he all but drank me in. His hand cradled my head as our kiss deepened. Slowly, his hand traced down my neck to my shoulder, pushing aside the strap of my gown.

My heart jumped into my throat, racing like a rabbit. His lips pulled away with a reluctant tug. "Don't be nervous." He kissed my bare shoulder. "I just liked you too much without the straps." His eyes tunneled into mine. "Indulge me?"

I nodded and he slipped the other strap off.

Fingers, soft as baby's flesh, traced the contours of my collar bone and shoulders. My chest rose under his touch, craving the gentle feel of his caress, chasing the movement of this fingertips.

"You are divine," he whispered into my neck before gifting it with more of his tender kisses. "But we really ought to go inside," he murmured.

My eyes fell closed from the sudden emptiness of losing his touch. When had I gotten so addicted to him? Two days ago he made my flesh crawl, now my skin was humming under his fingers. "Why?" I breathed.

"Because if I don't stop kissing you, I might never let you go."

I opened my mouth to protest, to tell him we could stay under the stars a bit longer, but he was right. As the rush of adrenaline coursed away, my courage went with it. *What in Hades was I doing? And why was I liking it so much?*

CHAPTER 25 — PSYCHE

I stirred when I felt covers tucking in around me. Flitting my eyes open, I could tell dawn was just running her rosy fingers across the horizon, spreading a hint of light through my window.

"I have to leave," Aris whispered before sealing his lips against mine.

That's right. We do that now.

A flush raced across my body, leaving me hot and cold at the same time. If I hadn't been so exhausted, I might've pulled him back to me; refused to let him go. The touch of his lips against mine was an addiction I didn't want to kick.

His lips brushed my temple as he pushed the curls back from my face. "Sleep tight, Love. I'll see you tonight."

As I drifted back to sleep, replaying the past two blissful nights we'd shared, something he said jumped out at me. When I'd asked if he was really a harpy's child, he'd said "yes and no."

That meant something.

Then I thought back to the gardens and the way Alexa had said his mother was such a harpy. I'd thought that was a pretty dumb thing for her to say at the time. I mean, if he was a son-of-a-harpy then obviously his mom was a harpy.

But what if they were using harpy as a metaphor?

What did that make him?

***

"So, Alexa," I asked when I finally pulled my tired carcass out of bed and plodded to the dining room for breakfast, "I was wondering how your magic works. I mean, how come you can be invisible?"

"I don't know," she answered. "I just think it, and I am. Same with going visible. It's just a matter of intent."

"Would you be able to make just part of yourself visible?" I plopped onto a couch and grabbed a bowl of strawberries. "Like, if you wanted to show one of us *mere mortals* just your hair, could you think that too and make it happen?"

"How naive do you think I am, Psyche?"

"What?" I bit into the strawberry and widened my eyes, trying to look innocent.

She heaved a heavy sigh. "I cannot tell you anything that would give away his identity." She recited the words in monotone as if it was some credo she'd been forced to memorize.

"Oh come on," I said, biting into another berry. "You can't blame me for being curious. I mean, if you were *interested* in someone, wouldn't you want to know everything about him?"

"You have got to be the most stubborn person I've ever met."

"Well, wouldn't you?" I insisted.

I heard Alexa drift over to the window. "Sure I would. But that doesn't mean I'm going to tell you anything."

"Just some clue. Give me something," I said,

160

setting the strawberries aside and moving over to her. "All I'm really asking about is what powers a nymph has, right? You should be able to tell me about yourself."

"No," she said.

"No?"

"No, I can't just show part of myself. I'm either all the way visible or not."

Feeling around for Alexa's shoulders, I gave her a quick hug. "See, that wasn't so hard." She snorted. "Okay then," I continued, "could a demi-god be partly invisible if he wanted to?"

"I don't know, you'd have to ask one," she said. "Go eat your eggs before they get cold."

Not a chance. I had too much new information to digest to want food.

"I'll come in for a snack in a bit," I said. "I want to visit the gardens before it gets too late." I practically ran away from Alexa.

Plucking a hibiscus flower, I twirled its little stem between my fingers. The soft pink blended into a muted blur as the petals spun as fast as my thoughts. Working with my new information and some pretty solid assumptions, I was narrowing down the list of possible identities.

I crossed gods off the list -- the only one I knew of with wings detested the sight of me. And the feeling had pretty much been mutual. No way my mystery guy was Eros.

It seemed unlikely that Aris was a demi-god since Alexa had answered my question about whether they could be partly visible: "*I don't know, you'd have to ask one,*" *she'd said*. I didn't think she'd lie to me, and her answer implied she didn't know any demi-gods, which would include Aris.

I abandoned my initial theory that he might be a hero since I'd never heard of a hero who had wings, or could create palaces, or disguise himself.

Which left nymphs. Wouldn't it make sense for a nymph to have another nymph in his employ? And I now knew they couldn't be only partly visible, which explained why he had to hide the rest of himself under a cloud to show his eyes.

Of course, I could still be falling for a monster, but I didn't think so. Not anymore. Not after *feeling* those lips...

Sinking onto a bench with a sigh, I brushed the flower under my chin. *Damn, I wish I knew more about nymphs*. Could one be mischievous enough to frighten the gods? Was there some metaphor there that I was missing? Not like the Oracle was known for clarity, but still. I felt like I was so close to something and still missing it.

And I was also bothered by the fact that I'd never seen Alexa create anything. She had amazing hearing, but I hadn't noticed any other powers. Was she hiding those too? Or maybe there was some super-nymph that I'd never heard of. Like a nymph prince who was more powerful than the others.

"Ugh," I tossed the flower into a manicured hedge and lay back across the bench, folding my arms over my eyes. Now I was inventing nymph royalty. Very productive.

CHAPTER 26 — EROS

Eros and Hermes sat by the river, watching a group of water nymphs splash and frolic. "So they don't interest you?" Hermes asked, nodding to the girls.

"Nope." Eros leaned back and rested on his elbows.

"Still not gonna undo the arrow then?"

"Why would I?" Eros asked.

Hermes looked at the nymphs again and wagged his eyebrows. Eros winced. "Them? They're nothing."

"Guess things are going good then." Hermes said. "You take my advice and use your arrows on her?"

"Nah. She deserves better."

Hermes shrugged. "Yeah, well, not all of us can score with whatever girl looks our way."

Eros barked out a laugh. "Right, like you've ever had problems."

"I'm just saying."

Eros sat back up and stared at the river. "Actually, she can't see me."

"What?" Hermes's eyebrows shot to the top of his head. "Is she blind or something?"

Eros brushed his palms together to wipe away some dirt. "No. I just – I can't take a chance, you know? My mom would…" Eros's voice trailed off.

"Kill her," Hermes filled in. "Yeah, that pretty much sums it up."

163

The gods sat in silence for a moment as the nymphs' light laughter played across the water. Finally, Hermes shook his head. "Man, I can't believe you're going the invisible route after what the Oracle told her."

Eros looked down at his feet. "I'm not exactly invisible either."

"How's that?"

"I created a shroud." He shook his head. "More like a black cloud really, nothing you can touch. It covers everything but my eyes. She can reach through it, but she can't see through it."

Hermes scowled. "That's just weird."

"What?" Eros asked with a shrug.

"She's gonna see a black cloud with eyes staring at her and freak."

"Well, it's working, okay?" Eros snapped.

"Whatever," Hermes shrugged. "Just don't blame me when she finally comes to her senses."

"Not gonna happen," Eros said as he hopped to his feet. "I can feel it."

CHAPTER 27 — PSYCHE

To my great disappointment, dinner returned to the dining room and Aris was very late. Slumped face down across the bed, I'd started drifting off to sleep when I finally felt his gentle touch across my shoulders.

My heavy eyelids pulled open. "You're late."

"I had something I had to take care of." His hands massaged into my shoulders and ran down my shoulder blades. "Trust me, I would've much rather been with you."

I thought for a moment of rolling over, but his touch was too potent. Moving away from it would have taken more willpower than I was willing to summon. His fingers sank again and again into my flesh, working away the knots created by this past week. And the room filled with the scent of lavender and verbena, relaxing me to the point where I had to work to keep from drooling on the pillow.

"Was it work?" I asked.

"Hmm?" His fingertips kneaded my shoulders and neck. I thought for a fleeting moment that if he could make my whole body feel this good, he could touch me wherever he wanted.

"That you had to take care of? Were you working?"

"Actually, yes. Sometimes I have a very demanding boss."

I didn't ask any more questions, but filed away his answer to think about later.

His skilled hands worked down my back, creeping lower toward my hips. Despite having been relaxed, I tensed again as he explored parts of my body no man had ever touched before.

"Relax, Psyche," he whispered close to my ear. "You know I won't hurt you."

"I know," I breathed, "but..."

A realization clicked into my foggy brain. I really did know he wouldn't hurt me -- ever. With the knowledge firmly in place, my heart brimmed with something I hesitated to label love, but was no less than all-consuming infatuation.

Rolling over, I wrapped my arm around his neck and I found his lips with my own. My muscles all but melted as his warm mouth sealed over mine. His touch turned from calming to impassioned, seeking out my hips and thighs with searching hands. As he lowered himself to me, his weight melded into my body as if we were shaped for each other.

He cupped my head in his palm as I searched out his mass of curls, grabbing fistfuls and pulling him nearer. My chest bloomed with emotion, layer after layer flowering with increasing intensity. Contentment, trust, need, passion. My tongue searched him out, trying to drink in the essence of all those emotions flowing like a current between us. And he answered my longing with such desire of his own that I felt like I'd combust under the heat of it.

His hand had just slipped beneath my one-shoulder strap when he froze. His head snapped up and his eyes seemed locked on the headboard.

"Damn," he cursed under his breath.

"What's wrong?" *Something had better be seriously wrong for him to snatch himself away right now.*

"I've got to go." He gave me a quick kiss on the forehead. "I'm sorry. Go to sleep."

Yeah right. Like I could go to sleep now? After that? And then like it had my first night, the command to sleep enveloped me and my eyes were powerless to stay open.

CHAPTER 28 — EROS

What an epic disaster he'd made of last night. When he felt Aphrodite calling for him, he'd panicked. He knew she couldn't see him.

He knew it.

And yet he'd freaked out anyway. He couldn't kick himself hard enough for letting that moment slip through his fingers.

Worse, he knew he'd be lucky if he weren't starting over from scratch tonight. He'd been around women enough to know you don't jilt them one night and share kisses the next. *Stupid, stupid, stupid.*

As evening drew near, Eros wandered through his Olympus home, too anxious for dark to do anything but pace.

When he passed his courtyard, the pleading whispers of a prayer tore him away from his own unrest. He hadn't planned on receiving prayers that night, but somehow this one had gotten in. A widowed mother called to him. Her broken voice tore at his heart as effectively as cut glass.   "Lord Eros, you blessed me once. The love I had with my husband was more than I ever dreamed. Amarus was my everything. My everything." Her voice caught in her throat as a sob bubbled up and burst from the woman's lips. Eros froze in place, transfixed by her desperation.

"But now he's gone, and my uncle will have me

married to another within a week. I know I must. My children need someone to support them. But how can I?" She paused and Eros heard her sniff. "Just make this alright. I need this to be alright."

Her prayer was simple enough. She wanted to be able to move on -- for her remarriage not to feel like a death sentence.

Eros stole a glance back at Psyche. She was bathing. Her damp hair floated around her in the tub like a chestnut halo. Her eyes fluttered closed as she sank deeper into the warm embrace of water. He didn't want to be late returning to her two nights in a row. But he knew with unwavering certainty that Psyche would want him to help. So he figured he'd spare a few minutes before dusk to help ease the pain of someone else's heartbreak.

When Eros found her, the widow was sobbing by her hearth. She was folded over it, head resting on her arms as her body shook with grief. Her younger children circled around the room, continuing their play, seemingly unaware of their mother's anguish. But her older two girls stroked her hair and tried to coax her to take a sip of water.

Eros stood in the corner, an invisible observer, and his heart ached for the woman. What would he do when he lost Psyche? She was mortal, after all, and someday he would lose her. He couldn't imagine the lifeless shell that would be left of him when that happened. If he thought he had pined for her before, now that he knew her, felt her, loved her, what would he do when she was gone?

Without another second's pause, he pulled an

arrow from his quiver and aimed. The woman gasped and raised her head, her eyes searching the room frantically. She'd felt the sting. Few ever did, but perhaps the sudden re-injection of love had tipped her off to the source of the unusual sensation.

Eros stayed invisible and made his exit. Under normal circumstances, he would've enjoyed watching the woman's metamorphosis back to a participant in the land of the living. But his Psyche was waiting.

***

He lit on the window sill and the bedroom went dark as the fire and candles extinguished. Still, his eyes cut through the night, looking for his precious Psyche. She didn't bound into his arms. Nor was she waiting on the bed. That would've been a welcome alternative.

In fact, she wasn't in the room at all. *What the...?*

He'd seen her in the palace when she was bathing. That meant she'd be headed to dinner and then back to the room. She had never *not* been there when he'd arrived. Granted, it'd only been a few days, but her absence that night made Eros's blood run cold. What if she intended to punish him for leaving her last night?

Or worse - what if Hermes had been right? What if Psyche thought better of kissing a darkened shape and had freaked?

He quickly scanned the dining room and kitchen, but Psyche wasn't there. She wasn't in the library or bathroom or any of the other myriad rooms in the palace. Alarm swelled in his veins -- she wasn't in the palace!

And then an even worse thought struck Eros: what if Psyche hadn't left on her own? Had his mother figured out where he'd been these past few nights? Had she looked for him as he flew out in a panic and he'd led her right to his new palace? If she had, Psyche was gone and there was no way he'd get her back.

Eros sank onto the edge of the bed and dropped his head into his hands. Whether she'd left on her own or not, Psyche was gone. He'd wondered only minutes before what sort of shell would be left of him without her, but he hadn't imagined he'd find out so soon.

His face crumpled and he struggled to suck in even tiny gasps of air as pain ripped through him. He wanted to fly off in search of her; to save her from herself or from his mother. But if she'd left on her own, he felt compelled to respect her choice. And if Aphrodite had her... well, Eros hoped she'd left on her own. A moan, more anguished than the widow's, broke from his throat.

"Are you okay?"

Eros's head jerked up and he turned to see Psyche standing in the doorway.

Rather than answer, he sped to her and plucked her off her feet in a consuming hug.

"You're crushing the flowers," Psyche complained.

"Huh?" Eros released her and took a step back.

"The flowers," Psyche explained, picking at the smashed bouquet to revive the blooms. "Since you're not here during the day to see them, I thought I'd bring the orchids to you." She offered him the tiny white and purple blossoms. "But I think they might be ruined now."

Eros took the delicate stalks and tossed them

over his shoulder.

"Hey," Psyche started to protest, but Eros drew her back into his embrace, silencing her with a kiss. "Thank you," he whispered as he rested his forehead against hers.

"It was nothing."

"Not for the orchids. For being here." He kissed her nose and her eyelids. "For being you."

Psyche rolled her eyes and smiled. "It's not like I have much choice on either one."

He wrapped one arm around her shoulders to draw her closer and cradled the back of her head in his other palm. "Don't ever leave me. Please."

Psyche threw her arms around Eros's neck and laughed. "Is that what this is about? I wasn't sitting here waiting for you to come in so you thought I'd left?"

"I don't know. After I rushed out of here last night ..." his voice trailed off. "There were a lot of reactions you could've had and most of them were bad."

"Yeah, well, you've got a demanding boss, right?" She winked. "Besides, I might be starting to like it here."

"Do you know how much I love you?" Eros brushed the tip of his nose against Psyche's and then kissed her again.

"I'm getting the idea," she answered, gazing into his dancing blue eyes. She ran her hand up his face and let her fingers trace through the mass of curls she now knew by touch. "Tell me something."

Eros's embrace loosened as he prepared for another round of the "who are you" questions. The ones he couldn't answer. The ones that drove the only remaining wedge between them.

"Why is everyone else here invisible, but you're not?"

An almost imperceptible sigh of relief escaped Eros's lips as he realized Psyche wasn't trying to re-walk a dead-end path.

"I mean," she continued, "you obviously don't want me to see you, so why not just be invisible like everyone else. Why the darkness and the night-only visits?"

"What makes you think I could be invisible?" he asked.

Psyche raised her eyebrows and looked around the room. "Umm... because you made everything here. I'm guessing invisible is doable for you."

Eros beamed at her. "You're right. I could do invisible. But I want you to see me. I want more than anything to be with you in the light."

"Then why..."

He laid his finger across her lips. "And since I can't do that, this is the next best thing. You can see my eyes, Psyche. Everything you need to know about me you can see in my eyes."

She studied them intently. "I can live with that."

Eros picked her up and spun her around. "I knew there was a reason I love you so much."

"Oh, wait," Psyche said, making Eros stop. "That reminds me. I've been wanting to tell you something."

Eros's heart thundered in his chest. Was she going to tell him the one thing that would make him happy forever? "Yes?" he asked, the word barely escaping his lips.

"Thank you."

Eros's heart sank, but he tried to smile. Her love would come, he assured himself. "For what?"

"For loving me enough to save me," she whispered.

"It has truly been my pleasure."

CHAPTER 29 — PSYCHE

By the time I fell out of bed the next "morning," the staff had already moved on to serving lunch. After grabbing a tuna pita, I met Alexa in the gardens. We were sprawled across the lawn and she was telling me about the time brother number seventeen hid a dead fish in sister twelve's dresser, when I heard wailing from far in the distance.

"You know, that pita looks really good. Come inside with me so I can get one?" Alexa asked in a hurried rush as she grabbed at my hand.

I didn't budge. "What's that noise?"

"It's probably a wounded animal. We ought to get inside in case it's dangerous."

I ignored her and moved closer to the sounds. And then I heard the wails more clearly. "My sister! Poor, Psyche. Poor, poor, Psyche!"

Chara. She must've come back from Mycenae to mourn me at the cliff. The relief of knowing she didn't hate me after all did little to diminish the heartache and guilt shredding my stomach. Here I was, happily oblivious in my new little world, and my family thought I was dead. I was the worst sister ever.

Alexa pulled harder on my arm. "Hurry, Psyche. Get inside the palace. Before it's too late." Her voice was urgent, pleading, frightened.

Still, I managed to shake my arm loose from her

grasp. "What are you talking about? That's my sister calling for me. There's no danger."

Scurrying toward my sister's laments, I followed her voice back to the cliff where my parents had been forced to leave me. Alexa followed in my wake, desperately pleading with me to turn back. But I couldn't stop. Chara was up there. She was so far above, and I was standing down where the West Wind had deposited me, hidden by a fresh forest of limbs and leaves.

"Chara!" I screamed at the top of my lungs. A heavy breeze rustled my dress and played my cry back to my own ears like an echo. I called out for her again and again, but each time the wind dampened my voice and kept it from rising.

"Zephyrus, stop that!" I screamed at him. "I need my sister to hear me. You let her hear me!" Tears and panic bit at me. I had to let her know Aris hadn't harmed me.

And then the wind was gone, as if it had never been whipping around my ankles in the first place. I called again to my sister and this time she stopped wailing.

"Chara! It's Psyche."

"Psyche! Is that you?" Chara's voice call back to me.

Alexa put her hand on my arm again. "Psyche, we need to go back. You don't know what you're doing. This is a mistake."

I ignored her.

"Yes!" I answered Chara. "I'm fine. Don't worry anymore, okay?"

"How can I get down there?" she called.

"Zephyrus," I commanded, "please bring my sister down here to me."

Stillness.

I waited for Chara to appear in the clearing, but she didn't arrive. The wind made no indication it had heard me.

"Psyche? Are you still there?" Chara called to me again.

"Yes! I'm trying to get you down here."

"Just tell me how. Where's the path."

"There is no path," I shouted back. "You need the West Wind's help. Zephyrus," I hollered again, searching the sky around me for any sign of a breeze, "bring me my sister!"

Everything remained still, but the Wind's booming voice shook me from inside as it answered. "Aris forbids it."

"He can't!" I sobbed. "He has to let her come see me. To at least see for herself that I'm still alive."

The Wind didn't answer. He'd given me my answer and moved on.

I racked my brain for what to do as my sister continued calling down to me. "I didn't understand. Did you say the path was to the west?"

"Can you come back tomorrow?" I shouted up to her.

"I don't want to leave you," Chara called down.

"I'm fine. I promise. Tell Mother and Father I'm fine."

"Father's sick," she called. "Can you come home?"

"I don't think-- I don't know." I could barely yell anymore over my tears. Father was fine when I'd left five days ago. What could've gone wrong already? "Come back tomorrow. You can visit. Please."

"Fine," she answered. "I'll be back tomorrow."

I took my time wandering back to the palace, barely hearing Alexa shuffling her feet behind me over my own sniffles. I had a problem. I'd promised my sister a visit even though I knew Aris had already forbidden it.

But why had he said no before I even asked?

CHAPTER 30 — EROS

He paced in the forest, barely hidden from view, waiting for night to fall so he could return to Psyche.

He'd known Chara would come. She'd prayed to Hermes for a safe journey to Sikyon. And Hermes had warned Eros. He knew if Chara was returning home so soon after her marriage, it could only be to mourn Psyche. Which meant she's be headed for the cliffs.

Eros did everything he could to try to keep Psyche and her sister from reuniting. He warned Alexa -- made her promise not to let Psyche near the hilltop. Alexa had assured him it wouldn't be a problem; Psyche only stayed in the gardens.

No one had figured Chara could wail so loudly.

Eros had kept watch over Psyche the entire day. He saw Psyche's attention suddenly snap toward the hills. He saw Alexa tugging at Psyche's wrist, pleading with Psyche to go back inside. And he saw Psyche's stubborn will win out as she shrugged free of Alexa and hurried to the base of the hill.

Watching the scene unfold had been tortuous. Eros wanted so badly to intervene. To save Psyche from herself. He knew in his heart that Psyche would demand a visit with Chara. What sister wouldn't under normal circumstances?

But things between Psyche and Chara weren't going to be normal any more. Chara's hatred for Psyche festered in the days following her arranged marriage.

Chara was miserable and she blamed Psyche. Her grief on the cliffs was real enough -- Eros could feel that. But she was more mourning the whole relationship they'd had. And sobbing for the misery that had become both their lives in such a short time.

When Chara and Psyche finally turned away from each other, Eros collapsed against the cool stucco of his courtyard wall. Chara was headed home; she wasn't going to try to find away into their valley. He wiped the sweat of his brow with the back of his hand and huffed. What good was being a god if all you could do was sit idly by and watch? He never wanted to relive another moment like that one.

But he also knew he wasn't entirely out of the woods yet either. Favinous had answered truthfully when Psyche asked why he wouldn't carry Chara down -- Eros, or Aris rather, had forbidden it. And for that decision, Eros figured he would likely suffer for awhile under Psyche's anger, disappointment, or grief. At least he hoped it was one of those more benign emotions. Because facing her hatred was something he would never be prepared for.

CHAPTER 31 — PSYCHE

I rushed through dinner and hurried back to my bedroom before the sun had fully set. When I entered my room, I stopped in my tracks.

The room was overflowing with fragrant, white flowers. Roses and lilies. Orchids and chrysanthemums. I leaned over a bouquet of roses and inhaled. Their scent was so perfectly sweet it was almost intoxicating. I pulled one of the long-stemmed beauties from among the others and traced it under my nose. It felt like softest velvet.

As I stood back to admire the flowers more fully, I noticed how the white petals glowed mysteriously in the candle light. How the heady aroma of fresh blooms wrapped around the room like a cozy quilt. It was sort of funny -- how he'd tossed away the orchids I'd brought him last night only to make it up to me with this. He definitely got points for style.

But then I remembered that he had forbidden my sister from visiting me. No matter how much I appreciated everything he'd given me, I couldn't let him keep me from my family. Especially not now.

Darkness was only starting to envelop the palace when Aris flew through the window and swept me into his arms. He kissed me deeply. Not passionately, but as if he were afraid he might lose me if he let go.

I looked up at his face, wishing for the millionth time that I could see the flawless features I knew were hiding there. All there was of him to see were his dazzling eyes. He'd said all I needed to know about him was in his eyes, but that didn't feel exactly true tonight.

Something was off and whether it was me or him or both of us, I didn't know.

Finally, he broke the heavy silence. "I need you to promise me something, Psyche." His hands gently shook my shoulders, as if his words were like flour that needed to be sifted into my brain. "Promise you'll never try to talk to your family again."

"What?" I wasn't sure what was worse, the fact that he'd been spying on me or the promise he wanted me to make. "Are you insane? They're my family."

"You should've let them think you were dead. It was safer."

"Is that the little string you're going to pull to get your way every time? *This isn't safe. That's not safe.* Safe from what? What do you think my family's going to do to me that's so dangerous?"

"Psyche, let me expla--"

"No, I want to finish," I said, pulling the petals off the rose I was holding. "You obviously knew Chara was coming since you'd already forbidden Zephyrus from bringing her down." The more I thought on it, the angrier I became. "Why are you trying to keep me away from her?"

Aris stepped back. He was probably stunned that I'd raised my voice at him. I had to admit it surprised me a little too.

Finally he said, "I did it for us."

"Us? There's only been an us," I said, indicating with my finger between our chests, "for like two days. How did you think cutting my family out of the picture would help us?"

"Because if I can't keep you safe, there is no us. Got it?"

"No, I don't. I feel like we're talking in circles. My family is not a danger to me." His eyes had turned metallic and I sensed I was losing, so I changed tact.

Clasping his hand in mine, I pulled him down to sit on the bed next to me. "You don't know what it was like for me today... to hear her up there, knowing Father is sick. All I want is for her to come visit for a day, just an afternoon even. She deserves to know I'm safe." I squeezed his fingers. "That you're keeping me very safe."

"Her visit won't make you happy." His answer sounded more like a sigh than spoken words.

"If she only brings bad news, I can deal with that. Heck, she could come down here, tell me she hates me and I'd be happier than I am right now. My family *needs* to know I'm okay."

"Psyche," he said, his fingers lacing into mine, "I don't want to fight with you." He reached over and stroked a strand of hair away from my face. "If you want to see Chara, then she can come. I won't stop her."

My eyes closed in relief. "Thank you."

"But I want a different promise from you instead. Deal?" he asked.

I couldn't bear to open my eyes and look at him when he was attaching strings to my last visit with my sister. "What is it?"

"Promise you won't tell her anything about me. Or listen to anything she says about me," he added. "Okay?"

"Fine."

That should be easy enough, since I hardly know a damn thing about you myself.

He leaned in, like he was going to try to plant one of his mesmerizing smooches on my lips. But I turned my head away. I was not ready to kiss and make up. On either front.

No kissing.

No making up.

Until I saw my sister tomorrow and knew he was making good on his end of the bargain, I wasn't ready to be done fuming.

"All the pollen in here is giving me a headache," I told him. "I think we better just call it a night."

His eyes looked misty. "I understand."

After planting a kiss on my forehead, he unfurled his wings and flew out of the palace. When I blinked, the flowers disappeared too. All except for the shredded rose I still held.

Falling back against the pillows, I realized he hadn't uttered his sleep command when he'd kissed me goodbye. *Of all the nights.* Between being keyed up from our argument and knowing I'd see my sister tomorrow, sleep didn't feel like it was going to come easy.

Sometimes I hated being right.

CHAPTER 32 — EROS

When Eros left, he gave one last longing look back at Psyche. *Could she keep her promise?* She was only human after all. She looked so small and fragile against her massive bed. He wanted to ignore her suggestion that he leave. Even more, he wanted break his own rules and stay beside her all the next day.

But it was just one day. It might be a hard day, but a day they would get through. And then things would be back to normal.

His powerful wings carried him back to his palace on Olympus. Eros pushed through the solid gold door and flopped down onto a pillow-covered couch. He'd planned to spend the night and all the next day on that couch, keeping silent watch to make sure Psyche's sister didn't interfere too much. But no sooner had he comfortably reclined, then he heard his mother's voice behind him.

"Out late again?" Aphrodite asked with raised eyebrow and a knowing glint in her eye.

"Mother!" Eros jumped up so quickly he nearly lost his balance. Only by jutting out a hand to the couch was he able to catch himself, but that caused a number of cushions to spill to the ground.

Aphrodite laughed, throaty and enticing. Her signature laugh.

"What?" Eros snapped at her, grabbing up the spilled pillows.

"Now is that any way to greet your mother?" Aphrodite purred. "You've kept me here waiting half the night."

Eros felt beads of sweat pop onto his forehead. *Did she know?* She couldn't have *seen*, but had she *heard?*

"You know, you've been staying out late quite a bit lately," Aphrodite said as she sauntered toward her son. "I'm afraid you're hiding something from me." Aphrodite ran her long, delicate finger down Eros's forearm. He couldn't help but shudder just a tad.

"What about it? I have a life, you know."

"Don't get so defensive, dear," Aphrodite said, raising her hand innocently to her chest. "You forget you're talking to the goddess of love. I know about *needs.*"

"I am so not having this conversation with you," Eros said as he plopped back down onto his couch. He folded his arms across his chest and closed his eyes, as if he could ignore his mother out of his house.

Aphrodite sat down next to her son. "I'm not judging you, son. I just don't want you to get hurt again."

Eros cut his eyes over to his mother, not sure where she was going with this.

"I just don't want you spending too much time with the *same* girl. As I thought you'd learned, it's not... judicious for us to get too attached to mortals." Aphrodite leaned in closer. "You won't be able to keep her."

Eros's eyes widened only briefly as he realized his mother had no idea about Psyche. She just thought he was having an overly-long affair with some anonymous mortal. He could work with that.

Eros curled up the corner of his mouth into a devilish grin. "Fine. I'll cut her loose. But don't expect me home still. There are plenty more where she came from."

"My thoughts exactly," Aphrodite said, "which is why I want you to meet someone."

No, no, no. She is not trying to set me up again. Please tell me she's not setting me up.

"You'll just adore Iris," Aphrodite continued. "She's bright and imaginative and she appears in the most beautiful places."

"She's a freakin' rainbow. For the last time, I am not dating her, okay?"

Aphrodite dropped the nice act. "Look around. It's not like there are that many available goddesses out there. You've already refused the one mortal I offered you. But you're getting too old to keep up this nonsense. If you don't settle down soon and stop being such a pest, Zeus is going to strip you of your arrows."

"I haven't shot at him in months. What's got him so worked up now?"

Aphrodite folded her arms across her chest. She looked out a window, decidedly not answering his question. "It's not him," she finally grumbled. "It's Hera."

"Why's she in a tiz?"

Aphrodite's jaw set, the tiny veins near her ears bulging.

"Why, Mother?" Eros pressed.

"She realized when I picked Psyche as my mortal daughter that there was more to her."

Eros sat up, suddenly much more interested. "And what's that supposed to mean?"

Aphrodite rolled her eyes. "Maybe Leda wasn't the only one who made a baby when a god came to visit."

"What are you --" Frustrated, Eros hopped up from the couch. "Just tell me what you're trying to say and stop making me guess."

"Poseidon is Psyche's father. When Hera figured that out, it reopened old wounds about Zeus siring Helen. As much as she hates you sending Zeus off to have affairs, the idea of him having any more part-human children makes her insane. And Psyche reminded her how very possible that is."

Eros' jaw unhinged. The love of his existence wasn't a full mortal after all. Did that change anything? And more importantly, how did that make Hera pissed at him? "Whoa. I wasn't even born for Helen and I was probably still a toddler when Psyche was born. Not. My. Fault."

Aphrodite stood and smoothed her long, white gown. "Yes, well, whether it's your fault or not, the proverbial heat is on you at the moment. I'd suggest you do something to cool all tempers involved."

Eros leaned back against the wall, arms crossed over his chest. "I can tell you already have something in mind, so lay it on me."

"You need to take Iris to the Olympian council meeting this afternoon."

Uh-uh. No way was he leaving the palace today. "Not today. Maybe some other time."

"I'm not asking. You *will* take Iris."

Eros ground his teeth. "You can't just come in here and order me around. I'm not your little puppet."

With startling swiftness, Aphrodite placed her palms against the wall on either side of his head, fencing him in. "You are nothing except what *I* say you are." An edge of contempt crept into her voice. "You have powers as the god of love only because *I* gave you some of my province. I will take it back as easily as I gave it."

Eros only blinked at her.

Aphrodite patted her son's cheek twice as she backed away. "The council then, at noon. I'll expect to see you and Iris there." Aphrodite turned on her heel and disappeared in a puff of sea foam and sand.

Eros hated when she left like that. He wiped away the salty taste of the sea spray from his lips and shook the sand from his tunic.

Slouching down on the couch, he tried to think of a way out. He'd completely forgotten about the council meeting. And of course, he had to go. Even if he wasn't taking Iris (a command he still might ignore), he didn't dare miss one of Zeus's monthly meetings. Especially since he'd just been warned that Zeus and Hera were already ticked at him.

But the timing couldn't have been worse. If Eros was at council, he couldn't keep an eye on Psyche and her sisters. He exhaled a burst of air as he realized his plans for the day would have to change.

Eros had no other choice really, which was a reality that made him even surlier than when he'd had to leave Psyche alone, waiting for her sister. The day was going downhill fast.

CHAPTER 33 — PSYCHE

Unable to lie in bed anymore, I threw open the shutters and looked out on the gardens, inhaling the still-cool morning air. It was thick with the scents of spring: rose petals and dew, grass and purity. Today would be a good day. I could feel it.

"Alexa," I called out. "Come enjoy this beautiful morning with me."

Alexa came to my side, but not with her usual promptness. "You called?" Her tone was sullen.

"What's with you? How can you not be happy on a perfect morning like this?"

"You've slept through every morning for the past five days. They've all been this nice actually."

I shot a critical look in her direction. "Seriously, what's with you today? Did I wake you up or something?"

Alexa snorted. "That'll be the day. When *you* wake *me* up."

"Did I do something to you?"

"You might as well have," Alexa snapped at me.

"I honestly have no idea what you're talking about. Either tell me what has you so upset or take your grumpy self somewhere else."

"You don't know what I'm talking about?" Alexa was almost shrieking, but her voice wavered in a way that told me she was on the edge of tears. "You're tossing all of us away just so you can have one more visit with your sister. Do you have any idea how much you've hurt him? How much he's sacrificing trying to make you happy?"

My heart was cut in two different directions. I hated hearing Alexa so upset. Hated hearing that he was upset. But I was also angry that she was injecting her opinions into my personal business. I'd already had this discussion last night and promised Aris I'd keep my sister's conversation on track. That was between the two of us and it was settled as far as I was concerned.

"Don't you dare try to second-guess me on this. My sister is visiting today and it won't be the catastrophe everyone seems to think it will be."

I heard Alexa stomp to the door.

"Before you leave," I called after her, "I'll remind you that you *will* treat Chara with the respect she's due."

"Yes, ma'am." Alexa slammed the door behind her.

What was happening around here? I'd gone a almost a week bonding with Alexa and Aris, certainly not fighting with either of them, and now they were both pissed at me. Because I wanted to see my sister? Hear about my sick father?

Well, they could just stay pissed then.

I skipped breakfast so I could get back to the mountain and greet Chara. Getting dressed took longer than usual because I didn't dare ask Alexa for help, so I ended up half-running to the front of the palace.

"It's time everyone," I called out to the servants. "Chara will be here soon. I need you to be on your best behavior. Alexa, will you come with me to get her?"

There was no answer.

"Alexa? Are you here?"

"The plans for your sister's arrival aren't quite ready. We weren't expecting visitors, you know. I ought to stay here to make sure everything is *perfect*." Sarcasm and resentment spilt out of Alexa faster than wine spews from a broken urn.

"Oh, okay. We'll be back soon then," I sang, hoping my happiness was as annoying to Alexa as her bitterness was to me. Did she not understand that I *needed* to hear about my father's health? It's not like I'd begged to see my sister just so we could sit around and drink wine all afternoon.

The massive front doors slammed closed behind me as I darted for the mountain. "Zephyrus! Is she here yet? Has my sister come back?"

With a sudden gust, my dress rustled around my ankles and the Wind nearly lifted me off of my feet. "Yes," he boomed, "but I'll be happy to make her leave again if you like."

"You bring her down to me this instant."

Zephyrus laughed. A booming, imposing laugh that shook me to the core. "As you wish."

No sooner had I reached the base of the cliff face than Chara was dumped at my feet. Zephyrus had apparently swept her off the hill and plunged her down with little care for her safety. As my sister sat dazed, trying to orient herself and fix her disheveled dress, I rushed to her side and threw my arms around her neck.

"Chara!" I gushed, kissing her cheeks. "I'm so glad you're here. You don't know how much I've missed you."

Grabbing her hands, I helped her stand. Chara

bent down to collect a small wooden chest she'd been carrying before being upended.

"Let me get that for you," I offered.

Chara looked relieved not to have to tax herself with the burden of carrying the chest anymore, even though it was no bigger than my hand. "It's for you anyway," she said. "Mother sent one of her honey cakes, but I ate half of it while I was waiting for you to get here."

Hmm... not exactly the sort of greeting I was expecting. Maybe she's still dazed from her cloud flight.

"Oh, well if you're hungry, let's go inside," I said. "We can have anything you like for lunch: oysters, quail, pork ..."

As I was listing off some of the finest foods I could think to offer, Chara suddenly stopped in her tracks. We had come around the tree stand and my palace stood in full view. It was still as pristine as the day I'd arrived, with the sun glinting blindingly off the golden roof and marble walls.

"*That's* your home?" Chara asked. Her eyebrows arched toward her forehead.

"It's something, isn't it?"

As we neared, the door opened invitingly. My doorman, Mathias, greeted us. "My ladies, welcome," he said.

Chara's eyes darted from side to side trying to find the source of the greeting.

"Sorry. I should've warned you that the servants here are invisible." I leaned in to whisper to her. "They're nymphs, so don't even think about asking to see them."

The door closed behind us and we stood in the massive entrance hall. "Is there anything I can get for you? Perhaps a glass of water or wine until lunch is served?" Mathias offered.

My sister looked too frightened to answer and just stared stupidly in the direction of Mathias's voice. "Thank you, Mathias," I answered for her. "We'll both have some wine."

"Of course," he answered politely. *At least I could count on him to mind his manners.* The light swishing sounds of his robe drifted away as he went to fetch our drinks.

"Let's go to the gardens," I invited. "It's a beautiful morning and the roses are blooming. It's my favorite place so far."

I led the way as Chara followed in my wake. When we neared the doors, they pushed open in front of us. Chara gave a startled screech.

"After you," Alexa said. I shot a stern look in her direction, warning her not to deliberately scare my sister again.

"Chara, meet Alexa. She's been like a sister to me while I've been here."

Chara's lips wrinkled uncomfortably.

"Not that she could ever replace you," I added hastily. "I just ... well, you know what I meant. She's just been really great."

Chara nodded with a twisted smile. "Of course. Sisters are always so good to each other, aren't they?"

Oh my gods. She hates me. She knows I knew about Rasmus and now she hates me. I'd said last night I could take it, but the reality slammed me harder than I'd expected.

"You've got to understand, Chara, I didn't --"

"What *is* this place?" Chara interrupted.

I laughed nervously, shrugging my shoulders. "Nothing. I mean, it's just a palace. What do you mean what is it?" I silently told myself to stop stammering. Alexa gave my hand a reassuring squeeze.

Chara marched out into the courtyard and took in the gardens. Then she stomped back to me, grabbing my shoulders a little too tightly.

"Tell me what's going on here," she commanded. Her eyes bore into mine and all I wanted was to look away.

Just then, Mathias came into the courtyard. Our drinks hovered on a silver tray, floating in his invisible hands. He handed each of us goblets encrusted with rubies and filled to the brim with red wine.

"Let's sit." I gestured to some padded stools that'd been placed in the courtyard for us. We both sat uncomfortably on the edge of our tripods and sipped at our drinks.

I swallowed hard. "What do you want to know?"

"Where's the monster who took you?" Chara asked as she glanced over her shoulder.

I laughed nervously. *Hadn't I just promised Aris we wouldn't talk about him? Crap. This wasn't going well.*

"He's not really a monster. The prophecy was a little off on that. But he's out hunting right now." That seemed liked a probable explanation. Father used to go out hunting for days at a time when he was younger. "Unfortunately, he won't be back in time to meet you."

Chara's eyes narrowed at me. "If he's not a monster, then what is he?"

My eyes widened as my heart thundered in my chest. I knew I had to steer this conversation in a new direction. And quickly. Alexa's hand pressed down on my shoulder. *What was she trying to tell me?*

Before I could answer, Chara made her own assumptions. "You don't know what he is, do you?"

"I, ah...well..."

"Shut up," Alexa hissed in my ear, so low only I could hear her.

"I knew you could be dense sometimes, but this defies all logic." Chara glared at me. "You know what the Oracle foretold."

"Yeah, well, maybe it's not as bad as we thought," I spat at her.

Chara shook her head. "Unbelievable. It's like you only see the world in shades of gold now."

The anger boiling in my veins actually started making me light headed. *Where was Mathias with the food?* I needed to eat something before I had a panic attack or something.

But Chara obviously wasn't done with her lecture. "You've been so fooled by all these riches, you can't see that you're living in a tomb. Come on, we're getting out of here now." She grabbed my hand and tried to beeline for the back door.

"That's enough!" Alexa screamed from behind me. "You don't know what you're talking about."

"The Oracle's never wrong," Chara spat back at her.

Alexa slid her arm around my shoulder

protectively. "Psyche, please don't listen to her. You've lived here. You know what's true. What's real. She doesn't."

Did I? I knew what I'd been told, but what did I really know? I knew that the Oracle had said I'd fall for a monster. Someone that even the gods feared. But I had plenty of evidence that he wasn't really like that. All those talks we'd shared. And kisses.

Had they made me forget the prophecy?

"You're wrong," I told Chara, even as confusion worked to crack my voice. "He's not a monster."

"Wise up, Psyche," she scolded as she dropped my hand. "Since he hasn't killed you already, he's probably just waiting for you to fatten up so you'll be a decent meal."

I covered my face with my hands as warm tears began to flow down my cheeks. "You don't know him," I cried.

"No, she doesn't," Alexa assured me. Her soft hands invisibly brushed the tears away. "And I think it's time she left. She's not welcome here if she upsets you this much."

"You're going to trust *her* over *me*?" Chara asked. "Has she ever even shown herself to you? She could be as much as monster as that thing you're living with."

My head was swirling. Alexa held me tightly, but I didn't know who to trust. I didn't want her arm around me any more and I shrugged her off.

"Stop, Psyche," Alexa implored. "Don't you see now? This is why he didn't want her to come. He knew she'd upset you with her ignorance. Don't let her do it, Psyche. Trust your instincts."

"Her instincts?" Chara laughed. "You mean the ones that told her to keep quiet about being friends with Aphrodite? Or the ones that refused a marriage proposal from Eros? Or how about that night at dinner." She looked at me with raised eyebrows. "The rumors about your little speech that night flew to me faster than if Hermes had carried them."

"Please, stop yelling," I begged. "Just let me think for a minute."

Alexa's voice was consoling. "Don't over-think this, Psyche. The only truth in the world is that Aris loves you."

"He did warn me," I confessed to her softly. "And I promised... I promised I wouldn't listen to anything she said about him."

"You are such a fool!" Chara yelled at me. "Why would he make you promise something like that unless he knew I was going to tell you the truth?"

I could feel my pulse jumping underneath my skin. As the jitters crept over me, my legs started to wobble. For my own sanity, this conversation had to end.

"I'm sorry you think that." I flicked my eyes to Chara before quickly looking away. "We really need to stop talking about this now though, okay?"

Chara's eyes would've sliced through me like a spear. "Maybe you're happy to sit around here waiting to be lunch, but I'm not. I'm leaving."

"Wait." I jumped in front of her before she could storm out. "You still haven't told me about Father. I'm far more worried about his health than mine. Can we please go inside and talk about it over lunch?"

As I turned to lead the way, a blinding pain flashed in my head and my vision darkened. The courtyard tiles felt like they were swaying beneath my feet as I struggled to maintain my balance. One hand shot to my head and the other reached out to find something to steady myself against. I couldn't fall over. But with the throbbing in my brain, I couldn't keep standing either.

Alexa had her arm around me in a heartbeat and Chara rushed to my side, but she only looked on.

"Mathias," Alexa called. "Come help!"

"My head," I moaned. Before I could even try to regain my balance, Mathias was in the courtyard and scooping me up into his arms.

"I think she's got a migraine," Alexa explained. "Take her to her room so she can rest."

As Mathias carried me inside, I asked him to wait. "I have to say goodbye to my sister."

I turned as best I could from Mathias's arms to look at her, but slammed my eyes again when the sunlight only increased the searing pain in my head. "Don't leave yet. At least stay for lunch. Maybe it will go away."

"Unbelievable," Chara muttered. "Fine. I'll eat lunch and then I'm leaving. If you're not up by then, I'll come find you to say goodbye."

As Alexa hissed something at my sister, plates and goblets floated into the dining room and Mathias carted me away.

He laid me carefully across my bed and propped my head and feet up with the silken pillows. Then he draped a scarf across my eyes to block out the light.

"There you are. Get some rest and forget about all that nonsense."

"Um-hmm," I mumbled in agreement.

But when I was alone, a sudden darkness of panic flooded me. My chest compressed as my head reeled with a suffocating dizziness. *What was I going to do? Who was I supposed to believe?* I'd sided with Alexa in the courtyard, but was back to questioning my decision. As my mind swam with questions, and the aching in my head intensified, I drifted into a restless sleep.

The next thing I knew, Chara was crouched beside my bed, urging me to wake up in a hushed whisper.

"Psyche, I don't have long. Alexa will come looking for me soon. Just listen to me."

I pushed up onto my elbows and blinked the sleep from my eyes. Chara's intensity was frightening.

"If you want to save yourself, then listen to me. Hide a knife and lantern under the bed. Tonight, after he's asleep, you kill him. And be quick about it. A beast like him won't give you a second chance to do what you need to do."

"I couldn't possibly... I told you. He's not like that."

"Just think about it. As mad as I am at you, I don't want to see you dead. You understand me?"

Just then the door flew open and pounded with a crash against the marble wall.

"What are you doing in here?" Alexa demanded in a thundering tone I'd never heard from her before.

Chara rose to her full height in a way I'm sure she meant to look proud and intimidating. "I was just telling my sister goodbye. And apologizing for upsetting her. Isn't that right, Psyche?"

I was shaking too badly to disagree. I nodded weakly since I didn't want another clash breaking out around me.

"Well, you should get some rest then. You'll need your strength." Chara's eyes bore into mine as she looked down at me. She was too tall, too imposing, looking at me that way. I wanted to pull the covers over my head and hide.

I wanted her to leave so the pounding in my brain would leave too.

"Travel safely," I said, waving a half-hearted goodbye.

Alexa closed my door again after Chara left and I flopped back into my pillows. I was so tired. And confused.

And achy.

I stared up at my ceiling and wondered if I was coming down with the flu. I remembered the terrible shudders and retching I'd had a few years ago and it was miserable. If Father was feeling this sick -- Father! I still didn't know what was wrong with him. That was the whole reason I really needed my sister to come in the first place.

Clambering out of bed, I hurried down the hall to catch Chara before she left. I was just rounding the corner into the entrance hall when I stopped dead in my tracks.

Standing at the gilded entrance doors, saying goodbye to my sister, was a perky-looking girl. Her dress was the sparkling blue-green color of the river where it meets the sea, and her amber hair flowed like rippling waves down her back. I would've known her voice anywhere. Alexa.

I backed into the hall to stay out of sight and listened. "So you see," Alexa was saying, "it's really better for Psyche that she not be able to see us. We're not sure she could handle it all."

My sister nodded and smiled knowingly.

What had Alexa just told her about me? How could she let my sister see her but hide herself from me? If Alexa had lied to me about it being bad luck to see a nymph, what else was she lying about?

Just then I had a sickening thought. *What if everything I thought was true, wasn't?* The architecture could be an elaborate rue to confuse me. My new friend a spy to mislead me. Maybe the only truth was what my sister had been trying to tell me after all.

How stupid had I been?

The clang of the front door pushing closed jolted me back. I couldn't let Alexa see me here. If I had any chance of surviving, she couldn't know what I'd just overheard.

CHAPTER 34 — EROS

Eros not only missed his chance to watch Psyche and her sister, but he wasted three otherwise perfectly good hours of his life listening to Iris chatter away in meaningless babble. His stomach nearly lurched when she pursed her thin lips together and batted her eyelashes in obvious hopes of receiving a kiss after Council. But Eros dropped Iris at her door, giving her only a quick, "See you at the next meeting," before launching himself back toward his Olympian palace.

Eros tore through the door and darted to his couch, perching on the edge. With his fingers tented together, he started scanning.

A swirl of purple mixed with cloud caught his attention first. Zephyrus was carrying Chara back up the mountain. Eros didn't know whether to be relieved that she was gone or angry that he'd missed the entire visit.

Before he could decide, his thoughts returned to Psyche. How had she held up?

Eros scanned through the palace courtyard and gardens. No Psyche. He searched the dining room and library with no luck either. He squeezed his fingertips more tightly together. Finally, he checked her bedroom, and there she was. He hadn't thought to find her there since it was the middle of the day. But now, his near-panic at not immediately finding her seemed foolish. She'd shown him just a few days ago that he didn't need to worry about her going missing.

Convinced that Psyche was asleep, Eros ignored the sunshine and flew down to his palace to find Alexa.

"Well," he whispered when he found her, "tell me what happened."

"Ack!" Alexa started, poking herself with her sewing needle hard enough to draw blood. "Look what you made me do!" Alexa stuck the wounded finger in her mouth. "Donth sneakth up on people," she said.

Eros let out a long sigh. "Sorry. So what happened?"

Alexa's eyebrows pinched together. "Weren't you watching?"

"I had Council today," Eros explained as he flopped into a leather-covered chair in the corner of Alexa's room.

"Well, you missed a show. Psyche's sister tried to turn her against you, like you thought she would. Chara made her so upset she got a migraine even. But Psyche was strong. She changed the subject and she'll be fine."

Eros exhaled the breath he hadn't even realized he'd been holding. "Is she okay?"

"It was just the stress. I'm sure she'll be better now that Chara's gone."

"Guess that explains why she's napping," Eros mumbled.

"Want to hear the really good part?" Alexa's eyes were wide with excitement. "Psyche was already resting when Chara left, so as I was showing her out, I showed her me." Her teeth sparkled from under her impish grin.

"I appreciate the gesture, but I'm not sure she

deserves what's coming now."

"You don't understand," Alexa whined. "She kept calling you a monster. And she tried to get Psyche to leave with her. She definitely deserves whatever bad luck she gets."

Eros crunched his teeth as he thought. Chara tried to take his Psyche away. He'd rather be shot than lose her. Finally, he nodded. "You did the right thing."

Perhaps sensing his tension, Alexa turned solemn. "Zephyrus didn't drop her on the way back up the cliff, did he? I wasn't trying to kill her or anything."

"I know," Eros assured her. "And no, I saw Chara make it back. But you know something is coming. No human ever escapes the bad luck that follows seeing a nymph."

CHAPTER 35 — PSYCHE

After seeing Alexa and Chara together, I slipped back to my room and flung myself face down onto my bed. I had to bite my pillow to muffle the sobs that threatened to tear from my throat in screams. Like frozen glass breaking apart, my heart felt like it had splintered into a million jagged shards.

It wasn't even that I now knew Aris was a monster. That seemed inconsequential in comparison to knowing that whatever feelings I was starting to have for him, he'd manipulated. Those tender moment we'd shared, the sweet promises he'd planted like kisses on my soul, were all lies. He'd promised to love me always and I had believed him willingly. How had I not seen he was just lulling me into a false sense of security?

I was suddenly so angry that I wished I could sink my fingernails into the baby-soft flesh on his perfect-feeling face and rip. To separate fistfuls of ringlets from his scalp. To dig below the black mask of perfection he wore and uncover the monster within.

I felt like I'd been living in the world's best dream for the past few days, only to wake up right where I fell asleep: trembling on this bed, waiting for a grotesque monster to come claim me.

Only this time, I would be ready.

Sitting up to wipe at my tears, I resolved that I'd had enough of simply sitting by and accepting the destiny life handed me. I would *not* offer up myself as a sacrifice, no matter what some stupid prophecy said.

Of all things, why did my sister have to be right about this? I closed my eyes, bracing myself for the trial ahead.

Chara had told me what to do. A lantern and a knife was all I needed. I could get a knife from the kitchen and I was pretty sure I'd seen a lantern in the library when Alexa gave me my official tour.

Locating them would be the easy part. Retrieving them unnoticed in a house full of invisible servants would be more difficult.

I pulled my legs up by my chest and hugged my arms around them. Resting my head on my knees, I tried to figure out how to get what I needed. The key would be distracting Alexa -- the traitorous witch. As soon as she knew I was awake, she'd want to gossip about how awful my sister was and she wouldn't leave. I'd scream if I had to listen to her badmouth Chara as if *she* was the evil one.

Maybe I could tell her I'd thought of a new dress design and I wanted her to get started on it right away. That I wanted to surprise Aris with it as soon as possible. She might buy that, but it wouldn't keep her far enough away. And if she needed any fabric, or thread, or whatever else goes into making a stupid dress, she might come out of her room and catch me sneaking around.

I needed her out of the palace.

And then it came to me.

"Alexa," I called, with acrid-laced sweetness. It was the best I could do.

She was to my door with her usual immediacy.

"Are you feeling better?" she asked with obvious

concern. Faker.

"You know what I'd really like?" I asked. "Some honey cake. Seeing my mother's honey cake today made me crave it, but Chara almost ate it all."

"That's easy enough. The chef can prepare as many loaves as you like."

I sighed and made a pouty grimace. "But that won't be the same," I whined. "Mother always uses fresh honey that she gets herself from the hives. Could you go get me some fresh... pleeeeeease?"

"Seriously?"

"It would mean so much to me. I'll be your best friend."

She sighed. "Ordinarily I'd tell you you're stuck with the honey we already have, but considering the day you've had..."

I made a show of clapping my hands excitedly. "Thank you, Alexa! You're the best. Take the chef with you to help. I don't want you getting stung."

In truth, I hoped she'd get stung by a million pointed bees' tails and her throat would swell closed. She was so much easier to hate than Aris. If it weren't for her, I might never have trusted him in the first place.

"Fine. Do you need anything before I leave?" she asked.

I rolled my eyes and waved her away with a floppy gesture. "It's not like I can't manage on my own."

The door started to close behind Alexa, but then pushed open again. "Are you sure you're feeling okay? Chara was really hard on you today. You're not acting like yourself."

"I'm fine," I said, a razor-sharp edge to my voice. "Can't I just crave honey cake after having the worst migraine in the history of the planet?"

"I'm sorry, Psyche. You just seem... never mind. I was worried, is all."

I glared up in her direction from under narrowed eyelids. "You don't need to worry about me. *I'll* be fine."

"Okay," she said, deflated. "We'll be back with the honey in a little bit. Maybe you should rest while we're gone." Alexa closed the door softly behind her.

"Maybe you should mind your own business," I grumbled, not even caring if she heard me or not.

I gave Alexa and the chef about ten minutes to clear the palace before I slunk down the hall toward the kitchen. This wasn't a room I'd been in yet, but at least I knew where it was. As I sized up the comparatively tiny room, with its jugs of wine, rows of spices and copper pots, I realized I had no idea where to look.

As quietly as I could, I pulled open drawers in the massive cabinet, rifling the contents in search of a weapon. It didn't take long to locate a gleamingly-sharp blade with a sturdy wooden handle. I wrapped my fingers slowly around the grip and held the knife up to get a feel for it in my hand. *Could I really do this? Could I really murder someone?*

What choice did I have?

After wrapping the knife in a linen kitchen towel, I slipped it under my belt, just over my hip. If I let my arm drop to my side, I could conceal my contraband well enough.

Leaving the kitchen, I turned left and crossed

through the dining room before winding down another long hall to the library. On the desk, right where I expected it to be, was the lantern I needed.

As I rushed past the stools on my way to the desk, I tripped on an unseen foot. In my haste, I hadn't noticed the floating scroll. It would've been an obvious clue that someone was reading there. My feet went out from under me as I fell forward. I knocked my head on the corner of the desk, whipping my head back. My neck crackled painfully from the jolt.

"Psyche, are you alright?" Mathias asked as he tossed his scroll aside and collected me off the marble floor.

I threw a protective hand over my injured right eye. A lump the size of a breaching whale felt like it was already pushing its way to the surface. I hadn't planned on crying again that day, but the pain was overwhelming. I couldn't help myself.

"I'll get you to your room," Mathias promised. "Alexa! Alexa, bring some ice for Psyche," he called.

"Unnn..." I groaned. "Stop shouting." His voice made my head throb. Again. "She's not here. She's getting me honey. I'll be fine, just let me lay down."

As Mathias laid me gingerly across the bed, he said, "This is twice in one day, Miss Psyche. You ought to take it easier on yourself."

I turned my back to Mathias as I rolled onto my side, curling into a ball. "Thank you, Mathias. That will be all."

"Of course," he said. I could hear him backing out of the room.

"Oh, Mathias, wait," I called, looking back over

my shoulder in his direction. "I was trying to get the lantern out of the library when I fell. Can you bring it to me?"

"Yes, ma'am. Do you mind my asking why you need it in here --"

"Yes," I cut him off. "I do."

It wasn't like me to be so abrupt, so rude. I hoped I wasn't giving away too much of my plan. But I couldn't help myself. As far as I was concerned, everyone in the house was in on the plan to fatten me for a human barbecue.

Mathias returned and placed the lantern on my vanity. "Will here do?"

"That's fine." I flipped my hand at the lamp before recovering my swollen eye. "Now please, my head is killing me. Make sure no one comes down here and bothers me."

"Yes ma'am," Mathias said, but without his usually paternal tone. My door banged shut with more force than a happy person would've used to close it.

As the pounding sounds in my head began to quiet, I was able to think well enough to realize that hitting my head had actually been a good thing. There was no better excuse for pushing Aris away than having a headache. It'd worked last night, after all.

I passed fitfully in and out of sleep. When I finally awoke, the last rays of the day were being sucked down into the earth, pulling a blanket of orange and pink in their wake. With a start, I realized I hadn't stashed my knife and lantern yet and popped out of bed. The sudden blood drain from my head made me so dizzy that I thought I was getting another migraine, but I managed to steady myself on the headboard until the stars disappeared from my vision.

Grabbing the lantern off the vanity, I untucked the knife from my belted waist. As I stashed the items under the bed, I hoped he had no reason to glance there tonight.

I didn't go to dinner since I didn't have the stomach for food. Besides, I figured there was a better than average chance that anything I ate would come back up again. So after stashing my contraband, I sulked in my bed and waited, willing the minutes to pass more slowly so I could put off the deed.

When darkness finally enveloped the palace, Aris appeared in his shrouded form, like always. But that night, his cloak had returned to feeling ominous rather than invitingly mysterious.

I winced when he wrapped me in his arms and my reaction obviously caught him off-guard. As quickly as he had embraced me, he released me and studied me with those piercing blue eyes of his.

"What's wrong, Love?" he asked. "Has your sister --"

"No." I cut him off. My sister was the last subject I wanted to discuss with him. I tilted my head and showed off the swollen lump above my right eye. "I fell is all. It just really hurts."

Without saying a word, he leaned forward and kissed my tender bump. Warmth coursed through the wound and the sensation made me lightheaded and less painful.

I searched his eyes for some trace of evil. Something to keep me committed to my plan when he otherwise seemed so innocent and loving. Despite my best efforts to hold it back, a single tear pricked its way over the threshold of my eye and spilled down my cheek. He gently kissed that away too.

"Is something else bothering you?"

I hesitated for a second longer than I should've before weakly answering, "No."

He tilted up my chin with the soft tips of his fingers and held my gaze. "I'll kill her if she caused you any pain."

"Stop it!" I screamed, batting his hand away from my face. "Do *not* talk about my family like that! How could you even say such a thing?"

I turned my back on him and hid my face in my pillow, sobbing again.

"Psyche, I'm sorry." He stroked my back. Every touch felt like a pinprick that I had to fight to keep from wincing over. "I wasn't thinking."

I twitched my shoulder in a gesture that I hoped said stop touching me, and told him -- again -- that my head really hurt and I just wanted to go to sleep.

"Do you want me to leave?" he asked.

"No," I answered, maybe too quickly, while snapping my head up to look at him. If he left, I wouldn't be able to kill him. "No, please stay. I feel better when you're here."

The lie had been easier to speak than I would've expected. And he seemed to believe me.

"Anything," he answered, giving my hair a final brush with his hand. "I'll always be here if you need me."

All I could think was: *not if I can help it.*

I was glad I'd napped all afternoon. Otherwise, out-waiting him to fall asleep would've been impossible. It seemed to take hours before his breathing settled into the rhythmic in and out that signaled he'd finally dozed off. I'd been faking the sounds of sleep myself for so long that I was in a nearly dream-like trance when it happened. My steady breathing had helped to calm and relax me though, so when I did hear him give a little newly-asleep snort, I was mentally ready to carry out my plan.

At first I was only brave enough to slip my left leg out from under the covers. I watched his cloudy form to make sure it didn't move or that his eyes didn't suddenly open. Then I let my toes touch the marble floor and slid myself to the edge of the bed.

When he snorted and shifted in bed, I froze contorted, half-in and half-out of the bed. *Real stealth. How was I supposed to explain why I was laying wrapped over the edge of the mattress if he woke up?* I held my breath and waited until his breathing returned to its steady pace.

Slowly, I slipped completely off the bed and crouched on the floor. Feeling around for the dagger and lantern, I silently wished I hadn't tucked them quite so far under the bed when I'd hidden them earlier. Sitting on the cool floor, I went over my plan for the millionth time in my head. Turn on the lantern, see the monster; drive my knife into his heart, kill the monster. It was that quick and easy. It'd be over before I knew it. I'll be safe again. I repeated that last thought like a mantra as I slowly rose from the floor.

I'll be safe again. I'll be safe again.

Holding the lantern in my left hand and the

dagger in my right, I crept around the bed until I stood directly over the sleeping black mass of monster. I closed my eyes one final time and then lit the lantern.

CHAPTER 36 — PSYCHE

The gentle light of the lantern cast its warm glow over
Aris. As I blinked through the sudden brightness, I saw
the light slowly piercing through his shroud. I braced
myself for the most horrid form I could imagine. Flaky
green scales, black oily wings, or razor-sharp claws. I
figured that if he could create the palace and all that
was in it, he could easily make me feel delicate skin and
curly, boyish hair.

So when the shroud began to fall away, revealing
flesh rather than scales, I sucked in a surprised gasp.
The light pierced his shroud more and more, revealing
all the features I'd felt under my fingertips as we'd
flown together, eaten together... kissed together.

His soft, delicate fingers rested easily across the
chiseled muscles of his chest. Tucked behind his back
were wings so white they seemed to glimmer. Before I
could stop myself, I reached out and touched the tip of
a satiny, white feather.

And suddenly, I knew.

Blood surged up my neck, pulsing and throbbing,
threatening to pop a vessel if I couldn't get my temper
under control. *How dare he be the one!*

I followed the light up his body as it cut through
the darkness and revealed his face. Sure enough, it was
the face I had no business not remembering, even if I
couldn't see it with my eyes.

With his head turned to the side in sleep, I could

see his perfectly-defined jaw line, his soft bow-shaped lips, his classically straight nose, and his long, dark eyelashes. Thick curls the color of dark amber fell carelessly around his smooth face.

My mind spun. *How had this happened? Eros had hated me. I'd hated him.*

Had he tricked me into these feelings, only to leave me a crumpled mess later? That had to be the plan. Aphrodite's. His. I didn't care. Attacking my heart felt like a worse betrayal than when I'd thought he was going to kill me soon.

And then an even more mind-boggling thought slipped into place. *I almost killed Eros. Correction* -- tried *to kill Eros. You don't kill gods. But still!*

When I realized what I'd almost done, I instinctively jerked back and the knife slipped from my grasp. It fell to the marble floor with a piercing series of clangs as it bounced several times before finally stopping. I stooped too quickly to pick up the knife -- as if picking it up could somehow take back the sound -- not bothering to think about the lantern I held in my other trembling hand.

As I leaned down, the light went out and blistering oil from the lantern sloshed over the sides. Our screams rang out through the night at the same time. I dropped the lantern and knife and howled from the painful burns on my fingers. Aris -- no, Eros, wailed too with the unmistakable sounds of pain.

I'd burned him.

In a flash of brilliant light, Eros illuminated himself. He hovered, wings flapping furiously, just over the bed.

"Is this what you wanted to see?" His voice thundered down at me.

"Actually, no," I snapped. "I can't believe you did this to me."

"Did this to *you*?" he yelled. His inner light surged brighter. "What exactly did I do except fall asleep?"

I folded my arms defensively across my chest. "You lied to me. You've been lying to me. Making me like you. Tricking me into kissing you." My stomach clenched at the thought. "I actually thought you... never mind."

"I can't believe you're so blind," he growled. "The *only* thing I lied to you about was my name."

I reached up to touch his arm, to pull him down to me so we could talk this through on equal footing, but he hovered just out of reach.

"I'm sorry," I mumbled. "I thought you were going to kill me. I didn't know."

"Of course you didn't know," he boomed, suddenly seeming angrier than ever. "That's been our deal from the start."

"Not *our* deal. *Your* deal," I shot back and climbed up onto the bed. If he wouldn't come down, I was going up. "All I've wanted since I got here was to see you. We wouldn't be having this problem right now if you hadn't been hiding."

"No, that's right," he said, trimming in his wings and dropping down to look me right in the eyes, "we wouldn't, because we'd be dead. My mother would've taken us both out by now for defying her."

Covering my eyes with my hand, I sighed. "So what do we do now?"

"We? There is no we. I've got to get out of here before --"

When I uncovered my face to see what'd made him stop mid-sentence, I realized his eyes were locked on something on the floor.

The knife.

His eyes were wide and round. In them I read horror. Fury. Grief.

His nostrils flared as he cut his penetrating glare back to me. He clenched his teeth so hard that I could see the veins stand out on his jaw. "What. Were. You. Doing?" He punctuated each word with anger.

I couldn't answer him. I didn't even want to admit to myself what I'd planned, how could I tell him?

Eros grabbed my face with both his hands, forcing my eyes to meet his. "Tell me what you were doing," he hissed. "All of our secrets are out now, right?"

I shuddered under his cold stare, but tried to explain as best I could. "I was falling for you, just like the prophecy said, and it felt so *right*," I started.

"Save it for a night when I haven't caught you slinking around with a knife."

Jerking my head out of his grasp, I hissed, "Do you want my answer or not?"

He was silent.

"Okay, just hear me out. I didn't believe my sister at first. She said you were going to fatten me up to eat or something." I snorted. *Of all the ridiculous ideas. How had I even thought that?*

He was looking away now, and I needed him to believe I was being sincere. Although it was Eros and not Aris, if he'd been telling me the truth about everything else, he deserved to know what was going on. I slipped my hands into his. His touch still sent blissful shivers rippling over my skin even though we were fighting.

"I knew you'd never hurt me. I *felt* that." I squeezed harder. "But after everything that happened with Al--"

He cut me off, dropping my hands and stepping away as he did. "How many times was I supposed to say I loved you before you believed it?" I looked down guiltily. "Before you'd stop planning my murder?"

"You're making this way worse than it needs to me." I blinked and a wave of tears spilled down my face. "Can we talk about this please? I'm sorry. I'm really, really sorry." Swallowing back the lump rising in my throat, I breathed, "I think I could've loved you."

Eros looked down into my eyes. Studying me, reading me. "I think you could've too."

His eyes moistened.

"You'll never know how much this pains me," he said. "Goodbye, Psyche."

His words were worse than having a spear run through my chest. That was it? After all the promises he made to love me forever and now he was telling me goodbye? The agony in my heart told me right then that what we'd had was more than a *chance* at love -- we'd actually had it.

And I'd literally been too blind to see anything but my own fear.

I opened my eyes to the sounds of his wings carrying him toward the window. I couldn't let him leave like this. This was not how things were supposed to end between us.

With a swiftness I never knew I had, I lunged from the bed and grabbed hold of his ankle. "You're not leaving," I told him. "Not like this."

Reaching down, he grabbed my wrist and pulled me up until I was crushed against his chest. His eyes were hard as we crossed the window threshold and floated into the garden.

"You're right. I can't leave you like this, can I?"

A tiny wave of hope swelled in me. Until he continued.

"Too much evidence." He dropped me into the dew-soaked grass and quickly soared out of reach.

"What?" I stammered.

"I'm sorry, Psyche, but you need to get away from the palace. Now."

And then the earth began to shake. The foundation to the palace buckled and gave way; the roof collapsed. A choking dust rose around me as I watched everything I'd come to know, to think of as my life in these past few days, reduced to rubble.

The sound of his heavy wing beats faded into the distance.

CHAPTER 37 — PSYCHE

As I looked off into the darkness, searching for Eros, I heard a familiar voice behind me.

"What happened?" Alexa wailed.

"Oh Alexa, you've got to help me!"

"What did you do?" she asked.

I looked down, unable to meet the eyes I knew were boring into my head. "I believed her..." my voice trailed off. I hoped that would tell Alexa enough of what she needed to know. How could I admit to more?

"And what? I've got to know how bad this is if I'm going to fix it."

I looked over her shoulder to the ruined palace. Nodding my head in that direction, I said, "It's bad." I gave a heavy sigh before I continued. "I didn't believe her at first. My sister said he was a monster but I didn't believe her. Not really. Until I *saw* you talking to Chara. And you were laughing at me." My voice had fallen into a tiny whisper.

I heard her suck in a sharp breath. "Psyche, I'm so sorry. You were never supposed to see me. It's horrible luck for you to have seen me. I mean really, really horrible."

"Then why? Why did my sister get to see you?"

"Because I was *trying* to give her bad luck. She was so awful while she was here, I thought she deserved it. And we -- well, me -- I wasn't laughing at you, sweetie. I had to give her some reason why you couldn't see me and she could." By now, Alexa was hugging me tightly and rocking me back and forth slowly, comfortingly.

"I'm so glad you made it out okay." I shuddered. "The palace crumbled so fast."

"He's got his mother's temper, but I don't think he'll hold a grudge against you for long." Alexa tried to sound assuring, but I heard plenty of doubt weighing in her voice. "You've got to show him you're sorry, and I'm sure he'll forgive you." She held me at arms-length. "What did you say to make him so mad anyway?"

"It's not so much what I said, as what I did."

Alexa was silent, meaning I had to continue.

"I thought he was going to kill me." I rushed through the rest of my tale hoping if I spat the words out quickly enough, the impact wouldn't be as bad. "So I got a knife and a lantern, and I looked at him, and I was going to stab him, but then I saw him, and I knew my sister was wrong and I panicked, and I dropped the knife and spilled hot oil on him and he woke up and saw what was going on and we fought and now he hates me."

"Crap," Alexa said, standing and letting go of my shoulders. "This is going to be very hard to fix. Not impossible, but close. I'll try to think of something, but you need to try to find him. Don't stop searching."

"Wait! Where are you going? You can't leave me too," I howled at her.

"I have no choice. He's calling me. I can't refuse."

Panic welled up from my chest. "Where do I go? I don't even know where to look."

"Ask the other gods for help where you can." Her

voice sounded further away. "Follow the stream through the forest to get out of this valley."

"Will I see you again?"

"I hope so." Alexa was now so far away that she was yelling so I could hear her. "And take these. They started the trouble, maybe they can help somehow." From out of the rubble of the palace, the knife and lantern floated to my feet.

"Come back," I screamed. "I need you."

There was no answer. Alexa was gone.

For a while I indulged in my typical reaction to bad news -- I cried. Hysterical, hiccup-inducing sobs. But when the initial flood of tears washed through me, I knew there was no point in sitting there bawling. It was time to start my search.

I tried not to think about the impossibility of that task. He was probably back on Mount Olympus by now and I had no way of getting there on my own. But Alexa had told me to search and I had nothing else to go on. So I tucked the knife into my belt, grabbed the lantern, and started walking.

To get to the brook as Alexa said, I had to pass through the gardens. I'd spent so many hours out here the past few days, loving the flowers and sculptures and babble of the fountains. Now they were a shadow of their former selves, looking utterly ruined in the early morning light. The flowers were dried and drooping. The sculptures were as crumbled as if Hephaestus had taken his tools and chiseled away the beautiful features. And the garden was eerily silent, like every living insect and bird had met extinction there.

Beyond the dying hedges of the garden maze I

found the stream Alexa had told me to follow. When I reached the tree line that marked the beginning of the dense forest, I turned to look back at my ruined home. The palace was gone. Not even the rubble remained. The cracked and broken sculptures had vanished. Not a single petal from the gardens survived. Nothing was left from my brief former life but an empty clearing sitting between the base of a jagged cliff and the entrance to this dark forest.

Sucking in a calming breath, I stepped into the trees and wound my way through the tangle of limbs. By the time the sun began to set, my feet ached as badly as my heart, and my stomach was close behind. When my legs literally wouldn't carry me another step, I sunk down into some cushiony moss at the base of a laurel tree. With my back against the trunk, I looked up into the leaves and watched the last rays of the sun trickle through the canopy.

I figured I must be having some sort of exhaustion-induced hallucination when the limbs of the tree slowly wrapped themselves around me in a prickly embrace. And then the tree spoke to me.

"Poor Psyche," the tree murmured in a voice barely louder than the breeze rustling her leaves. "Another of Eros's victims."

I was too tired to be afraid. My heart leapt into my throat for another reason. "Victim? Was I meant to be his target then?"

"Not like you mean. But he's careless. I am victim too."

"Will you tell me?" I asked.

Wind stirred through the leaves, almost like the

laurel was sighing through her branches. "I was a nymph. Daphne. Apollo loved me. I didn't feel the same." The tinkling whisper seemed to take great effort for the tree. "Apollo would've accepted my decision. But Eros stung him with an arrow. Apollo persisted; I ran. Father changed me to this tree. And Apollo still loves me. Eros's fault."

Turning onto my hip, I wrapped my arms around the base of the tree and hugged her back. The tree's embrace tightened as she hushed, "Sleep, Psyche. Sleep safe." And I did.

I didn't wake up until late the next morning. The tree's branches were no longer cradling me. In fact, this tree looked like all of the others in the forest: immobile. Had I dreamt the whole thing? If so, that was unquestionably the weirdest dream of my entire life.

I stared up at the tree. More to myself than to her, I said, "I'm sorry, Daphne. You deserved better."

As I turned to go down to the stream to get a drink before I set out for the day, she spoke again. "Almost home. You'll know my grove."

Home? I forgot about getting a drink and ignored the ache in my legs as I set off running. I knew of only one laurel grove and it was near my parents' palace. The grove I had visited with my sister when we made laurel crowns together as kids. *Could I really be that close?*

As I wound down the stream, it suddenly flowed into a river and hooked to the right. This had to be the Selinous River near my house.

As I followed its path, the land became treacherous. I was forced away from the sand-colored boulders and pale grey rocks that made up the steep banks. The river picked up speed as I pressed on, gurgling and spitting as it pounded against even more boulders and dropped down tiny rapids. I had no choice but to pick my way through the dense pines. The needles stabbed at my feet and tore at my already-battered dress. And yet I continued trying to run, hoping that each new bend in the river would lead me to the laurel grove.

By mid-afternoon, with the sun burning into my skin and my legs threatening to give way beneath me, the grove finally appeared. I was so relieved that my knees went weak. It wasn't much farther. I could make it.

With strength and speed a starving person shouldn't have had, I raced up the hill to my parents' palace. At first the guards blocked my way with their spears.

I looked from one to the other. "Belen, Demos, it's me, Psyche." I was instantly glad I'd taken the time -- unlike my sister -- to learn the names of the palace servants.

"You've escaped the beast!" cried Demos.

"Come inside, quickly," urged Belen.

Once I was inside my parents' home, it exploded in excitement. I was pushed and pulled from the embrace of this and that person until I landed with Maia. Like a calm inside the storm, Maia's arms brought familiar comfort and shielded me from the prying arms of the other staff.

Maia's eyes were full to the brim with tears, but she was smiling broadly. "Child, you've escaped," she said as she looked me over. "We were all so worried when Chara reported that you really were in the house of a monster." When Maia mentioned my sister, she nodded her head at the hallway behind me. I spun around and saw Chara standing. And staring.

If looks could kill, she would've been a crumpled pile of bones on the marble floor. "He was no monster," I told Maia, still staring down Chara with my most icy glare. I was about to unleash my pent-up anger on her when my mother and father bounded into the room.

"Psyche!" Mother yelled between hysterical sobs. "You're home. My baby's really home." She and Father nearly strangled me in a consuming embrace.

"I am." I pulled loose from her and turned to my father. "Are you okay? I've been so worried."

"Me? I'm fine. Had a touch of a stomach bug these past couple days, but I feel fine now."

A relieved sigh escaped my lips as Mother wiped at her tears and hugged me again. "I'm sorry," she bawled, "I can't help it. I never thought we'd see you again."

"I'm okay. Well, I *was* okay." I lowered my eyes to the floor as I felt everyone's stares settle on me. "I'm not so sure anymore."

"I don't understand," my father cut in. "You got free from the monster."

"You've got it all wrong," I protested. "He's not a monster." I pulled in a deep breath to steady myself, but the words still came out barely more than a whisper. "He's Eros."

I heard everyone in the room suck in astonished gasps.

Finally, Father stammered, "Well, what happened to you then? You look like you've been through battle."

"I haven't eaten in two days. Do you mind if we talk over an early dinner?"

The staff who'd been gathered around me immediately scurried like ants. I looked down at my tattered cloths and filthy body.

"A bath is probably in order too," I said to no one in particular.

"I'll get the water," offered Maia, and she too rushed off.

Maia was kind enough to bring me some cheese to snack on while I bathed, but I still hurried through the bath and quickly dressed to get down to dinner. As I ate, I gave the whole account of how I'd nearly murdered the god of Love and, in the process, lost what I now realized was probably the love of my life.

When I was finished, everyone just sat in silence. No one had any suggestions or advice for how to win back the love of an immortal. This was unchartered territory.

"So," I concluded, "I plan to start searching again just as soon as my strength is back. I don't see what other choice I have."

Chara snorted. "What, you think you can just walk up to Mount Olympus and knock on Eros's door?" she asked.

"Do you have a better idea?" I snapped.

"Yeah. Maybe you should let it go. You screwed up. Move on with your life."

"I screwed up?" I yelled her. "*Me?* This never would've happened if it weren't for you. You're the one who convinced me to kill him in the first place."

Standing up, my entire body shook with emotion as a new realization washed over me. "You did this on purpose," I stammered. "You did, didn't you?"

"Chara, is that true?" asked our father.

Chara rose off her tripod, her body rigid and fists clenched. "Rasmus is sweet, isn't he, Psyche? Of course, you know that. After your private chat."

I recoiled. The way she said 'chat' made it seem dirty. Her eyes narrowed into slits.

"Oh yes, I know all about it. You can imagine how guilty Rasmus felt about misleading me. He confessed everything like a shamed little school boy. Including the fact that you knew too."

"There was nothing I could've done."

"You could've told me," she shrieked. "You could've at least acted like a sister for one day in your life."

"So what?" I demanded. "You got to my house, saw I was happy, and decided to sabotage the whole thing?"

"Let's just consider it me repaying the favor."

Father came and stood in front of me, shielding Chara from my view. "Psyche, I think you need some rest." And then he turned to Chara. "And I think you'd better make yourself scarce."

Chara huffed before stomping out of the room. Mother moved to my side and pulled me into her with a one-armed hug.

"Come on," she offered, "I'll walk you upstairs. Your room's just like you left it."

As we passed together through the door, she

added, "I'm sure we'll figure something out."

Her words unwrapped a new layer of exhaustion and hopelessness. *Sure we will, Mom,* I wanted to say, *just like we figured out how to get me out of having to go to him in the first place.*

There were many things to love about my parents, but their ability to figure ourselves out of predicaments wasn't one of them.

CHAPTER 38 — PSYCHE

I woke up screaming. Not a bone-chilling, blood-curdling scream, but an aching, worst-misery-of-my-life scream.

"Shhh, sweetie," Mom comforted and pulled the covers up higher under my chin. "It was just a bad dream. Everything's alright now. It'll be okay."

When my eyes finally fought through tear-sealed crust to stretch open, I saw my mother sitting on the edge of my bed. She stroked my hair repeatedly, as if the motion was comforting to her too.

The lines under her eyes were deep with worry and I doubted she'd slept. I pushed myself up in the bed and latched onto her neck, hoping she was right about everything being okay. But I couldn't truly believe. The dream had been too real. And what I needed right now was *not* another wretched freaking prophecy.

As I remembered my dream, my heart felt newly pierced again, like someone twisting a spear deeper into my wound. I fell over onto my side and tried to fold up into myself. Desperate moans forced themselves through my lips as I struggled to hold on to the warmth and security offered by my mother's presence.

"Oh, baby," she soothed, rubbing my back. "Want to tell me about it?"

I shook my head weakly back and forth.

"The burden is less if you share it," she offered.

I half-turned back to look at her. "I saw him. He came back to me."

"In your dream?" she asked.

I nodded. "I thought he'd forgiven me. That he understood what I'd done. But then..." I choked as a sob began to swell in my chest. Could I even say the words I'd heard so clearly?

Mother ran her hand down my face. She looked so understanding, so knowing. Could she see that remembering this dream was tearing out my heart from its roots?

"He said he'd always love me." Air hitched in the back of my throat as my lungs struggled to function. "Then he said goodbye. And that would be for always too."

I curled back into my ball. I'm sure Mother tried to talk to me after that, but I wasn't listening. Or maybe she didn't. Maybe she knew me well enough to know I just wanted to be alone. Either way, she retreated, leaving me to mourn the loss of the love I didn't even know I'd felt until it was gone.

Strength eluded me after that. My muscles refused to drag me from bed; my brain refused to climb out of its darkness. I knew I was wallowing in self-pity, but I indulged myself. Never in my eighteen years had I been allowed to just lay about, feeling mopey or gloomy. I'd always had to smile, to be the bright and cheerful one. Now that I'd lost so much so quickly, I felt entitled to take a few days off.

When I finally emerged from my room on the third day, my hair was caked to my head and my skin felt tacky from not having bathed. A faint odor of decay clung to my skin like a damp sheet. I yearned for a long soak in the tub followed by a huge breakfast.

But first, I just wanted a hug from my mom. And confirmation that Chara had taken the opportunity to make herself scarce.

Mother was in the gardens. When she saw me, she set aside her embroidery and wrapped me in her arms -- despite my stink.

"Psyche, you're up," she chirped. "You must be starved. Do you want some breakfast?"

Before I could answer, she turned to Maia. "Maia, go get Psyche some eggs and sausage. And bread. Lots of it." Maia started to leave, but Mother called her back again, "Oh, and when you've done, get Psyche's bath ready."

It really was like she could read my mind.

"Of course," Maia answered before scuttling back into the palace.

Mother held one of my hands in hers and directed me to sit next to her. The air was warm this morning and we soaked up the sun as we sat in silence for awhile. Now that I knew my immediate needs were being taken care of, it took me a bit to work up the courage to ask about Chara.

What was I supposed to do if she was still here? I felt better after two days of self-indulged moping, but I wasn't sure I felt *that* much better.

Finally, I broke the silence. "Mother?" I asked.

She pulled her gaze away from some brilliant red flowers she'd been eyeing and looked over at me. "Umm..."

"What happened with Chara?"

"Your father sent her back to her City." Her gaze fell to her nervous fingers. "I think that may have been an always goodbye too."

I slid my hand away, unable to stand the damp heat rolling off her palms. I'd done this to her; destroyed any chance she may have had at rekindling a relationship with her firstborn child.

Someone should seriously be keeping a tally of the relationships I've destroyed, because I could probably win a medal at this point.

CHAPTER 39 — EROS

Eros had hoped that saying goodbye to Psyche, even if through her dreams, would give him so closure. Make him feel better.

It had not.

His shoulder still ached where the oil had burned him. But more than that, the physical pain was a constant reminder of the heartbreaking pain he felt every time he thought of Psyche. How was it possible, after everything he had done for her, given up for her, all the times he'd promised to love her, that she would betray him after just one visit from her sister? He'd thought she was slowly falling for him. Was any of it real?

And then came the waves of anger. How could a mortal, even if she was partly divine, even dream of harming him? The idea was unfathomable. Eros refused to really acknowledge the thought in the back of his head reminding him that Psyche didn't know he was a god because he hadn't told her. All the signs were there. She should've figured it out.

"Humans are so stupid!" he yelled at his house.

"You won't hear any disagreement from me," Aphrodite said, narrowing her eyes into a wickedly delightful twinkle.

Eros flexed his jaw and pressed his eyes firmly together, unwilling to acknowledge her entrance.

Aphrodite was the last person he wanted to see right now.

"Oh, come now, darling. You shouldn't be rude to me. You know that doesn't get you anywhere."

Eros let his head drop back as he breathed in deeply, trying to force his temper back down into wherever it was rapidly rising from. "I can't. Talk. Now."

"Tisk. You can always talk to me," Aphrodite chided, and reached out to lay her hand on Eros's shoulder. When her fingertips brushed his skin, Eros yowled in pain and spun around to face his mother. His eyes glowed with fury and agony.

"I'm asking you to leave," Eros spat through clenched teeth.

"Not until you tell me what happened to your shoulder. Did a mortal do that to you?" Aphrodite's voice seemed flooded more with vengeance than motherly concern.

Eros closed his eyes again and groaned, sinking down into the heaps of cushions on his couch. He shoved the heel of his palms into his eyes to block out the sight of his mother. "What does it matter? It's over."

"Unless you have killed the offender, this is *not* over." Aphrodite glared at her son, waiting for confirmation that the mortal had been appropriately punished.

Eros pulled his hands away to look squarely at Aphrodite. "I've doled out my retribution. I consider it over."

Aphrodite melted onto the couch beside her son.

"You didn't answer my question. Is the man who did this dead or not?"

"I don't want to talk about it," Eros protested, throwing his arm up over his eyes to block out his mother again. "Just leave. Please."

"Is he dead?" Aphrodite articulated precisely.

"No," Eros answered without uncovering his eyes, "*she* is not dead. But I won't let you hurt her." Eros sighed heavily, pain ripping at his chest as the words spilled. "I love her."

"What?" Aphrodite shrieked as she bolted to her feet. "You're in love with a mortal? Is that why you rejected my pick then? Because you already had some other little hussy lined up? I bet she's some prostitute the Senators are always fawning over."

"Stop! I will not let you speak about her like that." Eros's eyes blazed.

Aphrodite's breath caught in her throat as her eyes bulged. Expressions of shock, disbelief, anger, all flashed across her pristine face as she processed that her son really wasn't going to back down on this.

"Well, I suppose you ought to at least tell me who was so bold as to not only steal your heart, but nearly steal your life as well."

"I told you, it doesn't matter," Eros muttered.

"TELL ME!" Aphrodite screamed.

Eros looked up into his mother's eyes. Maybe it would be fun to tell her. Twist the knife a little deeper. It's what she deserved for not leaving him alone. "Actually, I think you might already know her." Eros's blue eyes glinted. For at least one second, he was going to enjoy wounding his mother. "Her name is Psyche."

Eros had barely spoken her name when Aphrodite slapped him. Eros slowly turned back to look at his mother while rubbing his tender cheek. Mother and son locked hateful gazes, each refusing to look away. Without breaking her gaze, Aphrodite snapped, "How dare you do this to me."

"How dare I? How dare I?" He sat up so he could get right in his mother's face. "How dare you send me out to ruin her life in the first place. She didn't do anything wrong. You can't punish her because I pushed her away."

Eros leaned back on the couch, arms crossed across his chest. Silence hung between them for a moment before Eros turned his icy, blue eyes back to his mother.

"It seems I'm in love with someone I can't be with and I have you to thank."

"How can you blame me for falling in love with someone I sent you to destroy? All you had to do was follow simple instructions."

"And I was on my way to do just that, when I *felt* her. I felt her heart, and her love, and her desperation, and all of the good in her. It was unlike anything I've ever felt before. I just couldn't shoot her. Not until I knew if she really was everything I felt." Eros took a deep, calming breath to steady himself. "And as I lowered my arrow, I nicked myself," he said, waving his hand at the tiny scar on his left knee.

"So out of all the deities -- and other humans even -- you picked her?"

"So what if I did? I'm un-picking her now. I assure you she's far more miserable now than if I'd followed your orders in the first place."

"We'll see about that. In the meantime, there's no reason for you to suffer. I'll simply undo the arrow." Aphrodite reached out to touch her son, but Eros slapped her hand away.

"Don't. I'll come to you when I'm ready. I deserve this pain as much as she does right now." That, and something else inside him wasn't ready to let go yet.

But before Eros could protest further, Aphrodite laid the palm of her hand on his forehead and hummed one long, sweet note. When she pulled her hand away, she looked triumphant. "There now. Feel better?"

The weight in Eros's chest lightened as the painful need to return to Psyche's side eased. It wasn't that he didn't still feel some loyalty to her, but the burning compulsion to be near her was gone. Perhaps, in time, he would be able to forget. Just as he'd forgotten Lelah.

Yes, once he'd found Psyche, the memory of Lelah all but disappeared. It could happen again. Heck, he could use his arrows to make sure it happened again.

Aphrodite patted her son's cheek as he blinked at her in shock. "You should rest. Mother has *things* to attend to."

"Don't hurt her," Eros muttered, already feeling himself drawn into sleep by his mother's command to rest.

"That's just the love hangover talking. You'll feel differently soon enough. Don't worry now. I'll take care of everything."

CHAPTER 40 — PSYCHE

Mother must've known she couldn't convince me to stay at home, so while I bathed, she had the servants prepare bags of food and fill flasks with water for my journey. When I emerged from my room refreshed and dressed, I found my favorite horse, Xanthippe, loaded and ready.

I stood frozen in the doorway to the palace. Mother and Father were behind me, pulling me back with their concern. But Xanthippe stood before me, pulling me forward with the allure of regaining Eros's love. I was on a precipice, torn between the safety I knew and the love I had lost. It was like being sent off to the cliffs again, feeling I might never see my mother and father and home again. But this time I knew the end destination and who would be waiting for me -- if luck was with me.

"Are you sure you won't let us send a guard with you?" Father asked from behind me. "The roads aren't safe for a woman alone."

I turned to look at him. His eyes were moist, welled with concern. Taking his hand in mine, I said, "I'm sure, Father. I've made my offerings to Hermes. If he can't protect me, there's nothing a guard could do."

Mother and Father exchanged pained looks, but they didn't force the issue.

"Just remember, Psyche," Mother added. "You're a powerful young woman. The gods will watch over you."

I gulped. What kind of crazy send off was that? "Well, I guess this is goodbye then," I said. "Again."

After kissing each of my parents on the cheek, I secured the lantern from my former palace to one of the packs and checked to be sure my dagger was securely tucked at my hip. A guard helped hoist me onto Xanthy's back and with a gentle kick, my mare headed away from the palace. I wouldn't look back; couldn't look back. If I was ever going to redeem myself, this was the only way.

There was really only one direction to go: toward Mount Olympus.

I stopped holding Xanthy back once I was sure no one could see us any more and we settled into a comfortable canter down the dusty, broken roads. I let Xanthy continue until she decided on her own to slow her pace. Her sweat-soaked sides heaved beneath my legs. When we came to a stream, we stopped and drank. After refilling my flasks with fresh water, I sat on a rock and watched Xanthy nibble at some weeds, uprooting the little flowers and leaves and devouring them in greedy bites.

Watching her, I was suddenly overcome with gratitude for the beautiful mare. Olympus was so far away; I would never make it without her. Not in this lifetime anyway. And she was oblivious to the danger I was dragging her into with me. If I failed in this journey, she would likely die with me.

Slowly I padded to the horse and wrapped my arms around her neck. "We should ride a little more. I think we can reach Corinth before sun down." I patted her mane and she nodded her head in what seemed like approval. I led her over the rock I'd been sitting on so I'd have an easier time mounting, but I was still glad no one was watching me as I fumbled onto her back.

Once there, my legs immediately protested. They already ached from our earlier ride and I realized I'd been foolish to try to cover so much ground in one day. Thanks to the crowds, it'd been forever since I'd ridden. My muscles were painfully sore and the insides of my legs were chaffed from rubbing against Xanthy's coarse hair.

"On second thought," I said, "maybe we better call it quits for today."

Looking around the deserted stretch of road, I wasn't sure the best place for us to camp. Would it be better to leave ourselves exposed to the animals of the woods or to human strangers who might come across us by the road? In the end, I figured Xanthy would be more likely to sense danger and wake us from an animal, so I led her from the road into the cover of dense pines.

After brushing Xanthy down and making sure she had plenty to drink, I ate some of the food my parents packed and then gathered pine needles to make a bed, rough and pointy as it was. Although the sun was only beginning to set, I was ready to sleep. The ride had taken its toll and I easily drifted off, knowing Xanthippe would stand guard.

Some time later, and I had no way to gauge how much later since the sky was midnight black, I woke to the sound of Xanthy huffing and pacing uneasily near the tree where I had tied her.

My fog of sleep immediately parted as fear took over.

I lay quietly for a moment, holding my breath, listening for sounds of an intruder. And then I heard what Xanthy's sensitive ears had picked up long before mine: footsteps shuffling through pine needles. The steps were coming closer.

I clambered to my feet and pulled out my knife as I protectively rushed to Xanthy's side. Whatever was coming, I wouldn't let it hurt my horse.

Perhaps because we were in the woods, it never occurred to me that the footfalls might belong to something other than an animal. Until I heard the voice call to me.

"There you are. I was starting to think I'd never find you."

CHAPTER 41 — PSYCHE

"Alexa!" I called, and ran headlong through the woods until I crashed into my invisible friend.

"I thought we were past this whole running into me thing," she teased as she hugged me.

"You came back." I was giddy as I held her in the darkness, unable to let go for fear she'd evaporate.

"I can't stay long," she cautioned. "I'm not even supposed to be here, but I snuck away."

My arms dropped away from her. "So he hasn't forgiven me yet?"

Alexa didn't answer, but she didn't need to. I already knew the answer.

"Did you tell him that I saw you? That's why I believed my sister over him?"

"Not yet, but I will," she said. "He refuses to see anyone right now. Heck, I'm under lock and key living with my parents again," she explained, as we walked through the woods toward my makeshift camp.

"Why'd you have to sneak away from your parents' house? Eros isn't there too is he?"

Alexa snorted. "No, he's back on Mount Olympus. But seeing as how this is partially my fault for letting you hear your sister in the first place, I'm sort of grounded."

"What?" I asked. "What do you mean you're grounded?"

I heard Alexa kick at some leaves. "Eros

could've gotten me in real trouble with the Olympian counsel for disobeying his order not to ever let you hear you sister's cries. He said he'd keep quiet about the whole thing if my parents promised not to let me come help you. So, like I said, I can't stay long."

As we reached my little camp, Alexa said, "I'm glad to see you have a horse. It'll throw Aphrodite off for a while. She won't expect you to be riding, and she's not a very good tracker."

My eyes grew wide and darted around the woods in panicked bursts. "She's coming for me?" I stammered. "She knows? But how?"

"She made him tell." Alexa paused before adding softly, "he didn't want to."

"But if she -- I'll never make it."

"Shhh..." Alexa hushed, wrapping an arm around my shoulder. "Don't give up. You *can* make it. I know you can."

"How?" I sniffed.

"You'll reach Corinth tomorrow morning. Just before you reach the gates, there's a shrine to Hestia. She won't want to pick sides in a fight, especially against Aphrodite, but if you can convince her that she's just keeping the peace until you find Eros, she might protect you as you travel."

"I don't really have anything to offer her."

"You can promise to give her something if you make it. It'll give her some added incentive to protect you." Alexa said.

"Alexa, what am I going to do without you? You *can't* leave me again. Please."

"Psyche, I told you. I can't stay. But you'll do

fine. I'm sure of it." She was already pulling her warm hand away from mine.

"Wait!" I called. "Before you go... does he...I mean...do you think that he...misses me?"

"He must," she answered. I could hear her footsteps moving away in the darkness.

"Will it be enough? To forgive me, I mean?" I tried to keep the panic from registering in my voice.

"Get some rest, Psyche. You have a long journey ahead of you still."

And just like that, the sound of Alexa's retreating footsteps was gone. The forest was so silent, I wondered whether Alexa had really come at all or if it'd been another dream.

Settling back down into my pine straw bed, I strained to pick up any noise that might hint Alexa was coming back. Or that Aphrodite was bearing down on me. But the only sounds filtering through the night air were the chirping of crickets and Xanthy's rhythmic breathing as she dozed.

When I awoke in the morning, the sun was only just beginning to rise. I quickly ate some crackers before leading Xanthippe back out to the rock and mounting. We hadn't ridden for more than an hour when I realized we were approaching Corinth. Little farm houses and grazing cattle showed we were nearing civilization.

Deciding to make sure I passed the town unrecognized, I pulled a shroud out from one of my bags and wrapped it around my head. I carefully tucked my curls into the folds of the fabric and pulled the sides out as far as possible to shield my face.

I was almost to the city gates when, just as Alexa

had promised, I spotted a small shrine. Around the marble inscription to Hestia lay clay pots, lamps, tiny sculpted animals and busts in the goddess's likeness. Tokens laid out by the farmers and pious visitors who came seeking favors. They reminded me again that I had so little to offer.

Just as I was about to dismount from Xanthy to make my prayer, I realized there was nothing, aside from the shrine itself, to use to get back up on my horse. I couldn't see praying to a goddess only to defile her shrine, so I decided to stay on horseback and hope Hestia wasn't offended.

Xanthy brought me right up to it and I stared at the relief image of the goddess. She looked so motherly. It was hard to imagine she was one of the virgin goddesses rather than a matron. Her shoulder-length, curly hair framed the broad face that sat atop her full shoulders and thick torso. Her head was draped in a cloak much like the one I was wearing to conceal myself, only the effect on her was to make her face more severe.

I'd never had much of a connection to Hestia in the past. Her domain was the home and hearth, things I hadn't had much concern for. Others had always cared for my palaces and kept the hearths going for me. I wondered whether I deserved her help now, before realizing that whether I deserved it or not, I had no choice but to ask for it.

"Hestia, eldest sister of Zeus, great mistress of the home and protector of the sacred hearth fire that keeps us warm, hear my prayer. I'm searching for Eros because I made a huge mistake. And I love him," I mumbled, swallowing back the guilt. "I regret that I have nothing to offer you in exchange for hearing this prayer, but am a lowly traveler in desperate need of your help. Your fellow goddess, Aphrodite, doesn't want me to find her son. I pray that you watch over me as I travel so that I have a chance to beg Eros's forgiveness. If you will help me, I promise to dedicate a shrine within my home to you and give thanks at it daily."

And there it was.

No flash of lightening or puff of smoke followed. Just the silence that hung in the air after I finished making the longest prayer of my life. Would Hestia give me a sign that she'd heard me or would help me? I waited a few minutes by the shrine for some indication the goddess was listening, but nothing happened. No birds flew overhead. None of the offerings on the shrine suddenly fell over. Even the wind was stagnant and unmoving.

There was nothing else to do except keep moving. I nudged Xanthy to move faster as we neared the gates of Corinth. I was still worried someone would recognize me, but the only person we passed was a shepherd moving his small flock of sheep to another pasture.

As we crossed the Isthmus of Corinth, the narrow stretch of land that separates the Peloponnese from the mainland of Greece, I exhaled a relieved sigh. We were still so far away, but being on the mainland made me feel closer to Eros.

From high atop the jagged, craggy cliffs, I looked down at the azure waters of the Aegean Sea. The waves pounded mercilessly at the base of the rocks, shooting crashing white waves up the stones like fingers grasping for something just beyond their reach.

I recoiled as I watched, moving Xanthy further away from the edge of the cliff. The sea was Aphrodite's domain; where she was born, where she played. I had the paranoid fear that the waves might actually try to reach up and tear me from my horse. Without spending time to rationalize away my fears, I urged Xanthy into a gallop so that we could quickly pass the ocean's edge.

We traveled on at trot for the rest of the day and as we neared the city of Megara, a cloud of dust rose up from the road in front of us. The shapes of four riders emerged from the haze, galloping wildly and barreling down on us.

Something about this band of riders made me uneasy. Maybe because they were moving so fast, maybe because there were four of them and only one me, maybe because these were the first people I'd encountered on the barren roads other than the shepherd, but something made my heart race as the riders approached.

I maneuvered Xanthy into the dry, crunchy grass beside the road to clear a path. The first three riders went tearing by so quickly that their following breeze pushed my shroud back from my face and my curls spilled down my shoulders. The fourth rider, catching sight of my face and hair, drew in his horse and called to his companions.

"Hold up!" he yelled, turning his horse back around and quickly closing the distance between us.

I fingered the handle of the knife that was still tucked away at my side and willed myself not to look back as the man rode up behind me.

"What's a pretty, little thing like you doing out here all alone?" he asked as he cut off my path with his own horse. The other three riders trotted up to his side, encircling us and backing Xanthy further into the brittle grasses. If their shields and cloaks were any indication, the men were Spartan soldiers, minus a commander.

My eyes flicked nervously from face to face. Their young eyes sparkled with menace and their lips curled up in snarling smiles. One of the men had an angry scar running from his ear, across his cheek, and down to his upper lip. Another had his left arm bound in a sling. They looked battle fresh and ready for another fight.

"You're Spartan warriors," I stated, using my most commanding voice. "Your men were friends to my great grandfather, King Alcander of Sikyon, in the Trojan War." I hoped my history knowledge would win some favor with the men. And also that they would have been too preoccupied with war training to have heard of me.

The man with the scar swung off his horse and grabbed a fist-full of Xanthy's mane. She snorted and tried to back away, but the man held her firmly as he bored his eyes into mine.

"*You're* a daughter of Sikyon?" he asked.

I nodded.

Before I could blink, the man grabbed my forearm and wrested me down from Xanthy's back while shouting. "Don't lie to me."

I landed on my knees in the grass, with my arm

251

still held painfully above my head. The other men laughed raucously from their horses.

"Princesses don't travel unguarded," he accused. I had to agree with his logic. Royal women didn't travel alone. Still, I scrambled for something to say that would make him believe me. And loosen his hold on my arm.

"Please, ask me anything," I begged. "Ask me about my parents, the City, anything."

He jerked my arm, making me wince. "What do I care about Sikyon? You could tell me more lies and I wouldn't know the difference."

"Please," I squealed. "There's got to be something."

The man yanked me to my feet and spun me around to him, leaning in so close that I could smell the stink of his breath. "What's your name?" he hissed.

Anything but that.

I didn't answer and he shook me, making my head jerk even though I was bracing myself against him. "Your name," he repeated, louder, harsher.

I bit my lower lip and took a deep breath while glaring at my captor. "Psyche," I finally answered between gritted teeth.

The men erupted in laughter. The one with his arm in the sling used his good hand to steady himself on another man's shoulder. The one with the scar, who was holding me, laughed in barks. He turned back toward his fellow soldiers. "You hear that, men? This girl thinks she's Psyche!"

More laughter followed. I felt a warm flush of shock and insult rise in my cheeks. Maybe I wasn't dressed in my finest clothes. Maybe I was traveling alone and unguarded. Maybe all of Greece thought I'd died last week. And maybe I didn't have my hair done and makeup on, but I *was* Psyche. Two weeks ago these men would've said I was the most beautiful woman in the world, and now they laughed at the idea.

In a burst of bravado, I tried to wrest my arm free, but he held on tight. My resistance actually brought him out of his fit of laughter. His eyes bored into mine, both threatening and mocking.

"Fine, if that's how you want it, *Psyche* it is."

I opened my mouth to protest that I was Psyche, but snapped it shut again. What could I say that would do me any good?

"Men," he announced to his three companions, "today we will have the good fortune of being entertained by Princess Psyche herself."

My eyes widened and I quickly searched their faces. My heart thundered in my chest as wicked anticipation registered in all their eyes.

My attention was jerked back to the soldier holding me when he began dragging me further away from the side of the road, where the grasses grew taller and thicker. The burrs scratched at my ankles as I tried to walk against the direction I was being pulled. His fingers dug into the skin of my upper arm.

I would've screamed, but only the other men would hear me. I was afraid it would just encourage them.

The other men were hanging back at the side of the road. Probably giving their leader a little privacy. I decided to stop resisting and allowed myself to be led another few meters into the grass, which was now waist deep. When he was satisfied with our location, the soldier yanked and twisted my arm in one quick movement that sent me sprawling to the ground. I quickly rolled over and started crawling backward.

The soldier undid his sheath, tossing his sword to the side. He was smiling down at me. The smile of a man with complete domination.

"You're no Psyche, but you're not bad," he hissed as he advance on me. He pulled his tunic over his head and kept walking. "I'm going to enjoy this."

Then he pounced, jutting his knees between my legs and holding my chest down with his forearm while he used his other hand to force up my dress. I used his distraction with my dress as an opportunity to pull out my knife from the folds of my waist.

I stuck the pointed tip right against his throat and pressed deeply enough to just barely slice at his skin. "Let me go and I'll let you live," I panted, half-crazed with terror.

The man used the hand that'd been pulling at my dress to wipe at the trickle of blood running its way down his neck. He examined the crimson smear on his finger and laughed. Then he swiped the knife from my hands so quickly I barely saw him move. Faster than Zeus's lightening bolt strikes, he had the blade pressed firmly against my throat.

"You be a good girl," he spat, "and maybe I'll let *you* live." He pressed the knife a little deeper for emphasis. I choked back a panicked scream, clamping my hand over my mouth to silence myself.

With his free hand, the soldier grabbed at the top of my dress and yanked. The fabric sank into the flesh of my shoulders like angry teeth before it began to stretch and tear. His scarred smile widened over crooked, discolored teeth.

And then he froze.

The knife fell out of his hands as he scrambled to his feet. He stood too quickly while his feet peddled backward and he toppled over, catching himself with one arm, before righting himself. That's when he started to sprint, pausing only to snatch up his tunic and sword as he ran toward the others.

"Let's go!" he called ahead to them. "Get out of here."

I watched the soldier run from sight before looking back over my shoulder, searching for any sign of the beast that had frightened him away. Pulling at my dress, I rolled over and laid low to the ground, hunkered in fear. I stretched my fingers out and gripped my knife, which lay forgotten in the grass almost beyond reach.

My heart continued to hammer; I could hear the whoosh of blood throbbing in my ears with every beat. But no monster appeared. No griffin, no chimera, not even a giant boar.

In the distance, the soldiers' shocked cries and the pound of their horses' hooves racing away called back to me. After those noises settled, I heard the breeze blow gently through the grasses. Then I heard a snort that I hoped belonged to Xanthy.

Since I couldn't see or hear anything that would cause me danger, I got up to a crouch, staying below the grass line. I remained scrunched down as I scurried toward the road, holding up my tattered dress as I moved. Before fully emerging from the cover of the grasses, I checked the road.

It was empty again, except for Xanthy.

I dashed up to her side, flinging my arms around her thick, butter-colored neck. She tossed her head and pressed her warm muzzle into my side. I'd never been so happy to see another living creature in all my life.

"I don't know what happened back there," I told her, relaxing my grip on her neck. "I just thank the gods that it's over."

Rummaging through one of the bags tied to Xanthy's back, I found the extra dress I'd stashed away. I'd planned on saving it so I would have something fresh to wear when I reached Olympus, but I had no choice but to wear it now. The ruined dress fell to the ground as I shimmied the new one on over my head. All things considered, I could have a lot worse problems than simply having to wear my clean dress before I meant to.

I dusted myself off, removing a few errant blades of grass and one spur that remained lodged in my skin. Then I looked around for something I could use to get back on Xanthy.

But there was nothing.

No rock, no wall, no discarded clay pot. Nothing.

"Well, I guess we'd better start walking," I said to Xanthy. "I move slower than you." The two of us set out toward Megara, and with each step I prayed to find some foothold that would get me back on my horse so we could gallop away from the emptiness of this stretch of road.

CHAPTER 42 — EROS

Since confessing to Aphrodite, Eros had spent his days in solitude. There was no one he wanted to see. Certainly no humans he wanted to help. He'd ordered everyone away, refusing to accept visitors.

Most of his days he spent curled up on the couch, trying his hardest not to look in on Psyche. Although the hopeless, painful love he'd held for her had been ripped away when Aphrodite undid the arrow, something raw still tugged at his heart. Eros convinced himself it was nothing more than leftover emotion that would be gone soon enough.

After several days passed, another visitor came to Eros's door. If it was possible, she was even more unwelcome than his mother had been.

Iris.

She was descending on him like a vulture descends on fresh meat.

"Don't say it," Eros sighed when she sashayed into the room. "You can't tell me anything I haven't told myself a thousand times."

Iris nearly pranced as she walked, with her long, overly-slender legs jutting out from under her indigo dress. When she reached Eros's side, she flipped her raven-violet hair and pouted while blinking her sunken brown eyes. "I just don't understand."

Eros rolled his eyes. "What?"

"I don't understand why you wanted that girl. She's a mortal."

Eros slapped his palm against his forehead. "Oh, *that's* what she is? Why didn't anyone tell me?" He knew, of course, that Psyche was actually only part mortal, but he wasn't in the mood to correct Iris.

Iris thumped her hand down on her outthrust hip. "You don't have to be such a jerk about it."

"You don't have to act like you're telling me something I've never thought of before." Eros's head fell down into his hands, where it remained upheld only because he was clutching fistfuls of his own hair.

Iris slid down next to him on the couch and wrapped her olive-tinted arm around his shoulders. "I'm sorry," she said. "I can't imagine being betrayed like you were. And by a human." Iris paused a couple of beats before whispering in Eros's ear. "I would never do anything like that to you."

Eros's head flicked up and he glared at Iris as he pushed himself far enough away that her arm could no longer hold him. "Is that what this visit is about? You still think we could be together?"

"Wake up, Eros." Iris hopped to her feet. "Hera wants us together. Your mother wants us together. You can't fight them."

"Yeah, except I love someone else, remember?"

"She's just a mortal. She'll die soon enough." Iris turned on her heel to storm out of Eros's palace, when Eros caught her by the elbow and spun her around. His blue eyes burned with metallic ferocity and he pressed his nose in close to Iris's.

"You will not say things like that about Psyche," he hissed through clenched teeth.

Iris easily jerked her arm free from Eros's grip and glared back, her eyes again dancing. "Fine. Then you won't hear it from me that she won't survive until nightfall."

"What are you talking about?"

Iris placed her hand on her chest in mock astonishment. "Oh, I thought you didn't want me to say things like that about Psyche." The edges of her lips curled in an involuntary smile.

Eros reached out to rattle the lithe goddess again, but she easily avoided his grasp. "Don't touch me. I'll turn you a putrid shade of green for a month if you ever lay your hands on me again." But as she spoke, her eyes lightened and she caressed her stomach, letting her touch run down to her thighs. "Unless I *want* you to lay your hands on me, of course."

"Tell me what you know about Psyche."

Iris took Eros's hand in hers, forcing it to trace the sultry path from belly to thigh that her own hand had just explored. "Kiss me."

"And then you'll tell me?" His brows narrowed to a point as he eyed her. He was unwilling to let his mouth mesh with Iris's thin, violet lips unless she assured him information in return.

"If you even still care afterwards," Iris said, forcing Eros's hand to her back as she pressed her mouth against his lips. She wrapped a leg around his waist and grasped thick clumps of his golden hair, drawing his body in closer to hers. Eros finally forced Iris away when she flicked her tongue against his lips.

"Enough." Eros wiped his mouth with the back of his hand. "What's going to happen to Psyche?"

Iris smoothed back her hair and straightened her disheveled gown. Then she studied her garnet manicure indifferently before finally answering. "Don't blame me. Your mother found her and called in a favor with Ares." She folded her arms over her chest. "I heard he was going to have her killed, but that's all I know."

Eros staggered back a step from Iris and his eyes glazed over. "She can't die." Eros's words were barely a whisper. "She's not supposed to die."

He thought back to how Charon had said he'd be seeing Psyche soon enough. Eros had been so enraged at the time that he hadn't thought it through, but now he realized that his mom must've been planning on killing Psyche all along. Setting her up with someone hideous was just a temporary diversion. Aphrodite had always wanted her dead.

Iris ripped him out of his thoughts as she tromped out of the palace. "Don't worry," she called out before stepping outside,"I'll forgive you for loving her first. I'll be much more understanding that she ever was."

Iris slammed Eros's heavy, golden door on her way out. He grabbed a copper urn, the nearest thing he could reach, and hurled it at the closed door.

Once the echoes of the clanging pot had settled, Eros slumped back down to his couch and wrestled with his thoughts. Would he go back on his promises to himself and look for Psyche? Even if he never wanted to see her again, he didn't think he could just let her die.

Without wasting time to think it through, Eros began scanning for Psyche. He quickly located her ambling on horseback down a dry road, flanked by even drier patches of grass.

He looked closely, studying her. She was dusty and her clothes were dirty, but nothing about her seemed harmed. Either he'd found her in time or Iris had made up the story in some demented scheme to torment him. Eros didn't really care either way. His muscles relaxed and the knots of tension in his shoulders unwound as he watched her. Even disheveled, she looked amazing.

And then he saw the cloud of dust on the horizon and watched as the Spartan soldiers stormed closer. *No.*

His mind raced as he watched one of the men accosting Psyche, dragging her from her horse and wresting her away from the road into the tall grasses. Even if he left Olympus now, he'd never make it to her in time. When the soldier threw off his tunic and pounced on Psyche, blind outrage flooded him.

"She's mine!" Eros hurtled his powers of creation across the skies to Megara. As Psyche lay defenseless, with a knife pressed against her throat, Eros's magic reached her.

To the soldier, her whole body appeared to quiver. Her shape shifted between monster and victim. Her hair flashed to coils of snakes. Her skin crackled, revealing deathly grey flakes and her eyes burned like fiery coals.

As the soldier staggered away, Eros knew he was reaching the only conclusion his eyes allowed. Psyche looked like a gorgon whose identity, concealed by a human mask, was falling away under the stress of his attack. The man would assume that if he looked in the gorgon's eyes, he'd instantly turn to stone. And so he ran. Ran from his own attack, leaving Psyche basically unharmed.

CHAPTER 43 — PSYCHE

A foothold for getting myself back onto Xanthy never presented itself, so I walked the rest of the way to Megara. I knew I should move straight on to Eleusis, but ventured inside for more water and help getting on my horse.

As I led her through the city streets, I kept my head down and moved quickly while looking for a public fountain. The crowd of Megaran citizens thickened, a jumbled blend of farmers, merchants, slaves and senators. Surrounded by all of these people, I started to worry that I'd made a mistake coming inside. What if one of them recognized me? Or worse, what if they attacked me like the Spartans had done?

When I reached the edge of the fountain, I filled my flasks. I glanced up for a moment and caught the gaze of another girl who was doing the same. Her hair was neat, and her lightly olive skin was clean, but she was wearing a dress that looked like it'd been made from the harshest, undyed lambswool. She must be a slave, filling flasks for her master.

As her eyes flicked to mine momentarily, she gave me an almost imperceptible nod. A sign of camaraderie.

The momentary insult was quickly overcome by the realization that "slave girl" was a good disguise. I'd be able to pass through the streets virtually invisible if I looked like a slave. No one would give me a second glance. A tiny smile tugged at my lips and I felt safer.

Until a sharp voice ripped me from my momentary security. "Girl! Your master's horse can't drink from the fountain."

I'd been so distracted that I hadn't noticed Xanthy stick her muzzle into the city's fresh water. I tugged at her determined neck until I pulled her head above the water line. Xanthy snorted, splattering me with cool droplets.

Only when I had righted my error did I look at the woman to apologize. "I'm sorry," escaped from my lips at the same moment I fully saw her face. It was severe, but illuminated with the light of suppressed laughter. And it was familiar. A second passed before I realized the woman's face looked the same as the relief image of Hestia I'd seen on her shrine.

My eyes widened and I bowed quickly. "My Lady."

She regarded me carefully, studying my face and clothes. Then she nodded and lifted her chin with an expected air of superiority. "You look like a good, little slave girl." Her eyes glinted. "I'll give you a piece of advice," she continued.

I let my eyes dart left and right to be sure no one was listening. The noble woman reprimanding the slave girl was going unnoticed.

"You ought to serve Demeter in Eleusis. It would be a mistake not to ask her assistance as well."

I nodded my head in what I hoped was a reverent-enough bow. "Thank you, my Lady. I am forever grateful."

One side of her mouth lifted in a half-smile as she leaned in close and whispered. "It's not your gratitude I seek, it's fulfillment of the promise you made."

"The shrine!" I blurted before slapping my hand over my mouth. Again, I quickly looked around to see if anyone had noticed us yet, but we still appeared safe. I lowered my voice. "You will, of course, have your shrine if I live through this journey. I would not go back on my word."

She raised one eyebrow accusingly. "Really? Is that what you told Eros?"

The air rushed out of my lungs like I'd been punched. Warm tears pooled in my eyes, threatening to spill over. I hadn't even cried from my attack, but her words stung worse than any physical assault.

I started to defend myself. "I never meant to hurt --"

"Smarten up, girl," Hestia cut in. "What you meant is apparent to everyone. You'll earn favor from no one lying about your true intent. Admit to your mistakes and you may yet be forgiven."

Her words were harsher than I would've liked, but I knew she offered them as a roadmap to redemption. I dropped to one knee and kissed Hestia's porcelain-smooth hand. "My Lady, I can never thank you enough."

Hestia shook her hand free and looked at me the way a teacher looks at a dimwitted pupil. "Get up before you draw attention to yourself," she hissed.

As I stood, I brushed the dirt from my knees.

"Besides," Hestia added, "I can't promise you'll

ever be able to build me that shrine. You can wait and thank me if it ever happens."

I stopped wiping at my dress and looked up at the goddess, my heart heavy with dread. Advice was obviously as much as I could hope for from her. I nodded. "Alright then."

Hestia backed away, disappeared into the crowd, and was gone. Although still a little shaky, I was ready to escape from this throng of people too.

The only thing I knew now was that I had to get to Demeter's temple in Eleusis. After finishing the flask-filling task I'd started, I grabbed Xanthy's mane and began to lead her away.

But I realized I still didn't have a way to get on her back. If I wanted to make Eleusis by nightfall, traveling on horseback was a must. I looked around the packed mall, seeing only people scurrying about their business like rats. But the fountain was empty. Would anyone notice?

Hopping onto the fountain wall that separated the people from the pool, I steadied myself with Xanthy's mane to keep from accidentally falling in. I easily flung my left leg over Xanthy's back and wiggled into place. With a nudge of my heels, Xanthy and I barged our way through the mass of people until we were safely back on the road leading out of Megara. Once outside the city gates, we headed north and began the trek to Eleusis.

Blessedly, the road was empty.

I waited until after dark to slip through the gates of Eleusis and wind my way toward the city center. We followed the well-rutted road and, as expected, it led directly to the agora. The empty market stands and discarded scraps hinted at the life that would fill the long, rectangular plaza again come daybreak. But in darkness, it was eerily lifeless.

On the far end of the agora I could make out the silhouette of a temple. A few solitary torches flickered from inside. Sliding from Xanthy's back, I approached slowly, feeling total reverence for the goddess as I stood in the footprint of her most sacred shrine.

To honor the goddess for her gift of agriculture, the Eleusians had built a temple that itself seemed to grow from the earth. Long slender columns, like stalks of wheat, lifted the massive triangular roof. Icons of the goddess, riding in her horse-drawn chariot, graced every wall.

Taking a deep breath, I left Xanthy behind and climbed the steep temple staircase. My leather sandals tapped lightly against the marble stairs. The only other sound was of the wheat field at my back as the wind chaffed the stalks against one another. The temple floor was so far elevated above the ground that I couldn't see inside until I was more than half way up the steps. When I could take in the full sanctuary of the temple, what I saw shocked me.

There I was, standing in the most renowned temple to Demeter in all of Greece, and it looked like a pack of wild pigs had been let loose inside. Shriveled ears of corn lay scattered across the floor with brittle, brown stalks of barley. Mixed in among the rubble were farmers' tools -- rakes, hoes, and sickles -- left strewn about like the farmers had simply tired of tending the field across the way and tossed the devices inside with little care for where they landed. In a far corner, one of the smaller statutes tilted precariously against the wall.

Even if I could've focused amongst so much rubble, I refused to ask for Demeter's help while her tribute lay in ruins.

I ran to the statute and wedged myself between it and the wall. At first I didn't think I'd have the strength to stand it back up, but by pushing with my legs, the statute eventually lumbered back onto its base with a thud that echoed through the cavernous sanctuary.

Then I started picking up the litter of tools. When I'd collected them all and arranged them neatly in another corner, I started working on the mixture of expired grains. Fortunately, I found a little grass basket, which I used to collect the debris.

When I thought I'd collected everything, I paused, surveying my work for a minute. There was satisfaction in cleaning. It wasn't just serving a goddess. It felt good to have made order out of chaos. Satisfied that the temple was once again tidy, I turned to dart down the steps and throw away the wasted grains.

I got little more than half way through my turn before bouncing off a warm, solid chest. The little basket crushed into her and sent the grains I'd worked so hard to collect spraying once again across the floor. I was about to yell at the woman for standing behind me, scaring me, and ruining my work, when I recognized the face of Demeter.

Why did goddesses seem to think it was a good idea to sneak up behind me today?

Immediately, I dropped to my knees, reaching frantically for the strewn grain. Before I could grasp even two pieces, she exhaled a gentle breath, like she was blowing out an already waning candle, and they were gone. Even the pieces I had gathered were gone. I looked up and Demeter was smiling.

But she wasn't mocking me. Her smile was gentle, motherly. The radiance in her eyes was so openly caring that I wanted nothing more than to be wrapped in her arms. While she didn't hug me, she did hold out a softly golden hand and helped me to my feet.

"Thank you, Psyche," she said. "You can't imagine how it pains me to see this, of all my temples, in such disarray. Autumn is one thing. I don't really even care then, what with the farmers so busy with their harvests. But I have come to expect better in the springtime." Her deep brown eyes sparkled as she spoke, taking in the sanctuary with obvious pride.

"I can't believe they ever let it get like this," I said, now angry with the Eleusians for failing to take better care of the temple.

Demeter waived away my concern. "They're busy with the spring planting. I suppose I can't be too cross with them for using my gifts." Then she moved silently through the temple, decorating every crevice with explosions of fruits and flowers.

Her copper dress swayed effortlessly as she moved. When a spray of mahogany hair worked itself free from her carefree bun, she simply tucked it behind her ear and continued her creations. It was like watching a dancer and artist rolled into one.

Having created the last of her cornucopias, Demeter dusted her hands off and turned her attention back to me.

"Now, am I correct that you didn't come visit me to brush up on your domestic skills?"

My gaze dropped away from her liquid eyes as I nodded. "I don't know where to begin," I stammered. "I've never made a prayer in person before."

She laughed softly and set her hand on my shoulder. "Don't worry. I already know what you've come to ask." She sighed. "I only wish there was more I could do."

I searched for an explanation in her dark eyes, unable to speak. Hope rushed out of me like water bursts from a cracked dam.

"I will do my best." A sad smile tugged up one corner of her bronze-tinted lips. "But just as I couldn't shield my own daughter from Hades, I can't protect you from Aphrodite forever."

"I don't need forever," I stammered. "Just long enough to get to Olympus so I can see Eros. If we can just talk once he's calm, I'm sure we can work this out."

"You'll never get to Eros unless Aphrodite wants you to."

I blinked blankly at her lovely face, unsure what she was telling me.

"You won't like it, but there is a way," she finally told me.

"Anything!" I blurted.

"You can't hide from her. You can't get past her. You just have to go to her." Demeter continued, "She's angry with you, on many levels at the moment, but she'll respect your courage. You've got to make things up to her before you get the chance to apologize to Eros."

My own weight was suddenly too heavy and my legs wouldn't hold. It was like the monumental roof above my head was slowly squashing me into the ground. I crumpled into a pile at Demeter's feet.

"Come on now, I just picked you up off that floor a moment ago," she softly chided. She scooped me up under my arms and placed me back on my feet. My knees started to buckle again, but a sharp look from Demeter forced me to get myself under control.

"This is not hopeless," she said.

I nodded my head with little, stunted movements. It was the best I could do to indicate that I understood, even though I didn't. Turning myself over to Aphrodite seemed about as sane as dancing in a fire.

"If I thought she was going to kill you, I'd spare you the anguish and take you down to Hades myself," Demeter said.

Some comfort. I didn't want to be tortured, banished, ruined or any of the myriad other things Aphrodite could do to me short of death. I just wanted to see Eros.

"Besides," Demeter continued, "I think she's calmed down since her first attempt."

Words failed me for a second time in as many minutes. *Aphrodite has already tried to kill me? Like, really and truly kill me -- not just curse me and ruin my life?*

"Buck up," she said, closing my unhinged jaw with her finger. "You'll be fine."

The constancy in Demeter's eyes was impossible to ignore. That's when I realized, I was standing before a goddess of Olympus, who was telling me, as gently as she could, that I'd run out of options. I bit at the corner of my lip as I considered what to do next.

"Okay," I finally said. "How should I find her?"

Demeter's smile spread across her face, penetrating all the way up to her eyes. "I knew I wasn't wasting my time with you," she beamed. "I don't know that you're particularly brave, but you clearly love our little Eros." Then she added in a hushed voice, leaning in closer so her words couldn't be overheard, "Devotion like yours cannot be ignored, even by an Olympian. Remember that."

"I will," I promised.

"Excellent." Demeter stood tall again and grasped my hand in hers. "Come on then. I'll take you."

"Wait. Right now?" I pulled my hand away. "What about my horse?" I asked, faltering for any excuse to stall. "I can't just leave Xanthy here."

I wasn't ready to reunite with Aphrodite that very minute. I figured I'd have at least another night before facing the goddess I was convinced wanted me dead. *How'd we gone from being like family to her wanting me dead?*

"Hmmm." Demeter pressed her index fingers against her lips and looked thoughtful for only a moment before revelation flashed across her face. With a wave of her hands, she simply said, "The horse will come too. Problem solved."

I didn't even have time to shut my gaping jaw again before Demeter grabbed my hand and gently tugged me down the steps of her temple. Xanthy had her head and half her body stuck into the sacred wheat fields. She was munching away, but Demeter didn't seem to care. With an effortless and fluid motion, she grasped my waist and plopped me onto Xanthy's back. Then Demeter swung herself up behind me and clasped two fistfuls of Xanthy's mane, steering her out of the chest-high stalks of wheat.

I felt her nudge Xanthy forward into a trot, and then we were flying. It wasn't flying the way a bird flies though - or the way Eros flew. There was no effort, and no soaring or gliding. It was more like being a feather caught in the wind, floating, twirling, falling. Only with unimaginable speed. It was exhilarating and terrifying at once.

Demeter laughed like a giddy child behind me. "Isn't this great? I *love* not having to rely on wings to get around."

I hugged myself tighter to Xanthy's neck even though I was pretty sure Demeter wouldn't let me fall. I had to disagree with her though. I'd flown on wings and found it to be a superior, and far less nauseating, way to travel.

In less time than it would've taken me just to get back out of the gates of Eleusis, we landed on Mount Olympus. The air was cooler, the ground rockier. A chill ran up my spine, making me shudder.

Demeter slid off Xanthy's back with the fluidity of water. "Come on, dear," she said as she pulled me down. "You can stay with me tonight. Tomorrow we'll go to Aphrodite."

CHAPTER 44 — EROS

Eros stayed awake that night, swarmed by memories. His mind replayed Psyche's stories a hundred times -- from the first ones she'd told him over cheesecake to the ones leading up to their fight. They were stories he'd made her tell so that he could remember her while they were apart. Now the stories prevented him from forgetting.

As he tossed, alone in his bed, he heard Psyche's gentle voice; remembered her delicate laughter as she recalled something funny. And then when she'd finally kissed him, her lips burned their impression into his. The short time they'd spent together crashed around him, pouring over his head like drowning waves.

When dawn finally broke, Eros rolled over and pulled his blanket over his head with a groan. He knew Aphrodite had removed the sting of love's arrow. But he felt hungover on the love just the same, like it was an intoxicating liquor that left him wanting more even after it had run through his system.

He closed his eyes against the intruding light. More memories filled the lightless void. He could see her eyes flutter. He felt her soft fingertips on his cheek. Psyche's breath whispered in his ear.

"Enough!" Eros pushed the blanket away and sat up. His feet swung to the floor as he brushed through his tangle of curls.

"This is enough," he told himself. "It's time to get

back to work."

He shuffled out of bed and into his open courtyard. Besides forcing Psyche from his mind, work would help with some other problems he'd been avoiding.

His first and most immediate non-Psyche problem was that Zeus was going to open up the heavens on him if he didn't start answering some prayers. His second, and more troubling problem, was that his mother was determined to see him with Iris. But, if he used Iris to help with problem one, he'd also get Aphrodite to back off for awhile on problem two. He could work that angle if he had to.

From his courtyard, Eros began tuning in to prayers. At first the words ran together like the background buzz at a large dinner. Working through the jumble, he managed to separate the requests into discernible snippets.

"And I swear if you make him stay away from the prostitutes, I will be all the woman he needs." Eros didn't even have to look to know who was making that request. She'd be a middle-aged Senator's wife, the bloom of her youth slowly wilting as she fussed over children and arranged gatherings for her ungrateful husband. He'd heard a thousand prayers just like it before. He was sympathetic, but uninterested.

"Ever since I heard about Zeus appearing to Ledo as a swan, I've been obsessed with the idea of him coming to me in disguise. Maybe a lion or snake. Can you use your arrows to convince..."

Um, definitely not. Next.

"...and I know you usually make people fall in

love, but could you make this girl *stop* loving me? I know I'm good looking, but she won't leave me alone, no matter what I do to her. Like when I tripped her and she fell into a pile of horse crap. Didn't matter. She just kept following me around stinky. It's getting hard to get the pretty girls to notice me because they actually think I'm with her."

Eros chuckled. "Look in a mirror. It's probably not your shadow-girl driving them off," he murmured. For a second, Eros considered making the man fall in love with the pesky girl as punishment for being so proud. But love, even if unwelcome, would make the dope happy. Staying miserable and hounded would be better.

Next.

Then Eros heard a voice that was sweet and young, yet nearly strangled with fear. "Today I will marry a man I've never met. Mother tells me he's only twenty years older than I am, so it could be worse since I'll be his second wife. But I'm so frightened."

Eros scanned quickly for the girl, finding her curled in a chair by her window.

"I've heard he loved his first wife before she died and I'm worried there'll be no room in his heart for me. I know our marriage is political now, but I pray that it'll develop into more. Please, Lord Eros, if you can open my husband's heart to me, I will forever be in your debt."

The girl closed her eyes and dropped her head onto the knees. Eros almost felt the torture in her heart. Now *that* was a prayer worthy of answer.

And he knew how to use Iris to grant the wish.

All he had to do was wait for Iris to arrive. Even after their tiff the day before, Eros was sure he hadn't seen the last of her. As expected, she floated into Eros's palace as soon as the midmorning sun began streaming its warm, yellow rays through his windows. Eros wasn't even close to liking her, but he figured he owed her at least tolerance for tipping him off about Ares's attack on Psyche. Of course, Iris didn't know she was sparing Psyche's life, but Eros was still begrudgingly grateful.

"Hello, Eros," Iris purred. Today her skin tone had a touch of blue. Not deep like a blueberry. Just a thin cast of blue, like she was freezing from the inside out. "Maybe she is," he mused. "She usually gives me the chills."

She titled her head to the side and narrowed her eyes. "What? You look like you just remembered a good joke."

"I was just thinking of the work we have to do today. It should be fun."

"Work and fun don't usually mix," Iris said. A wry smile pulled at her lips. "But I'm intrigued by the 'we' part of it."

Eros told her about the young bride and his plans for granting her prayer. Not unsurprisingly, Iris agreed to come along. Once at the bride's home, the gods disguised themselves as wedding guests. Blending in with the throng of strangers filling the streets outside, they waited for her wedding procession to begin.

"The bride will lead us right to the groom," Eros whispered to Iris. "It'll save us having to look for him ourselves."

"I guess we wouldn't want to accidentally find the

wrong groom," Iris said with a grimace. Eros raised his eyebrows and nodded in agreement.

Before long, the young bride emerged from her parents' home. Her gown was made from a fine red silk and embroidered with a Greek key pattern in gold along the hem. Her light brown hair and wide hazel eyes looked plain against the elaborate wedding costume. Nothing like Psyche had looked that first night... Eros shook his head to rattle out the memories.

"Poor thing," Iris said. "She's scared to death. It's written all over her face."

Eros nodded. "Some prayers just have to be answered." Then he slipped further into the crowd to follow the wedding procession as it made its way from the bride's former home to the groom's. Iris hugged in close behind him.

When the procession started singing, Eros joined in. Iris shot him a sideways look that asked why he was participating in a human ceremony.

"I'm blending in, remember?" Eros smiled and winked. "You sing too."

As they walked and sang, Eros' hand inadvertently brushed against Iris's fingertips. Her hands weren't icy like Eros had expected.

When they reached the groom's house, Eros grabbed Iris's elbow and skirted sideways around the crowd. "Come on," he whispered. "Everyone will be going inside for the banquet. We can slip around back."

From the courtyard, Eros easily picked out the young bride in her screaming red gown. Beside her was a man Eros suspected was the groom. The dome of his bald head shined in the late-afternoon sun. Eros's suspicions were confirmed when the man began vigorously shaking the paw of a formidable-looking man and promising to take good care of his new bride.

With much-practiced ease, Eros pulled an arrow from the quiver and drew back his bow.   No one noticed as the silver arrow exploded with a burst of starshine into the man's back. The yellow-white crystals momentarily sprinkling the air were lost on all but Eros and Iris.

"That should do it," Eros said, slipping his bow back over his shoulder. "Prayer answered." When he turned to look at Iris, her jaw hung open and her eyes were frozen on the spot in the man's back where the arrow had vaporized.

"What'd you think was going to happen?" he asked with a satisfied smile.

"I -- I don't know," Iris said. "How did they not see? It was so beautiful."

"They're human. They only see what their eyes can comprehend."

Some thought tugged at the back of Eros's mind. He tried to bring the thought forward, but set it aside when it didn't easily surface.

"Come on," he said, tugging at Iris's arm and leading her out of the courtyard, "it's your turn to work some magic."

Iris looked up. The sun shone unmercifully from a pristine blue sky where only a smattering of clouds puffed here and there. She shook her head.

"I need more clouds. Rainbows don't work in pure sunlight."

Eros stopped. "What do you mean?"

Iris shrugged. "I can't just make rainbows appear anywhere. I need sun *and* rain clouds."

Eros's eyes flattened. "You might have clued me in to that little detail before you agreed to help." He threw up his hands and raised his wings to fly.

"Wait!" Iris said. "All we have to do is get Helios to drive behind one of the clouds." She pointed to a rocky grey-colored cloud near the horizon. "That one has rain in it. It would work."

"Oh. So all we have to do is get the sun to fly off course and we're in business. Sure. No problem." Eros rolled his eyes.

"For a god, you aren't very clever about using your gifts," Iris said. "Helios would gladly take a jaunt behind that cloud if something tempting enough were up there."

Eros and Iris looked at each other. "Who?" they said in unison, then laughed together.

"A girl would have to be pretty dazzling to get the sun's attention," Iris said.

"Of course!" Eros said. "Aglaia." The Grace of Radiance. "Helios would be drawn to her even without my arrows."

Iris gave him an quick, excited hug. "Perfect! Now how do we get her up there?"

"*I'm* the one who's not very clever?" Eros asked. "I can make him think Aglaia is up there, but the illusion won't hold when he tries to talk to her. Can you work quickly?"

Iris burst into the air, calling back for Eros. "What are you waiting for?"

With a jump and a flap of his wings, Eros sped

past her. "Work fast, remember?"

Iris answered with a laugh as the gods sped toward the lone rain cloud.

When they got to the cloud, Eros reached for his arrows and Iris perched on the edge like a diver about to jump into the sea. Eros's arrow caught Helios in the shoulder and his head snapped around toward the pair.

Helios's gaze tightened on a hologram of dancing light. The mirage took shape in the figure of a sparkling girl whose hair moved with the wind and whose eyes flashed with the brilliance of the stars. A perfect duplication of Aglaia. She tip-toed across the air toward the rain cloud.

"It's working," Iris whispered as Helios turned his solar steeds toward the girl.

"Get ready," Eros said. "Helios won't stay enchanted after she disappears."

Helios's chariot drew closer, shooting spikes of heat toward the gods as he neared. Iris flinched. "I can't believe I'm doing this for a human."

In a flash of searing light, Helios was behind the cloud. Iris dove, drawing her palate of colors across the sky as she fell. Her rainbow illuminated the sky and just for a moment, Eros thought he saw a red-dressed girl looking up in awe.

As Iris touched down behind a hill and tucked away the tail of her rainbow, an accusing boom of a voice call out. "Eros!"

Iris had only just spun around to look when Eros tore down from the sky and swooped her up in his arms.

"Let's go," he said, furiously flapping his wings

back toward Olympus. When Eros set Iris down back at his palace, they both burst out laughing.

"I assume Helios wasn't pleased?"

"You could say that."

"Aren't you worried?" Iris asked, wide-eyed.

"Nope. He can't hurt me. Besides, that was fun." Eros looked at Iris. "Thanks for playing along with me. I needed that."

Iris took a step closer to Eros. "I could be a lot of things you need."

The smile fell from Eros's face, but kindness remained in his eyes. He ran his hands down Iris's delicate arms and clasped her hands. When had her hue changed from blue to pink?, he wondered. She looked almost edible flushed with a more natural color.

"I'm just not ready yet," he breathed, looking down at their hands laced together.

Iris pulled one hand free and raised Eros's chin until his eyes met hers. "It's okay. I said a lot of things yesterday that I shouldn't have... If you can forgive me, I can wait. Deal?"

Eros looked off in the distance. "I forgive you."

Iris raised up on her toes and kissed Eros on the cheek. "Good night."

He watched her sultry aura of shimmering colors trail her out the door.

That night, alone in his palace, Eros relaxed with the pleasant tiredness that comes from a satisfying day. He'd answered a prayer *and* used his arrows on a god other than Zeus. What more could he ask for?

The thought was barely out of his head before Eros regretted it. He could ask for Psyche to have loved him enough to trust him. He'd forgotten her while he was out playing with Iris, but memories of her came crashing back in the solitude of his home.

Eros was angry with himself for being so easily amused by Iris. Yesterday he had hated her, but today... not so much. And he was shocked to think he could so easily be drawn to her after the devotion he'd held for Psyche. Was giving Psyche up really as easy as wiping away the magic of his arrows?

As Eros mulled it over, the little flicker of a thought he'd ignored back at the wedding crept to the surface.

They're human. They only see what their eyes can comprehend.

Even if she had some divine blood running through her veins, Psyche was still human. She could only see what her eyes could comprehend. "Yeah, so," he goaded himself. There was something there. What was he missing?

Eros thought through everything that had happened leading up to Psyche's betrayal. They'd fought. Then made up. Psyche's sister came to visit, but Alexa said Psyche hadn't listened to them.

And then he remembered. Alexa told him she'd shown herself to Chara. And when Psyche was trying to explain herself, she's started to say something about Alexa, but he'd cut her off.

What if Psyche had seen Alexa too? Psyche's eyes would only comprehend betrayal. She'd see a palace built on lies. A supposed best friend stabbing her in the back.

Hope too painful for words grabbed Eros's heart

and squeezed. He had to find Alexa. If his hunch was right, Psyche was the one who deserved his forgiveness.

Perhaps he would need some forgiveness of his own.

CHAPTER 45 — PSYCHE

When I woke up the next morning, my mind instantly clamped down with the fear of facing Aphrodite. There was nothing to do though except busy myself with getting ready.

Demeter floated in with her carefree nonchalance as I wound my hair neatly into a bun. When she opened her hand, a tiny white daisy materialized. She tucked the delicate flower behind my ear before taking my hands in her own.

"You can do this," she assured me, squeezing my palms.

I closed my eyes and exhaled while bobbing my head and forcing a tight smile. "I know," I said and bit my lip. "Might as well get this over with, huh?"

I didn't mean a word of it, of course. I'd have taken any excuse to delay.

Demeter straightened the flower behind my ear. "No time like the present," she confirmed. Her dark eyes danced again with motherly assurance.

Unable to stop myself, I threw my arms around the goddess. Everything about her was comforting. Her skin smelled fresh like the Olympian air and her smile radiated warmth. She encircled me with her own arms as I shuddered against her.

"Oh, Psyche," she sighed as she rubbed my back. "You *must* believe that everything will work out. All is lost if you lose hope now."

I stepped back and blinked at Demeter. "I don't understand," I muttered, now furiously chewing the corner of my lip.

"When you stand before Aphrodite to apologize, she'll know your heart better than you do. If there is *any* hesitation in there, she'll sense it."

Gulping, I nodded. *This had better be the best apology of my life.*

"And the same is true when you tell her you love her son and deserve his forgiveness," Demeter continued. "You must go to her with the conviction that you *are* Eros's destiny. You do believe that?"

"More than anything," I whispered.

"Then you can do this." She tilted her head so she could look at my downturned face. "Putting it off won't make it easier."

I looked up into her eyes. "I believe that too," I muttered with a sigh.

Demeter's laugh was as light as butterfly wings. She squeezed my hand once more and led me out of her palace.

Xanthy was grazing in the flower-filled field beside Demeter's home. I headed toward her but Demeter stopped me. "Leave Xanthy with me."

Stopping short, I swung around to meet Demeter's command. My heart broke. I didn't want to leave my horse behind. She was the only link I had to humanity on this mountain of gods.

Demeter glided up to me. "I'll take good care of her until you return," she promised. "Now come."

When her hand touched mine again, we fell into Demeter's sickening flight, floating and diving through the glorious morning air. But this time our flight was quick, and we landed with a gentle touchdown on a gilded path. I followed the glinting metal under my feet up to the entrance of a palace.

Her palace. It was grotesquely ornate, and nothing like the down-to-earth persona she'd had when visiting me. But now it made sense why Eros thought I'd like golden everything -- he'd been raised in it. The palace dripped with golden columns, golden doors, golden statues. It made my stomach sour and I glared at it from behind furrowed brows.

"Yeah, we all think it's a little over-the-top," Demeter whispered in my ear, "but don't you dare let Aphrodite catch you making that face at her home."

I wiped the dissatisfaction from my face just before Aphrodite's gilded door opened.

"Demeter, is that you I hear out --" Aphrodite stopped mid-sentence when she saw me. The goddess stood in her doorway, seeming to fill it with her aura. She was even more astounding on Olympus than she'd been back in my home. Soft blonde ringlets cascaded down her back and spilled around her shoulders. Her eyes sparkled like the ocean waves from which she was born. Her delicate porcelain skin seemed to radiate light.

As Aphrodite glared at me, a small, cruel smile tugged at her lips. When the smile broke, she chuckled, then laughed, then tossed back her head with maniacal laughter that rang out like cries from a flock of hungry gulls.

"You see the irony, don't you *daughter*?" Aphrodite spat when her laughter subsided. "All you had to do was listen to me in the first place, and we'd both still like you."

My shoulders slumped. She was right, of course. She'd tried to bring me and Eros together from the start and we'd both refused. His heart had obviously changed once since then, but I feared it'd changed back already.

Scrambling forward, I dropped to one knee beside her golden-sandaled foot. Being so near her was overwhelming in a way it'd never been in my room. For one, she no longer needed my lotions: her own scent was as calming and powerful as being surrounded by blooming jasmine. But there was a charge vibrating off her skin, threatening to shock like an eel. I closed my eyes and pressed my forehead against the back of her hand.

"Get up," she snapped at me. "You're embarrassing yourself."

Obeying, I slowly rose, never letting my gaze tear from hers. "You know me," I whispered. "Once, you liked me enough to consider me your daughter. To marry your son. I know I've messed that up now, but *you* know it wasn't supposed to happen this way." I pulled her hand over my heart. "You know I acted with the best of intentions, even if I was stupid."

For a second, I thought her armor would crack. A smile tugged at her lips and she looked at me like she could almost see us being friends again. But the tone of her voice told me I'd misread her.

"That, my dear, was before I realized you were just as much of a slut as your mother."

"How dare you!" I screamed. Immediately, I

clamped my hand over my mouth.

"What did you just say to me?" Aphrodite grabbed my arm, digging into my skin with nails like talons. "How dare I? I tried to set you up in a legitimate marriage and instead you just ran off and slept with my son behind my back."

"We never slept together, I swear it." The muscles in my arm began to cramp as she squeezed tighter. "But I wasn't talking about me anyway. I meant my mother. Please. Leave her out of this."

"She can't be left out. She started it the night she slept with Poseidon." She squeezed again before freeing my arm and I stumbled back a few steps.

My mom had done what? No, Aphrodite was lying. She had to be. Mother loved my father. She wouldn't betray him like that.

"I wondered if he could make a daughter as lovely as Zeus had." Aphrodite snatched one of my curls between her thumb and finger. "It seems he can, only you're not a blonde."

Whoa. What? The world went blank as I pulled inside my head. *Was that even possible? If she was telling the truth, Father wasn't my father at all then. Which could explain why Mom was so upset when she found out Aphrodite had made me her daughter. And why...*

"That's why you picked me then." My eyes filled like warm pools. "Not because you liked me, but because I was already part immortal."

"Let me put the question back on you, Psyche. Have you ever heard of an immortal spending her free time with a full mortal? And I'm talking about more than a night here."

I shook my head "no." Gods hung around with other gods and demi-gods. As a rule, they only meddled with people's lives, not participated in them.

"Then I believe you've answered your own question."

After that, I couldn't meet her eyes. I couldn't even ask to see Eros. There was too much information to process and I wanted to escape and think it over. Turn it in my brain like an odd-shaped rock and study every side.

"I can feel you're struggling with this, Psyche. I understand."

Aphrodite's changed tone got my attention. It must've resonated with Demeter too, because she took the opportunity to drift to my side and slide her hand into mine.

"Here's the problem, as I see it," Aphrodite continued. "You're my niece by Olympian standards and I did actually like you. But first you refused my command and then you tried to kill my son. I'm pleasantly surprised that you didn't sleep with him, but that's not enough to redeem yourself."

"Please," I begged her. "All I want is a chance to talk to Eros and tell him how I feel." My voice trailed off as I remembered the horror of our last night together - the raw emotions sweeping every arc from fear to desertion to betrayal and even to love. "He deserves to know I love him."

"Don't tell me what he deserves." Aphrodite's voice hissed out with a chill as she rose and stormed down the stairs. "What he deserves is a wife who won't try to stab him while he sleeps."

"I know," I admitted. "I know. And maybe I'll never win back his heart, but I need him to know that he won mine."

Aphrodite paced. "Demeter, we've got a problem. You brought her to me, so it's your problem too. I *think* I'm calm enough not to want her dead anymore, but I can't just let her go back to Eros. Or even run around with everyone thinking she's still my daughter. What am I supposed to do?"

"Hmmm..." Demeter shifted from one foot to another. "Perhaps a test? If she passes, you let her talk to Eros. If not, you can turn her over to Ares."

My eyes probably could've doubled as fat olives as big around as they got at that suggestion. *A test?* I had no skills outside of being able to read, how on earth could I pass any sort of test? And who knew what dreadful, unspeakable things Ares would do to me before I died.

Aphrodite shrugged. "It worked for Heracles, I suppose. What'd you have in mind?"

CHAPTER 46 — EROS

Eros started looking for Alexa with a simple scan of her parents' home and land. After all, they'd agreed to keep her under lock and key in exchange for him not going to the Olympian Council. In retrospect, he realized he might've been a little harsh.

But he didn't spot her.

Running a hand through his soft curls, he exhaled. "Where are you, little nymph?"

He plopped onto his couch and settled in for a more detailed scan. Eros started with some of Alexa's favorite siblings. Perhaps she'd gone off to visit them. But her metal-working brother and flower-guarding sisters were alone. One by one, Eros checked all fifty of her brothers and sisters, but Alexa wasn't with any of them.

Where on earth?

Eros broke from his scan to close his eyes and think. He knew she wasn't working (he'd fired her himself) and she wasn't with family, so where did that leave? He thought through vacations in Crete or lazy baths in salt spas. None of those things felt like Alexa. He'd never known her to even want a vacation. Could she still be holding on to her job even though work was forbidden?

Yes. Of course. Alexa would cling to her friendship with Psyche no matter the cost. Eros realized he had to find Psyche if he wanted to track down

Alexa.

The last place he'd seen Psyche was outside Megara, where he'd saved her from the soldiers. That was less than two days ago. She couldn't have gotten *that* much further.

"On horseback," he muttered, "she would've passed Eleusis, and might be past Athens, but she couldn't have made it to Thebes yet." That narrowed his search radius. All he had to do was scan the roads between Eleusis and Thebes, and he would find her. As a last resort, he could check the cities too, but Eros was sure he was close.

He was so confident that he started flying to Thebes, scanning as he flew. He planned to work his way backward, certain Psyche was moving as quickly as she could toward Olympus. As his wings beat furiously against the afternoon sky, he scanned the dusty roads.

By the time he reached Thebes, he'd scanned the entire length of road with no sign of her.

"What am I missing?" He dropped down onto an empty stretch of road. Eros thought back through his mental calculations of how far Psyche could've traveled. Even galloping non-stop, he didn't see how she could be past Thebes already.

As he rested, he scanned inside Eleusis, Athens and Thebes. Still nothing. Eros kicked a stone laying on the edge of the road, sending it careening into a strand of trees in the distance. How could she just be gone?

"This isn't possible!"

A quiet echo played back to his ears. *Possible, possible, possible.*

Aching gripped Eros as realization washed over

him. His knees weakened and he took a staggering step backward. "Mother."

Eros unfurled his wings and shot into the air. "Mother, where is Psyche?" he screamed as he hurtled back to Olympus.

CHAPTER 47 — PSYCHE

Aphrodite led me down to a river on the west side of her estate. My feet skidded on rocks and pebbles as I struggled to keep up with her stride. When we reached the river's edge, my toes squished into the mud, making my sandals so slippery that I fell back onto my butt.

"I still like my idea of sorting grain," Demeter added. "She's not a weaver, but nothing says 'domestic' like success in the kitchen."

Aphrodite looked down at me as I scrambled back to my feet. "No, this will do." Then she set about explaining that all I had to do was cross the river and shear a clump of golden wool from each of her sheep before noon.

I blinked and nodded as she explained, trying to show how intently I was listening, but focusing more on what she wasn't saying. Something about the test seemed surreally easy -- easier than sorting grain -- and that worried me. *Were the sheep impossibly fast? Maybe they secretly had wings like Pegasus and would fly away?* I had to be missing something.

"Understand?" Aphrodite asked.

When I nodded, she smiled grimly. "Good. Then I hope to see you back here before noon."

Aphrodite pranced back up to her palace, gossamer white gown and blonde curls flowing like enchanted waves in her wake. Demeter gave my shoulders a quick squeeze before following her.

Nope - definitely not a good sign.

Once they were gone, I turned back to my task. Now that I looked at the sheep closely, maybe this wouldn't be so easy after all. The animals weren't so much fluffy, timid sheep, as massive, snorting rams. Their golden fleece sparkled only half as bright as the solid gold, spiraling horns that rose dangerously from their foreheads. Beady black eyes seemed alive with the heat of simmering coals and all of them were locked on me.

Gulping, I slipped the knife out from my belt. I moved slowly, cautiously, wading step by careful step toward the bank on the meadow-side of the river. Even though it was still early, my palms were already starting to sweat. The knife passed to my left hand as I tried to dry off my right, but my dress was muddy from my little tumble. I leaned forward ever so slightly, touching the soft green grass of the meadow, drying my damp hand.

Never did I take my eyes off of the biggest ram. As luck would have it, he was the closest to the river. And as I approached, he lowered his head, bobbing his horns in warning. When I touched his meadow, he stomped his massive hoof, sending a divot of grass flying behind him with no more effort than if he'd been pawing sand.

"Easy, boy," I said. "It's alright. I'm not going to hurt you."

Even if he could understand me, my knife probably spoke louder than my words.

Sliding my right foot onto the bank, I slowly rose

out of the water. I hadn't even straightened my knee when I was hit and launched back into the river. Water rushed into my mouth and nose as I gasped. For a moment, I thought I might drown in a measly meter of water. When I forced my head above water, choking and sputtering, I expected to see the ram standing on the bank, preparing to wade in and strike again. But he hadn't moved. He was still stomping his little patch of earth into oblivion.

I pushed a soggy clump of hair from my mouth. "What the..."

And then familiar arms wrapped around my shoulders, hugging me in a tight embrace. "Don't hug me back," Alexa said. "She may be watching."

"If she's watching, how would she explain me flying into the river just now?" I asked. But I really didn't care. I was just relieved to have my friend back, whether it caused me trouble with Aphrodite later or not.

"Did you see yourself sliding around on the bank earlier?" Alexa giggled. "It's not much of a stretch for her to think you did that all on your own."

"Maybe so." I pursed my lips together. "Mind telling me why I needed to crash in the first place?"

"Um, because the sheep would've killed you, silly. You can't just go walking up there and whacking off pieces of their wool now." I felt Alexa sit down in the water beside me as I looked at the shimmering beasts.

"But I have to collect their fleece before noon. I can't --" A sob caught in the back of my throat. "I can't *not* do this."

I pushed myself up to stand but Alexa tugged my

arm out from under me. Without support, I toppled back over with a splash.

"Uh oh, looks like you've sprained your ankle," Alexa told me. "You better scoot back to the shore and rest for awhile."

I didn't understand, but I didn't argue either. Like an injured crab, I pulled myself backward through the water with my hands and pushed with my left foot, making a show of not using my right foot at all.

"Okay, now what?" I asked Alexa as I scooted my dripping self out of the water.

"Now, you sit," she answered. "Look at your foot, roll it around, but don't stand on it. You might as well dry out in the sun while you wait."

"Wait for what?" I pounded my fists on the shore as I glared at the big ram, who'd gone back to chewing grass. "I don't have time to sit around here. It'll take me forever to get wool from all of those sheep."

"Do you have time to die?"

"No." My lower lip jut out in a very immature pout.

"Then just trust me, will you? The rams nap late in the morning. They'll all go lay in the shade under that oak on the far side of the meadow. Zeus could drop a thunderbolt on top of them and they wouldn't wake up. You'll be able to collect all the wool then with no problem and be on your way... long before noon."

Instinctively, I reached to hug her. She batted me away with an invisible hand.

"Stop! You'll give us away."

"Oh, right." My hands fell back to my sides. "You're still the best, even if I can't hug you."

"Yeah, I know." Alexa pulled herself up beside me on the bank and stretched out on the warm grass. I plucked blade after blade of grass, tearing them into little pieces and pitching them into the river.

"How do they do it? The rams, I mean. They look strong, but strong enough to kill?" It wasn't the question I really wanted to ask, but it broke the uncomfortable silence.

"Well, if the flames they shoot from their nostrils don't burn you up, they'd run you through with their horns. Maybe both. I guess they have to be vicious or everyone would be running around with golden clothes."

"She tried to kill me, then." I peeled another blade of grass into strips. "I mean, Aphrodite sent me out to this field to be burned and staked."

Alexa rubbed my hand.

"I'm sure that wasn't what she hoped would happen. It's just, the tests given to demi-gods are never easy." Her voice seemed to blend with the flow of the river and my vision got watery as my eyes teared up. I still had so much to think about when it came to my family and every spark of a thought burned.

"Maybe I should just let him go," I mumbled. "After everything that's happened, everything I am, I don't deserve him."

"Don't be ridiculous. Knowing who your real dad is doesn't change a thing about who you are." Alexa smoothed a strand of hair back from my face. "I told you the first time we met that you deserved everything in that palace -- and that includes him."

Rubbing at the bridge of my nose, I pushed away

any tears that had managed to escape. "I just don't know if I can do this right now."

"You're tired, is all." Alexa squeezed my shoulder. "See, the sheep are starting to lie down. They'll be napping in no time. You can do this."

We sat in silence as the dozen golden sheep meandered to the oak and lumbered down to rest. One by one, their horns tore into the ground as their heavy heads fell over in sleep. As they dreamed, their hooves stuck at the dirt and sparks jumped from their nostrils.

As I watched, Alexa squeezed my hand. "You should go now," she said. "They sleep soundest when they've first dozed off."

My knife was still stuck in the bank from when Alexa had knocked me off my feet and it'd gone flying. I plodded over to it and pulled it loose from the mud. After washing it in the river and drying it on my dress, I inspected the blade to make sure it was perfectly clean. "Wouldn't want to get mud on Aphrodite's golden wool," I muttered under my breath.

Alexa laughed. "Don't forget to limp. You sprained your ankle, remember?"

"Whatever. Aphrodite can think whatever she wants about me falling into the river. I'm not going to fake a limp around flesh-eating sheep."

Sloshing out of the river, I climbed onto the far bank. At first I took careful steps, trying not to let the grass crunch under my feet. But the closer I got to the rams, the more I just wanted to be done with the task and get out of the meadow. When I was within a few meters of the animals, I started running until I got to the farthest one away. My plan was to start far and work my way closer to safety.

I knelt by the back of the first ram to stay out of the way of his feet and flames. Of course, that put me within easy striking distance of his massive horns he if threw his head back for some reason.

For a moment, the horns paralyzed me. With fear or with awe, I don't know. They were much more intricate and deadly than I'd seen from across the river. Instead of being perfect spirals, the horns came to a razor-sharp point along the top ridge. And the tips looked sharper than any needle I'd ever seen. Yet the horns were still beautiful, laced with delicate carvings that corkscrewed around in intricate patterns.

What are you doing? If you don't hurry up, you might get to feel the horns and not just look at them.

I grabbed a fistful of fleece from the back of the ram and started slicing. Trying not to tug on his skin, I sawed the knife as fast as I could until the clump fell loose in my hand. The soft, glittery fleece squished between my fingers.

One down, eleven to go. I duck-walked to the neighboring sheep and started sheering away a clump of his fleece. With each patch I removed, I got more confident. Sawing faster, tugging harder, just trying to get the task over and done with.

But as Alexa had warned me, demi-gods don't get easy tasks; things only went that smoothly until the eleventh sheep. My left hand was about overflowing with puffs of golden wool by then, and I lost my grip on the tuft of fleece from the ram I was working on. I was crouched down on my toes and leaning over the sheep, so that when I lost my grip, I fell face-first across his belly.

Now Alexa may have thought that nothing could wake the sheep while they napped, but she was wrong.

The ram leapt to his hooves, leaving my face to fall into the dirt as my feet were tossed up in the air. The knife slipped from my hands and the clumps of wool scattered. I rolled over and found the ram's face nearly pressed into mine. His black eyes glinted with rage and he snorted sparks that singed the ends of my hair.

"Easy now," I whispered. "I don't want to hurt you." I wiggled my right hand carefully through the grass until I felt the knife handle on my fingertips.

"Ngeeeeeeeee." The ram bellowed and raised up on his hind legs. I grabbed the knife and rolled as the ram came down and struck the ground with a thundering blow. While he shook his head and refocused on me, I managed to get up onto one knee and plant my other foot on the ground.

The ram charged, snorting blasts of fire as he lowered his head and aimed for mine. Just before he reached me, I fell to the side to dodge his blow. As he passed, I plunged the knife as deep as I could into his side. He wrenched it from my hand as he barreled past, leaving me defenseless.

I scrambled to my feet as the ram skidded to a stop and turned to face me. Blood like crimson dye spilled across his golden wool where the knife jutted out from his side. He pawed the ground impatiently while looking first at his injured side and then at me.

Again, he raised onto his hind legs and bellowed. I was worried he'd figured out my duck and roll trick, but I knew I couldn't outrun him either. With no time to think, I ran at the sheep and jumped as high into the air as I could when he charged, hoping I'd at least clear the razor-like horns. Because his head was down in his charge, I did manage to make it over the horns, but my feet and legs came down awkwardly.

My left leg slid down the ram's side and my right leg was caught up underneath me, pinned between his back and my body. I toppled forward and grabbed whatever I could get hold of to keep from crashing into the ground. With one hand, I caught his tail. With the other, a chunk of wool. As I fell, the wool popped off in my hand and I spun backward off the sheep, holding on by only his tail. The sudden shift in my weight knocked the ram off balance and he crashed sideways into the ground, driving the knife deeper into his side.

I hurried back to my feet, ignoring the trails of blood oozing down my own legs after that fall. My heart thundered as I tried to think of a new way to dodge his next charge. Jumping hadn't been my best idea. As I slowly backed away from the ram, I realized he wasn't getting up.

His side heaved with each labored breath. The ram expelled a final, fiery breath and then was dead.

Two thoughts crossed my mind at the same time. *I did it! I'm going to finish this task.* and *Crap! I just killed one of Aphrodite's golden rams.* No matter how much sparkly wool I hauled in, she would not be happy about this.

The clump of wool from the dead sheep was still clutched in my grasp. *Well, that makes eleven.* I scurried back to the place where I'd spilled the other ten balls and quickly gathered them back up. Praise the gods, none of the other rams had woken up during my fight. Just one more sheep to sheer and I'd be done.

When I turned to go to the last sheep, I realized I didn't have my knife anymore. How was I supposed to cut off a lump of wool with no knife?

Running back over to the dead ram, I tried to roll him over, but he was too heavy. I even tried sliding my free hand under his carcass to get my knife back, but it was no use. I couldn't wiggle my fingers enough under his massive weight to even find the handle. For all I knew, it was lodged so deeply in his side, I wouldn't be able to get it out anyway.

Frantic, I looked around for some tool. I hadn't come this far, shorn eleven sheep and battled to the death with a fire-breathing golden ram to fail now. I toed some rocks by my feet, but none of them had a sharp enough edge to cut through fleece.

As I stared at the twelfth sheep, another ram rolled over and butted his head right into its flank. The horns! I could use the horns as a knife. Tip-toeing around the two animals, I reached down and gently grabbed a tuft of wool right under the horns.

Please just don't let them wake up. I sawed one ram's wool off using the other's horns. If the other ram so much as raised his head, I'd lose my hand. But the horn was so amazingly sharp, it severed the wool like a hot knife cuts through butter.

With twelve tufts of golden wool in my hands, and the sun starting into sink almost directly overhead, I sprinted toward the river. "I did it!" I yelled to Alexa as I crashed into the water, splashing and tripping with every frenzied step. I scrambled up the bank, panting and dripping wet. "Did you hear me? I did it!"

But it wasn't Alexa who answered me.

"Of course I heard you," Aphrodite answered. She'd materialized out of nowhere and stood towering over me as I stooped to catch my breath. She unraveled the ball of fleece from my fingers and inspected it.

"You got all twelve, I see."

"Yes," I panted, still trying to catch my breath. Even through gasps though, I noticed I was smiling and Aphrodite was not.

"Is that your blood I smell, or have you injured one of my rams?"

I lifted the hem of my tattered dress and looked down at my legs. Angry red scratches and dried blood still lined my shins, but I'd stopped bleeding. That was probably more than I could say for the sheep.

Dropping my dress, I stood and looked up at Aphrodite. "Probably a little of both. One of your sheep attacked me."

"Then the only way you could be here is if you killed it."

My shoulders slumped. This didn't sound like it was going to be good.

"I'm sorry, Psyche. But your task was to sheer the sheep without harming them."

Um, how'd I miss that instruction? Maybe while I was focusing on trying to look like I was paying attention but not actually hearing a word she was saying.

"Since you bested the ram, though, which is more than I expected, I won't call off our deal just yet. I'll give you another task."

I wasn't sure whether I should be grateful or pissed. I'd had a hand-to-hand duel with a killer sheep and collected twelve tufts of wool, just like she asked, but I wasn't any closer to seeing Eros.

Then again, I wasn't any closer to being turned over to Ares either. I guessed I had to take what I could get for now.

CHAPTER 48 — EROS

Eros raced back to Olympus, wishing for something more powerful in his quiver. If Aphrodite had so much as scratched Psyche's perfectly tender skin, he wasn't sure he'd be able to hold himself back. A week ago he'd cowered at his mother's vengeance, but that was before he owed Psyche an apology. Before she became his everything again. Now, he wasn't prepared to let anything stand in his way. Even his mother.

As he flew, Eros spotted a brilliant burst of color descending on him.

Iris. What was she doing here? He didn't have time for her now. Still, he slowed his flight, flapping his wings only enough to keep him airborne.

"There you are, Eros. " Iris stopped herself on Eros's chest. "I've been looking all over for you. I was thinking, maybe today we can find prayers to answer in a town where it's already raining. That'll make things easier."

Eros put his hands on her shoulders and gently turned her out of his way. "I can't today. I've got to get back to Olympus."

Iris's lips pursed as she set her jaw. "I suppose this has to do with Psyche?"

"I'm sorry, Iris. She might be in danger. I have to go."

Eros flapped his wings to continue his flight to

Olympus, but Iris reached out and caught his wrist. "Wait."

Eros glared at her and she released his hand.

"I mean, let me help you," Iris offered. "You think she's with your mother, right? Why don't you let me go to Aphrodite? You can wait in my palace, and I'll figure out a way to borrow Psyche so you can see her."

"You'd do that for us?" Eros's lip curled up in a soft smile. "You'd really help us?"

Iris shrugged. "No, but I'll help *you*. This isn't for Psyche. I'm just trying to help my friend."

Eros crushed Iris into his chest. "I don't know how to thank you."

Iris clutched Eros's hand and launched into a flying sprint toward her palace, moving so quickly she almost dragged Eros behind. "Oh, I'm sure you'll think of something," she called over her shoulder.

Chapter 49 — Psyche

"You're trying to kill me!"

I blurted out the words before my brain registered that it wasn't smart to yell at a goddess, even if she was sort of your quasi-mother.

"On the contrary," Aphrodite responded, twirling a golden coin over and under her fingers, "I'm saving you." She flipped me the coin and I caught it over my head. "The coin will ensure you get safely into Hades."

"And what about coming back out?" I demanded.

Aphrodite laughed, throaty and indulgent. "Smart girl. You did pay attention during our visits." She materialized another coin and tossed it to me.

I put the coins into a little wooden box and tucked it under my arm. For my second task, Aphrodite told me to take the box to the Underworld and borrow some of Persephone's beauty. To hear Aphrodite tell it, the stress of everything that'd happened between me and Eros had melted away some of her eternal glamour. And somehow, although Aphrodite was already prettier than everyone else anyway, Persephone would gladly give up some of her own beauty to make Aphrodite feel better.

In my opinion, that wasn't likely. Never mind that humans don't go into Hades and come out alive — or come out at all for that matter.

So, setting aside the fact that my task was basically

doomed to failure, all I had to do was get Charon to ferry me into Hades, sneak past Cerberus the three-headed guard dog, find Persephone, convince her to give me some of her beauty for Aphrodite's benefit, get back past Cerberus, and get Charon to ferry me out of Hades. Oh yeah, and I had to get half-way across Greece before even meeting up with Charon.

No problem.

"Don't be so traumatized," Aphrodite said, probably noticing the glazed-over, scared-half-to-death look in my eyes. "You're a demi-god, remember? You can do it. Besides, I'll take you to Charon myself."

My heart lightened by the weight of a feather. There was still a ton of crap to get through, but at least one part of this trip would be easier. "Thank you."

The words were barely out of my mouth when she grabbed my wrist. Salt water rushed into my mouth and my face was pelted by sea spray. I choked back the panic of drowning and tried to crunch the sand out from my teeth.

As quickly as the ocean assault began, it was over. As we regained our footing on solid ground, Aphrodite looked refreshed, her cheeks glowing. When I reached up and felt my own hair, I was convinced I looked like I'd just lived through a hurricane. *Great.*

Our new location was obvious even though I'd never been there before. There's only one way to get into Hades and that was through the gates in the Alcyonian Lake.

Aphrodite's hand lingered on my wrist before she released me. "Here you are then," she said. "See you on the other side."

"How will I get back? To Olympus, I mean."

"When you make it out, I'll come fetch you."

When. She'd said when, not if. Could it be that she was actually rooting for me now?

With another burst of sea spray, she was gone. And I was alone staring out across the endless blackness of the lake.

From a distance, I heard small splashes coming toward me. As I watched, Charon emerged from the mist, plunging his pole into the water as fast as he seemed capable of moving. He paused only once to rub the sheen of sweat from his forehead with the back of his hand.

He stopped paddling when his boat neared the edge of the lake, letting it glide into the bank. His yellowed teeth were exposed beneath a wide smile. Despite being covered in grime, there was something soothing about Charon. I saw kindness in his brown eyes and no trace of menace in his smile.

"Psyche, you've finally come to join me," he said as he held out his weathered, crooked hand.

I smiled back, although weakly, and took his hand as I stepped into the narrow wooden boat. "I don't plan on staying, but I could use a ride if you don't mind."

Charon covered his heart with his hand and sighed. "You are as I've dreamed. So perfect," he murmured. "Even Helen didn't come to me until she was an old woman. But you..." He caressed a strand of my hair between his fingertips. "No wonder Eros didn't want to give you up."

That got my attention. I locked eyes with

Charon, no longer caring that he was fondling my curls. "What do you mean Eros didn't want to give me up?"

"Ah, there is so much in the way of the gods that you don't understand. Do you even know why Eros brought you to him in the first place?"

I shook my head. "Sit," he said, "I'll tell you while I paddle."

"Oh, your coin," I remembered, opening the little box and taking out a golden coin.

He took it slowly from my fingers and then sniffed it, long and deep. His eyes rolled into the back of his head with pleasure. When he opened them and saw me watching, he explained. "It smells of you and Aphrodite combined. Truly divine. I will… treasure this." He tucked the coin into a pouch and plunged his staff into the water, pulling us away from the bank.

I sat nervously on a narrow bench at the back of the boat. "About Eros --" I prompted.

"Ah yes. Eros came to you at his mother's bidding. He was supposed to make you fall in love with a monster. But you bewitched him."

"That's impossible. The first time we met, he couldn't stand me."

"Don't be silly. He just didn't want to be hurt again." Charon paused again to wipe at his brow. "Anyway, he came to shoot you with one of his arrows, but when he saw you, he simply couldn't do it. And he nicked himself with the arrow instead."

Memories flooded back on me. "Then that wasn't a dream? The archer in the garden was Eros." I was somehow relieved by this information, like knowing it'd been Eros and not the most deranged prophetic dream ever meant I wasn't going nuts.

But just as quickly, another realization popped in behind that one.

"If his arrow..." My lower lip started to tremble and tears welled up in my eyes. I bit my lip hard to stop the teary aqueduct from overflowing. "He didn't *really* love me then. Not on his own. It wasn't real."

"Does it matter why he loved you? You won the heart of a god."

"And I lost the heart of a god. If his love wasn't real to begin with, what chance do I have that he'll take me back?"

Charon stopped paddling for a moment and looked back at me. "I'd say your chances are better than average."

"Thanks," I said, only half believing him. After we sat in silence for a moment, I asked, "What did you mean when you said he didn't want to give me up?"

"Aphrodite went into a real rampage after you refused her son. First she sicked Eros on you, but that wasn't enough. So then she promised to send you here to me. Of course, I figured you'd be dead when you arrived. But I think I like you better alive." His chuckle came out hoarse. "You are heavier this way though."

"Oh... sorry." *Was I supposed to apologize for not being dead?* "Charon, can I ask you, how do you know all of this?"

"I hear things," he said. "Of course, most of my information came from the gods themselves."

"So you actually talked to Eros -- about me?"

Charon ducked his head as we entered a cave. The light nearly extinguished behind us. I could barely even see Charon just ahead of me in the boat, still pulling us forward. "Eros stood right where you stood on the bank of that lake. You can be sure he was quite angry when I told him his mother intended to send you my way."

"How long ago was that?" I moved to the edge of my seat, anxious with anticipation.

"It's been weeks. Before you went to him."

I dropped my head. So much had changed in the past few weeks. Maybe he hadn't wanted me dead then, but I still had no clue whether he cared now.

Lost in thought, I gazed down at the water, barely visible in the darkness. It sounded like we kept brushing against branches as we slid through the water. I strained my eyes to see what we skimmed against. The water swirled like an inky pool and gray wispy figures began to emerge. Their long, snakelike fingers clawed at the sides of the boat, but had no more effect than if we were brushing past a weed. I watched in horror as their soundless mouths opened in screams and their hazy eyes chased us as we passed.

"Wh...what are those?" I asked, barely able to speak myself.

"You're no longer in the land of living. Those are shades, lost forever in the Acheron River."

"I don't understand. Why aren't they in the Underworld?"

"No coin," he answered. "You don't think I haul dead people down this river for free do you?"

I looked back down again at the shades and watched them slip beneath the water. Like clouds of smoke blown away in a breeze, they disappeared under the surface. "You can't just leave them here," I said, scrambling forward in the boat to get closer to Charon. "You must have so many coins already."

Charon turned on me, rocking the boat more than I liked, and locking me with an icy glare that was visible even through the blackness. I backed cautiously to my seat in the rear of the boat, knowing I'd overstepped some invisible line.

Still.

"Maybe these souls died on the battlefield and weren't recovered," I pleaded. "Or maybe they died at sea. Or maybe... maybe their families were just too poor to spare a coin to line your pockets. It's not fair for you not to take them."

Charon threw his staff into the boat, where it clattered against the sides. "So now you're going to tell me how to do my job? Fine. You row the damn boat." The boat bucked as Charon thumped himself down on the seat.

I sat in stunned silence until the boat bumped against the wall of the cave. Without Charon steering, we were adrift on the river. Never mind that I'd never paddled a boat before, I certainly wasn't going to sit around in a dark cave waiting for the current to dump us back in the lake.

Reaching forward blindly, I felt around the boat until I grabbed Charon's staff. The weathered wood felt smooth, almost polished, from the years of use. I plunged the staff into the water, striking the bottom of the river, and used it for balance while I stood. It took all of my weight to move us forward against the current. With a heave, I quickly moved the staff forward, digging again into the silt on the river bottom, and put my weight into pulling us forward.

After just three pulls, I was starting to feel breathless. I didn't know how much farther we had to go, but I was already doubting I could make it.

"You're not so light... yourself," I panted at Charon between breaths.

Charon snickered. "Must be my heavy heart from drowning all those poor souls in the river."

His sarcasm fueled my determination, giving me strength when I thought I didn't have any left. "You're just... a lonely old man," I heaved. "But not too old ... to change your ways." I paused from my rowing, resting my head against the staff. Charon was looking back at me, waiting. I shoved the boat forward again. "You're never too old ... to change."

"What do you know about being old? Or about change for that matter?"

"I might not be old... but I know I've got some things to change if I make it out of here." I shoved the boat forward again, but this time it slid to a grating halt.

"Well, what do you know?" Charon asked. "You actually made it the rest of the way. I'm impressed."

I was so relieved to not be paddling, that I staggered out of the boat and fell backwards into the sand. Sprawled on the cool shore, my chest heaved and my hammering heart slowly returned to a more normal pace.

Charon knelt down beside me. I heard the sand near my ear crunch under his boots. "How about a deal?" he asked. "I'll promise to start bringing some souls into Hades without coins -- *if* they have a good excuse -- if you'll do something for me."

I closed my eyes and sighed. What choice did I have? Didn't I owe it to a world full of impoverished shades not to damn them to eternity in a river?

"Sure," I answered.

His calloused fingers closed around mine. "Good. Let's get going then." With an easy pull, Charon raised me to my feet and let me go.

I shook my head in confusion as we began walking. "What's the favor?"

"You're giving me a vacation while I accompany you through Hades. As the daughter of Aphrodite, I think you've got enough clout to get me the afternoon off."

"That's it? That's really all you want from me?"

Charon turned and looked at me. His eyes were dull, tired. "What more could I want? I'm getting some time off to spend with the most beautiful woman in the world. Isn't that enough?"

"Shush! Aphrodite's mad enough at me as it is. Don't you dare get me into any more trouble with praise like that."

Charon started walking again, leading me toward a far-off light. "I didn't say you were the most lovely immortal, did I? I'm not stupid."

We walked in silence for a little while, coming

upon torches that lit a narrow path. Shadows began to dance across Charon's face as the flames flickered. The effect made his face appear angry one moment and concerned the next.

I took a step onto the path, but Charon grabbed my arm and pulled me back. "Wait," he called.

Screeching and hopping, I looked down at my feet, afraid I was about to step on snakes or into a pit or something. Charon chuckled at my graceless little dance.

"For the record," he told me, "Eros would be a damn fool if he didn't take you back."

CHAPTER 50 — EROS

Rubbing the sleep from his eyes, Eros blinked back the blinding rays of morning sun. He wondered where he was for a few seconds until the memory from the night before settled in.

Seeing Iris's palace in the daylight was disorienting. Curtains were purple, couches were orange, pottery was green. And not muted, pastel versions either. These were full-on, ultra-saturated colors. The explosion of hues gave Eros a headache and he rubbed at his sore temples.

He'd felt like this before, but only after way too much wine. And he'd only had a few sips of ambrosia while he was waiting for Iris to come back. But he didn't remember her returning. In fact, he didn't remember anything after sipping from her cup.

"That harpy drugged me," he realized.

He picked himself up off the floor. Somehow he'd ended propped against a couch, meaning he'd spent the night asleep on the ground. This would not weigh in Iris's favor if he ever caught sight of her again.

"Iris!" he called to the empty palace. "Iris, are you here?" He slowly circled the room to make sure his voice carried to every part of the house.

When Eros's own voice echoed back to him, it was clear he was alone. "Good," he muttered, "because I might have to kill you if you were here."

When his anger ebbed, Eros remembered why he was at Iris's in the first place. She'd promised to help him find Psyche. But now neither woman was here. Damn it.

Eros pushed through the drug-induced stiffness in his wings as he bolted into the morning sky. As fast as he could manage, he flew to Aphrodite's palace and pounded open the door. The golden portal crashed into the marble wall behind it, shaking the entranceway.

"Mother, don't make me come looking for you. Get out here." Eros clenched his hands into fists so tightly his biceps shook.

Aphrodite sauntered into the room as if nothing were unusual about her son's visit. "Ah, there you are. I was expecting you yesterday, but I guess you found other ways to occupy your evening." Aphrodite half-smiled, twirling a ring on her finger.

Eros eyed his mother. "*You* sent Iris to drug me? So I wouldn't get here sooner?"

"Umm..." Aphrodite answered with a sigh and brushed her fingertips along Eros's shoulder, touching the remnants of withered flesh that still hadn't fallen off after the burn. Eros jerked his shoulder back reflectively. "How *is* your scar healing?"

"As you can see, it's fine. Almost gone," Eros said through clenched teeth.

Aphrodite arched her eyebrows and turned her back on her son. Taking hold of her door, she removed it from where it'd come to rest against the wall and quietly closed it. Then she looked at the large crack that ran through her marble wall, running her fingers over the crevice. "Something else I'm going to have to clean up after you make a mess of it, I see."

"Enough. Where's Psyche?"

Aphrodite strolled over to a padded stool and dropped down into it. She pursed her lips and looked at the ceiling as she sighed. "Hades."

The word worked better than a swift punch to the kidneys. Eros staggered two steps backward, clutching his gut in agony.

"You asked."

Eros continued backing up until he found a stool to sit on. "How? How'd this happen?" He gripped his hair in his hands and rocked himself in denial. "I saved her from the soldiers. I saved her. She got away. I saw it."

"I didn't say she died," Aphrodite finally answered, after letting him marinate in misery for a few moments. "I said she was in Hades. I took her to the Alconian Lake yesterday and Charon ferried her in."

Eros's eyes bulged as his hands fell away from the death grip he had on his hair. "You did *what*?"

"It's a test. I'm sure you've heard of such things; Heracles had twelve of them." When all Eros did was glare, Aphrodite continued. "Psyche's actually getting off easy with only two."

"Why'd you do this?" Eros demanded. "You loved her once too. We were all supposed to be family. Why can't you just let it go?"

"I'm trying to, Son."

"Excuse me?" Eros's eyebrows strained for his hairline.

"I tried to bring the two of you together once and if you'll recall, you both refused. How am I supposed to just act like that never happened? Or that you didn't follow through on my curse? Or that she threw my divine gifts back in my face? And then that she tried to kill you?" Her head lolled back against the cool marble wall. "I still want the two of you to be together if that's what will make you happy, but things are more complicated now."

As a god himself, Eros appreciated his mother's need to avenge her reputation and her family. Her instincts weren't the prettiest side of her nature, but they all had them. No slight on Earth ever went unnoticed on Olympus.

"When she makes it out, does that settle the score?"

Aphrodite's lips pursed together. "I'm still not sure."

"Will you at least agree to call off Iris?"

"The trip to Hades and back is a long one." Aphrodite went to her son and lifted his chin. "Don't light a torch under Iris's pyre just yet."

***

Just like his visit two weeks ago, Eros was left waiting when he reached the Alconian Lake. He paced along the bank, his steps falling with the graceful impatience of a caged lion. His eyes remained fixed on the cave entrance, but the only thing to see was the current of the river flowing out.

He forgot his pacing when he heard faint splashes on the lake. Every muscle in his back coiled into rigid ropes as he stood frozen on the shore. The splashes grew louder. Charon would be coming out of the cave any second.

Please let Psyche be in the boat.

CHAPTER 51 — PSYCHE

I'd forgotten. There's a reason Hades doesn't need a gatekeeper to keep trespassers out or shades in. His name is Cerberus, and he's 90 kilograms of nasty, three-headed, slobbering, growling dog.

We hadn't been on the path into Hades for long when I heard Cerberus's snarl in the distance. But it wasn't the snarl that scared me. It was the vicious, angry barks followed by terrified screams. Since I was still a little hesitant of killer animals after my morning sheep encounter, I half-hid behind Charon as we plodded ahead.

"We don't have far to go now," he assured me. "Just stay with me, and you'll be fine."

The stench of decaying feces and sulfuric dog-breath wafting through the craggy tunnel confirmed Charon's warning that we were nearly to Cerberus.

When we rounded a corner, I was suddenly face-to-face with three sets of bone-crunching jaws. Saliva splattered against my cheek as one of the heads chopped in my face. My shrill screech echoed the ones I'd heard earlier and I staggered backward into Charon. The ferryman easily caught me and pushed me safely behind him.

Cerberus strained against his heavy chains, snarling and snapping, threatening to bite Charon's head off. But Charon never flinched. He just stood his ground, inches from the snapping fangs, and glared back at the over-grown mutt.

"I don't suppose you have a honey cake in that box of yours, do you?" Charon asked me, never looking away from Cerberus.

I barely heard him over the thundering of my own pulse. Facing Cerberus was bad enough, forgetting the only thing that would distract him was a monumental disaster. Sweat broke out across my upper lip as panic set it.

"No. Now what?"

"Check the box to be sure."

"But I didn't ask Aphrodite to give me a --"

Charon cut off my hysterics. "Check the box."

I snapped the lid open, thrusting it forward so Charon could see it was empty. Like I told him it would be.

Only it wasn't empty.

"Well, what do you know? There's a honey cake in the box," Charon said as he pulled the cake out and closed the lid before flinging the cake in the opposite direction of our path.

Cerberus leapt and spun in the air, throwing himself at the cake. I watched in horror as the heads snapped at each other, drawing self-inflicted blood, in their battle for shreds.

"Come on." Charon grabbed my hand and we lunged forward. He was ridiculously fast for an old man. As I worked to make my feet catch up, my sandal hit something slick and I went down.

Charon's hands latched under my arms and lifted me, but not before Cerberus noticed we were stopped.

The beast turned mid-air as he jumped. When his paws struck ground, he was already sprinting toward us. Charon spun me out of the way, but Cerberus still managed to snatch a chunk of my dress in his fangs. The heat of his rancid breath burned through the cloth.

With every bit of strength I could manage, I pushed myself forward while Charon continued to pull. Seconds passed. We were deadlocked. Cerberus's growls rumbled through the cave. His head snapped side to side as he tried to jerk me free from Charon's protective grasp.

And then came a distinctive tear. The same ripping as when the soldier had shredded my dress, exposing my flesh. Only this time, the sound was the best thing I'd ever heard.

As a swatch of cloth separated from the dress, I tumbled just beyond the reach of his jaws. Savage barks split through the cavern, deafening in their intensity.

"Let's go," Charon screamed over the snarls. We raced down the path until we could no longer hear the hungry heads fighting one another for their chance to spill my blood.

It took longer than I cared to admit, but my breathing finally slowed enough that I could talk. "How'd you know that'd be in there? The honey cake, I mean."

"Even Aphrodite has to abide by *some* rules." Figures. Charon didn't sound winded at all. "If she wants you to run an errand for her in Hades, she at least has to give you the tools to get inside."

"But she didn't tell me. I mean, if you hadn't been here, I never would've known."

"Just part of the test," Charon said. "Be glad you have a tutor that lets you cheat."

"Please tell me I'm not overhearing evidence of cheating going on," a lovely, young voice piped up. "Especially if it's cheating death. We tend to frown on those sorts of tricks."

Her willowy body materialized on the torch-lit path. Charon immediately bowed to the woman, then took her delicate hand in his. Down here, this could only be Persephone, Queen of the Underworld.

"Of course not, your Highness," Charon chuckled. "At least not the accusation of attempting to cheat death."

Her eyes danced as a wry smile tugged at her lips. "In that case, I'll pretend I didn't hear a word." She squeezed Charon's shoulder tenderly. "It's good to see you again, old friend."

"You know how it is. I never get a day off to come visit," Charon complained.

"And yet, here you are." Persephone's eyes turned to me. They were deep brown, like Demeter's, only shockingly intense. She studied me, perhaps sizing me up, but I didn't get the sense I was being judged.

"Perhaps I understand why," she said, eyebrows raised, still watching me with those eyes. "Charon, aren't you going to introduce me to your... *friend?*"

Charon cleared his throat. "Of course. Queen Persephone, this is Princess Psyche, Eros's fiancée. Psyche, Queen Persephone."

Persephone's face instantly brightened. "I didn't know Eros was engaged!" She flung her arms around me and squeezed, welcoming and sisterly. "I'm so glad you came down to meet me. I'm long overdue to return, but I didn't know I'd missed such important news."

Charon frowned. "That's true. You are overdue." Persephone was only supposed to spend fall and winter in Hades. Come spring and summer, she returned to Earth to visit with her mother. "Is everything alright?"

"Oh yes!" she gushed. "If I didn't know better, I'd think Eros had been down here spreading some of his magic. Hades has been such an amazing husband lately, I haven't wanted to leave. And mother agreed spring could still come as long as I'm happy." She shrugged her shoulders. "So, here I am."

I looked around the dimly-lit pathway and jagged, rock-lined walls, wondering how she could possibly want to stay here when spring was exploding in the gardens outside. But then I thought of the nights I'd spent in Eros's company, cocooned in darkness and bursting with emotions I couldn't name. It wouldn't have mattered where we were, as long as we were together.

As if picking the image of Eros out of my brain, Persephone asked, "So, Psyche, where is that fiancé of yours? Is he too scared to come down into Hades himself?"

"Actually, Charon exaggerates. We're not really engaged. Aphrodite tried to arrange our marriage but -- you know what? It's a long story. Let's just leave it at I love him."

Persephone tilted her head and a spray of honey-colored hair tumbled onto her lean shoulders. "I seriously need a messenger to bring me news from

Olympus so I'd have a clue what's going on."

When she snapped her fingers, three tripods appeared and the cave illuminated under added torch light. Not that light helped any. Now I could see the stalactites hanging like fangs over my head and the filmy, grey ooze slowly creeping down the walls.

Persephone, however, seemed totally unaffected by her nightmarish reality. "Come, sit. I have all the time in the world."

So I told her, in as condensed a version as possible. But there was really no way to sugar-coat what I'd done or why I was there. As I reached the end of the story, I rubbed my hand nervously over the top of the little wooden box.

"And so Aphrodite sent me here as my final test. I'm supposed to bring back some of your beauty for her."

Persephone snorted. "For *her*? What does Aphrodite need with more beauty?"

"I'm sorry," I apologized. "I hate to ask, but I have no choice."

"So let me get this straight," Persephone said, "if I say 'no' then it's my fault you don't get to see Eros?" She flung her hands into the air and let them fall back to her sides with a thump. "That woman is unbelievable."

"I think I have an idea." Charon rubbed his chin with his crooked fingers. "Aphrodite never said Psyche had to get *face* beauty." Persephone and I looked between Charon and each other. "The Queen could give Aphrodite beauty from her big toe, and Psyche would still have completed the task."

This time, Charon was on the receiving end of one of Persephone's jubilant hugs. "Charon, you're a genius. I love it!"

"It won't hurt her, will it?" I asked. "I mean, her face isn't suddenly going to look like your big toe or anything, right?"

Charon and Persephone burst out laughing. "I wish," Persephone giggled. "I'd give her my whole foot to see that."

"No," Charon explained, "when she opens the box to receive Persephone's beauty, it will simply go to her toes. Nothing to worry about."

"But what if she thinks I tricked her?"

"There's nothing we can do about that," Persephone said, already unlacing her sandal. "The real test is whether you make it out of here alive after having convinced me to part with some of my beauty. What type of beauty you bring back won't be that important."

She freed her foot from the sandal and held out her hand. "Here, give me the box."

Placing it in her hands, I crouched forward on my stool to see how she went about extracting beauty from an appendage.

"Oh Psyche, you can't watch this part," Persephone said. "The essence of divine beauty would probably kill you. Once I give you this box back, whatever you do, don't open it."

I shook my head fervently from side to side to show how clearly I understood. No way was I going to open that box. Death by beauty was not what I needed. Talk about ironic.

Persephone opened the box as I backed away. "Wait," she called. "You forgot your other honey cake." She removed the cake from the box and held it out to me.

"Oh yeah."

"I'm not sure how far away you need to be," Charon said. "You'd better start back down the path. I'll catch up."

"What about Cerberus?"

"I didn't tell you to go all the way back by yourself, did I? Now get."

I nodded reluctantly. Bile rose in my throat as I thought about having to brush my fingers against the oozing slime to feel my way back out of the cave. "Okay," I croaked.

I started to leave, but then turned back. "Queen Persephone?" Her dark eyes met mine. "Thank you. For everything. You don't know how much this means to me."

Persephone just nodded and smiled kindly. She didn't need to answer. I knew she understood.

Slowly, I paced down the path that led back to Cerberus. If I moved slowly enough, I didn't have to touch the walls after all. I just shuffled my feet and leaned back, hoping if I hit a wall, my toes would stop me before my face collided.

As I moved, I squeezed the little cake tight in my fist, not caring if it crumbled, so long as I didn't lose it. *How much further should I continue without him? What if I ran into Cerberus alone?* We both needed to use the same cake for our escape. I was still trying to figure out my next move when Charon ran up beside me.

The torches rushed to life along the path as he returned, chasing away the inky blackness. I didn't think I'd ever be so grateful for the smell of burnt olive oil and the sting of smoke in my eyes.

"That was fast."

"Here you are, my dear," he said, holding the wooden box out to me.

I reached my hand out slowly to take the box, but then pulled back. "Are you sure I can touch it? Persephone said it could kill me."

He thrust the box toward me as if to say take it. "The only danger is if you let the beauty out of the box. So don't."

"Got it," I confirmed and grabbed the box.

"Better hold it with two hands just to be safe," Charon noted.

I held up my other hand to show that it was coated in mushed honey cake. "Mind holding this then?" I asked with a grimace.

Charon snorted. "What'd the cake ever do to you?"

"Let's just say I was keeping a tight grip on it to make sure it didn't get away." Charon raised his eyebrows without comment and peeled the sticky, crushed cake from my hand. "I didn't figure Cerberus would notice if it was a little mashed up."

"I've seen worse come through here. As long as it's quasi-edible, it'll do the trick."

After wiping my sticky fingers on my dress, I gripped the box in both hands. For good measure, I also tucked it into my chest and clutched it there. When we got back to Cerberus, Charon launched the cake remnants and the hound greedily bounded after it.

"Let's go," Charon called to me and we both scurried past Cerberus's lair. I gripped the box tighter as I ran, even though it made me hunch over slightly and run a little slower.

We were barely past Cerberus when Charon started to slow. "Let's keep going," I begged. "I just want to get out of here."

"Of course. Why would you want to stay with me when you have Eros waiting for you?"

"No, it's not that." I stopped and turned to face Charon. "That's not what I meant at all. You've been wonderful and I couldn't have done this without you." I uncurled one hand from the box to touch his shoulder. "Besides, I don't know whether Eros is waiting for me or not."

Charon looked away like he didn't believe me.

"Really," I said. "I just want to get this box back to Aphrodite. I feel like I've got death in my hands and I don't want to touch it anymore."

When Charon looked back, he was smiling. "I suppose I'll see you again eventually anyway." He reached out and stroked my cheek with his knobby fingers. "I've had fun though and I thank you for my day off."

"*Fun* probably isn't the word I would've picked, but I'm glad you came with me," I answered. "And I'm serious. I couldn't have made it without you."

He gave me a light pat on the back. "Alright, enough with the sap. Let's get out of here."

We both trotted back to Charon's boat and he steadied it while I climbed inside, still clutching the box to my chest. Charon pushed us out into the river before climbing aboard himself. As soon as he was standing, he plunged his staff down to the river bottom and we were moving away from Hades.

I couldn't help but sigh with relief as the shore was lost in the blackness of the cave. Persephone had been wonderful, but nothing else about Hades gave me any reason to look forward to the day I'd have to return.

As we glided through the darkness, I tried not to peer into the murky water. I didn't want to see the hapless shades drifting like submerged clouds below the surface. But when I let my focus drift, something caught my attention and I had to look.

A pair of shades took shape. One was a woman who held her baby up to the surface. Her paper-thin lips pled the same silent word over and over until I was sure I could read what she was saying. Please. Please, she begged, and the infant's body broke through the surface.

"Charon!" I screamed. "Stop. We have to save them." Working more on impulse than reason, I set the box down on the floor of the boat and reached out to the shades. I scooped the baby up into one arm and grabbed the mother around her wrist with my other hand. They were like holding solid air. They had shape, but no weight. When I pulled the mother up, she easily came over the edge of the boat without so much as making it tip.

By then, Charon had stopped paddling and turned on us. "What are you doing? Put them back. Now."

CHAPTER 52 — PSYCHE

Charon loomed over us in the small boat. The shade mother took her weightless child out of my arms and cradled him while cowering on the floor. "Please," she cried as she stroked her baby's withered head. "At least let my son pass on."

"Charon," I pleaded. "We had a deal. You promised to help some of the shades in the river. Why not let these be the first?"

He just stood there, motionless. In the darkness I couldn't read his expressions to gauge what he was thinking.

"Please. For me?" I asked. Seconds ticked by without an answer.

Finally, Charon grumbled, "It's lucky I like you, or you'd be in the water with them." But before he was even done grousing, he'd begun pulling the boat forward again.

Remembering why I was even on the river in the first place, I bent down to retrieve the wooden box from the floor. When I leaned over, the mother kissed me on the forehead.

"Thank you," she whispered. "I don't know who you are, but may the gods be with you always."

For the rest of the ride, I watched the mother and child huddle together. Their obvious love was so consuming, I moved to the floor of the boat, just to be nearer. In fact, I was so engrossed by them, I didn't

335

notice we'd emerged from the cave until our boat scraped to a stop on the shore.

That's when I heard Eros's voice calling my name.

Hearing him again was like getting my heart back. My chest had been empty without him and now it swelled. I jerked up and saw him half running, half flying toward me. His arms were outstretched, his lips pulled in a smile so wide it consumed his face.

I scooped the wooden box off the floor of the boat and scurried over the side and onto the sandy shore. Clasping the box tightly in one hand, I ran full speed toward him.

We quickly closed the distance to each other and I was only a few steps away from launching myself into his arms when I noticed a ribbon of color descending on me. The radiant hues tangled around my feet, tripping me as I ran. I was moving too fast to keep from falling. As I toppled, my chin smashed into the packed sand and the box skidded out of my hand, bouncing away.

I watched, eyes wide, as the box tipped onto its side and the lid cracked open. Scrambling on my hands and knees, I scurried to the box, hoping to close the lid before any of Persephone's beauty escaped.

The last thing I remembered seeing was an illuminated fog circle up out of the box as my hands closed around it. The mist swirled around my head, filling my nose and mouth. When I gasped, the mist pulled me under the surface of my own consciousness. And everything went black.

CHAPTER 53 — EROS

Eros's heart skipped a beat when he saw Charon's boat emerge from the cave. At first, he didn't see Psyche crouched low in the boat. An involuntary pull set his feet in motion, dragging him slowly toward the approaching ferry. Even if Psyche wasn't on board, he had to see the boat, talk to Charon, figure out what happened. If nothing else, he would find out how to get into Hades so he could see Psyche one last time.

When Psyche's head bobbed into view over the side of the boat, Eros exhaled a breath he hadn't realized he's been holding. His footsteps quickened as he hurried to reach the spot on the bank where Charon was mooring his boat.

"Psyche!" he yelled, now running and flapping his wings to push him faster. "Psyche!"

Relief washed through him as Psyche's eyes met his and she scrambled to get out of the boat. He was amused that she wouldn't leave without the little box that must be holding Persephone's beauty. As if his mother could stop him now. He would have her again whether she fully completed Aphrodite's task or not. He opened his arms wide so he could wrap them around Psyche the very second she was close enough to embrace.

Soft and low, Charon muttered, "You don't deserve her, boy. Take good care of her, or someone else will."

The warning was too low for Psyche's ears, but Eros heard. He cut his eyes away from Psyche for a second to glare at Charon. What business did the old ferryman have telling him to take care of his love? Anger almost blinded Eros for a moment, but Psyche's steps were so close, he quickly regained his elation.

Eros looked back at Psyche in time to see her eyes dart right. In a burst of rainbow-tinted speed, Iris swooped down on Psyche, wrapping up Psyche's ankles in her vibrant tail. All he could do was watch as Psyche slammed into the ground. Overcome by rage, Eros lunged after Iris, but missed catching her.

"Damn it, Iris!" Eros shouted after her. "This is enough."

He ripped his bow from his shoulder and snatched an arrow from his quiver. Taking aim at the sky, Eros said, "Helios," and released the arrow. It shot into the sky and exploded in a burst of silver fire when it hit the sun god's chariot.

Iris immediately stopped running and looked to the sky. Her violet eyes sparkled as her expression changed from vengeance to adoration.

Shooting toward the clouds, Iris left a glittery trail of color in her wake.

Satisfied that he was finally rid of Iris, Eros slung his bow back over his shoulder and hurried to Psyche. He knew he should've gone straight to her and dealt with Iris later, but his temper had gotten the best of him. Especially after the stunt she'd pulled last night by drugging him. If it hadn't been for Iris, Eros could've saved Psyche from having to go into Hades at all.

As he reached her, Eros saw that Psyche wasn't moving.

"Psyche. Psyche, are you okay?" He skidded to a stop by her shoulder and kneeled. The sand pressed into his knees as he reached down and scooped Psyche into his lap. Eros rolled Psyche over so he could see her face and cradle her head. Her expression was still and peaceful, a mask of tranquility.

Eros rocked her and stroked her hair. "You'll be okay, Psyche. Everything's okay now. You hear me? You're safe with me."

"That's where you're wrong, boy," Charon said. The old man leaned on his staff as he approached. "The box is empty."

Eros's jaw fell open when he saw Charon holding Psyche's box, but he couldn't stop rocking her. "No, I'll protect her." Eros whispered his conviction more to himself than Charon. Tears burned at his eyes. "She has to wake up. I need her."

Charon crouched down and looked at Eros from across Psyche. "I didn't want to see her back so soon either." Charon's old blue eyes misted as he looked away and back out over the lake. "She did everything right. It wasn't her fault the box opened."

Eros stopped his rocking to concentrate. "How do we fix this?"

Charon slowly stood and tossed the box to the ground. "She's a mortal. There is no fix. She should be dead already."

"But she's not," Eros said. "I can feel her heart beat. And she's breathing. She's not dead." Eros looked down at Psyche and resumed his rocking. "I won't let you die, love. Hang on with me until we figure this out."

"Maybe we can take her back to Persephone and ask her what to do," Charon said. "As fast as you fly, you could get her into Hades in no time."

Eros's face blanched. "I won't take her in there. They can't have her yet."

Charon glared. "So you have a better idea then?"

"Enough fighting boys." Queen Persephone's warm, silken voice interrupted their argument. Her brown eyes flickered with calm and confidence as she looked between the two men. "I see we have a little problem here."

"Yes, Your Highness," Charon said with a bow. "Your beauty escaped, but it wasn't Psyche's fault. She didn't open the box."

"I know," Persephone said, waving Charon away with a dismissive flip of her hand and gliding to Eros and Psyche. She knelt down beside them and brushed Psyche's cheek. "I actually wanted to see Aphrodite freak out when Psyche made it back." A sad smile tugged at the corner of Persephone's lips. "I saw it all."

"Can you help her?" Eros asked.

Persephone shook her head. "I really don't understand what's happened to her. Charon's right, she should be dead already." Persephone looked down and scratched her forehead. "Was there anyone in her bloodline who was divine?"

"Yes. Yes, actually." Eros's arms wrapped tighter around Psyche's shoulders. "Poseidon's her father."

Persephone nodded. "At least the necessity for a test makes more sense now."

"Perhaps, my Queen," Charon added, still

standing outside of their circle, "you could take your beauty back."

"I don't see why not." Persephone sat, crossing her legs. "Here, give her to me." She gestured with her arms for Eros to slide Psyche over.

Eros's muscles flexed as he lifted Psyche from his own lap and placed her head on Persephone. His fingertips lingered before sliding away from Psyche's soft curls.

Persephone tilted Psyche's head back and opened her mouth. Eyes closed, Persephone exhaled through her nose and leaned forward, wrapping her lips around Psyche's. With their lips sealed, Persephone drew in a deep breath, pulling the ghostly beauty back out of Psyche.

Psyche coughed, dry and ragged, rolling off of Persephone's lap as she gasped for air. Braced on all fours and back arched, Psyche's body raged against the poisonous beauty, coughing up every last wisp of the luminous mist. Eros stroked her hair, feeling helpless, as he watched her battle for each breath.

After a last short bark of a cough, Psyche took a deep breath and sat back onto her heels. "Hi," she said, biting her lower lip.

Eros surrounded Psyche with his arms, pulling her into his chest. He kissed her temples, forehead, nose, eyes, and cheeks, taking in every feature of her face with his lips.

Eyes moist with tears, Psyche pulled her face away from Eros and looked deep into his eyes. "I'm sorry," she whispered. "I'm so, so sorry."

Eros pulled her head back into his chest, stroking

her hair. "I'm sorry too. I should never have left you."

Eros felt warm tears spill down his chest and realized Psyche was crying even harder. "What'd I say?"

"I'm just so happy to see you again." Psyche shook her head and wiped the tears from her cheeks. "I was scared you'd hate me forever."

Eros tilted Psyche's chin up with his finger. "I told you I'd *love* you forever, remember?"

Psyche nodded, a smile breaking across her face brighter than the morning sun.

"I meant it," Eros said, "forever."

CHAPTER 54 — PSYCHE

My head was still spinning from coughing up ragged death. It took me awhile to even remember where I was or why I was laying on the bank of a lake surrounded by deities. And when did Persephone get there?

Before I knew what was happening, I realized Eros was with me and then we were apologizing to each other. And he was kissing me.

His soft lips were warm against mine, brushing me gently at first as if finding me for the first time. Then he kissed me deeper, pushing at me with longing and passion that took my breath away.

I rose up on my knees, throwing my arms around his neck and leaning into the kiss. Eros dropped his arms to my waist, pulling me closer, as his lips pushed even deeper against my own.

Persephone cleared her throat, reminding us that we weren't alone.

My cheeks burned and I buried my head in Eros's shoulder to hide my face. Eros scooped me into his arms and stood, carrying me as easily as if I were a baby.

"Persephone, Charon," Eros nodded at both of them. "I can't thank you enough for taking care of Psyche for me." Charon glared. Persephone beamed, the creases that only come from true smiles circled her lips.

"You know me," she said. "Just like my mom. I

love new beginnings."

Eros looked at me and winked. "What do you say we get out of here?"

But before he could launch, Charon cut in. "What about Aphrodite? Psyche still owes her some of Persephone's beauty."

"You let me worry about my mother," Eros answered.

Before I knew it, we were flying together. His powerful wings beat the air as we soared like eagles back to Olympus. I clutched his neck tighter as I looked down at the ground. The sensation of flying with him was totally new, and surprisingly more scary, than it'd been at night when I couldn't see how far the ground was below us.

"I won't let you fall."

I gazed up into his crystal blue eyes, instantly lost in the wonder that I'd lived to see them again. "I know," I answered, letting a smile tug at my lips. "But that doesn't mean I have to let you go."

Eros's dimple beamed as he smiled back at me and raised his eyebrows. "Mmm... don't you dare let me go." He nuzzled his lips against my forehead, blessing me with kisses.

It wasn't until we were landing that I noticed we weren't at Aphrodite's palace. As Eros set me on my feet, I took in the new mansion. This palace was twice as large as Aphrodite's, and thankfully not constructed of solid gold. But it was still ornate.

"Welcome to the center of Olympus," Eros whispered. Power radiated from the building with such force that I shuddered. Eros squeezed my hand and pulled me close. "Don't worry. They're going to love you," he promised as he started up the stairs.

I wanted to follow, but my feet wouldn't move. Eros stopped when my arm was fully extended. I had to tug my hand free to keep from being pulled over.

He looked at me, one eyebrow arched.

Would I ever tire of seeing *his expressions?*

"What's wrong?" he asked.

"Something doesn't feel right." I shook my head and bit at my lip, unable to explain any better.

Eros came back down beside me and wrapped an arm around my shoulders. "You're probably feeling their immorality. It's stronger here than anywhere." Eros ducked his head so he could meet my eyes at level. "But that's why we're here. Only they can make you one of us."

He stared into my eyes as the weight of his words sunk in. Fresh tears pushed their way to the surface and I clasped my hand over my mouth. "Really?" I whispered from behind my fingers. "How?"

"If Zeus and Hera say you can join our ranks, then you're in."

I turned my head into Eros's shoulder and threw my arm around his neck, full of hope and excitement.

And fear.

"What if they don't want me?"

Eros tilted my chin up with two fingers and kissed my nose. "Who *wouldn't* want you?"

The warm rush of blood filled my cheeks. "I thought maybe you."

He pulled me into his chest with both arms. "I'll make you a deal. Let's forget the last two weeks ever happened, okay? We've both done things we wish we could take back, so let's put that behind us and start again."

I only nodded my head, unwilling to break the lyrical echo of his sweet words.

"Your life starts over today. You'll be immortal. We can live here, on Olympus. I'll build you a new palace, whatever you want."

I wrapped my arms tighter around his waist. "I just want to be able to look at you every minute of every day."

"Done," he said.

"And not have to hide from your mother," I added, raising my head to meet his sparkling eyes.

His soft fingers stroked away a strand of hair from my face. "You'll never have to worry about her again."

"Then what are we waiting for?" I grabbed his hand and together we ran up the stairs and into Zeus and Hera's palace.

As soon as we crossed the threshold into their home, the two gods appeared before us, seated in ornate golden thrones at the back of the room. We skidded to a stop and Eros bowed. Quickly following his lead, I did the same.

"I didn't think I'd see the day Eros dared to set foot in this house," Hera said. Zeus shifted in his chair.

I could see Hera's large eyes focused into narrow slits from across the room. My own eyes widened as I looked to Eros for an explanation for our less-than-hospitable greeting. He leaned over and whispered in my ear. "I might have had a hand in some of Zeus's more recent affairs."

"Ha!" Zeus said, pointing at Eros. "I told you I couldn't help myself. I told you Eros made me do it. Now do you believe me?"

Hera cut Zeus a look that silenced him and he sank back into his throne.

"This is quite a mess you've made for yourself, Eros," Hera said.

"Yes, Your Highness," he replied, bowing his head and refusing to meet her gaze. His muscles were taut like he was about to spring, but everything else about his posture spoke of submission.

"But this visit isn't really about you, is it?" Hera eyed me with her dark doe eyes.

As if sparked to life, Eros grabbed my hand and rushed forward. "No, Your Highness. I'm here for Psyche." I had to scurry to keep up until we stopped at the base of Hera's throne.

Her expression softened as we approached and her eyes sparkled with the hint of a smile. But Zeus' gaze was not so embracing. As he studied me, his caterpillar-thick eyebrows twitched, as if they were somehow a reflection of the thoughts bouncing around his skull.

"So," he finally said, turning to Eros, "what is it exactly that you want from us?"

Eros bowed again, lowering his head to Zeus. "Sire, I want Psyche to be one of us." He squeezed my hand. "So she can be mine for eternity."

Zeus laughed so horsely it sounded like a cough. "After all you've done to me? You've nearly ruined my marriage ten times over with your arrows." He rose from his throne, towering over us. "What makes you think I'd do anything to help you?"

I watched Eros's face, saw his jaw clench and unclench as he searched for words. Silence radiated louder than words through the marble halls.

And then Hera moved in close to her husband, laying her hand on his shoulder, peering down at us with the same imposing height. But Hera's eyes sparkled with warmth rather than anger. "Hmmm.... Zeus?" she asked, easing the tense silence.

Zeus moved his eyes to his wife without turning his head away from us. "I know that tone."

Hera chuckled and rubbed Zeus's shoulder. "I seem to recall you agreeing that the boy should settle down. Besides, I think this might actually work to our advantage."

Zeus snapped his head around to look Hera dead-on. "You mean you want to help him?" Zeus pointed an accusing finger at Eros. "What happened to you wanting to pull his wings apart feather by feather?"

From the corner of my eye, I saw Eros wince.

Hera smiled. "I think the boy's service to my cause might suit me better than plucking his wings apart. Wouldn't you agree, Eros?" Her eyes narrowed as she tilted her head, waiting for Eros's answer.

Eros dropped to his knees before her. "I will serve your every command, my Queen." He raised his head, eyes pleading. "Tell me what you want and I'll do it."

Hera reached down and took Eros's hand in hers, then pulled him to his feet. When he was standing, Hera reached out with her other hand for me. As she joined our hands together, she said, "Honor Psyche as your wife. Love her each and every day, because she has proven herself worthy of your love. In loving her, you do your greatest service to me."

His eyes grew wide as he turned to me, clutching my fingers tighter. "Marry me, Psyche? Please?"

"Consider your decision before you choose, Psyche." Zeus's sage voice startled me. *Why wouldn't I choose to be with him?* "Loving an immortal is a commitment for eternity -- not just a few decades." He smiled at Hera before continuing. "And I must warn you, our Olympian family is a little, shall we say, dysfunctional from time-to-time."

"I can handle dysfunctional."

"And eternity? With me?" Eros drew my attention back to him, pulling at my heart like a lasso.

"I can't imagine anything better."

Eros dropped my hands and clasped my face, drawing me into him. He kissed me like he was trying to drink me in. When I pulled away, breathless, we rested our foreheads together.

"Love you." I smiled up at him.

He tucked an errant curl behind my ear. "And I love you."

"We still don't have an agreement yet," Zeus cut in, invading the momentary bliss. "I have a condition of my own."

I felt the blush rising to my cheeks as I stared at my feet.

Eros answered. "Sire?"

"You are never, ever to use your arrows on me again. Are we clear on that?"

Eros swallowed. "Absolutely, my King. I was young, and impulsive --"

Zeus waved away the words with a stroke of his hand. "Never mind excuses. Just promise me... on Psyche's life."

Eros looked at me, then back at Zeus. "On Psyche's life, I promise never to shoot you again."

Zeus strolled back to his throne and reclined. "Good. And one more thing,"

We waited in silence for the king to speak. Waited for him to make some demand Eros couldn't agree to.

"I think my wife would prefer you use your arrows only for true love. No more affairs. Your mother's realm of passion is strong enough without any extra help."

Hera moved in close to her husband and kissed his forehead. "Thank you, Love."

Zeus reached up and grabbed her tiny hand in his, pressing her fingertips to his lips. "Anything for you," he replied, his pale sea-glass eyes nearly pouring over with emotion.

As the two of them radiated love, the feeling permeated the air. I turned to Eros, encircling his neck in my arms. My heart ached at the thought of just *seeing* him as I held him in my arms every day, I wanted it so badly.

I might have stayed wrapped up in him forever, but Hera broke the spell by clapping twice. Her signal brought a bevy of nymphs dancing in from another room, carrying with them overflowing plates of fruit and pitchers spilling a syrupy liquid.

One girl handed out golden cups to everyone

while another followed behind, filling the glasses. "Cheers," Zeus said, raising his glass.

Hera raised her glass to me. "Welcome to Olympus, Psyche."

Eros smiled so broadly that his adorable little dimple peeked out from his cheek. His crystal blue eyes danced as we intertwined elbows and drank.

The ambrosia coursed down my throat like liquid warmth, filling me. As the heat spread, running into my fingers and tingling my toes, my skin itched with tiny jolts of lightning. I was simultaneously numb and more alive than I'd ever been before.

Eros's arm curled around my waist to steady me as I swayed, eyes closed. Absorbing the energy of immortal life wasn't what I'd expected. It was better and worse in one wonderful, overwhelming instant. When my eyes fluttered open again, I felt almost normal. But stronger. Like I could run from Olympus down to the tip of the Peloponnese and never tire.

And I was ready to focus the buzz of my new-found immortal energy on Eros.

As I reached up to put my arm around his neck, my dress pulled at my arm, not giving me enough room to move. I looked down at myself and saw the dress no longer fit right. It was pulled tight against my chest, cutting deep into the skin under my arms.

"What in the world?"

"Allow me," Eros said, unfastening the clasp at my shoulder that was holding my dress up.

My eyes widened as I glared at him. "Not right here," I whispered in a panic, nodding my head toward Zeus and Hera. "There are people here."

Eros rolled his eyes and chuckled before kissing my nose. "Lighten up, will you?"

Without exposing my chest, Eros let the dress fall open in the back. Free from the constraints of the dress, a pair of magnificent blue butterfly wings unfurled from my back. They were nearly indigo in their richness and outlined with a delicate, lace-like black trim.

I craned my neck and arched my back, straining to get a better look at the new attachments. "I don't understand..." I said, scowling in confusion at the beautiful wings.

"Your love gave you wings, Psyche," Hera said, waving her hand through the air and fluttering her fingers as she spoke. "Now go. Fly together. I'll see you at the next Council meeting."

Eros held my dress in the back to keep it from falling off as we left. We half skipped, half flew out of the palace as I tested my new wings.

I was so enthralled with the prospect of flying, that I didn't notice Aphrodite blocking our path until we'd nearly slammed into her.

Eros yanked my dress back to help me stop and we both giggled as I barely got my balance in time. Surprisingly, Aphrodite looked just as amused as we were.

"I thought I might find you here," she said before wrapping me in her arms.

Yeah, totally lost. I thought we were basically mortal enemies. She had tried to kill me on more than one occasion after all.

"Mother," Eros barked. "I don't know what

you're up to, but you need to forget it. You won't hurt her ever again."

Aphrodite never bothered looking at her son. "I know." Her smile poured over me like liquid sunshine. "Finally, something works out the way I'd planned."

"This?" I asked. "You planned on all of this?"

"I'm sorry, dear, but you were more mortal than not," she said. "And mortals are nothing if not predictable."

Closing my eyes was the only way to make my brain focus. She'd planned all this? How? Why?

Her hand tightened on my shoulder. "When you two seemed bent on refusing each other, I *had* to come up with a Plan B." She leaned in close, a co-conspirator sharing a secret. "My son may have told you, but I generally get what I want."

Eros's feathers ruffled. "So why try to kill her? If you wanted us to be together?"

"Don't you see? I didn't *want* her dead or she would be. What I wanted was for you to realize how much you still loved her. Forcing you to save her from the soldiers worked perfectly."

Eros slipped his hand into mine. "And sending her to Hades? What'd you get out of that?"

"You mean other than a little retribution for refusing my Plan A?" Aphrodite eyed us both pointedly. "I got proof of Psyche's love. She was willing to risk death for you, son. And now no one, not even Psyche's sister, will be able to take that truth away from you."

The feeling of being Aphrodite's puppet was unsettling, but I couldn't argue with the end result. Eros and I were together, immortal, and we both knew with unwavering certainty how deeply our loved flowed. I guessed this was one of those times where the ends justify the means. Even if they were pretty sucky means.

Leaning forward, I kissed her cheek. "In that case, thank you. For everything."

"You can save your mother-daughter bonding for later," Eros said, gently squeezing my fingers. "There's something I want you to see now."

A smile pulled at my lips until my cheeks almost ached. "What is it?"

"Our new life."

EPILOGUE — PSYCHE

The dream wakes me up again. It's been the same three nights in a row. My sister dissolves into dust and bone before my eyes and I never get the chance to tell her I'm sorry for all that happened between us. And I know someday that will happen. She will die and I will not. But before that day comes, I will apologize to her. Assuming she lets me anywhere near her.

The more I wake though, the easier it is to forget the one problem that's followed me into immortality. As I lay curled on my side in bed, I can feel the sun's warm fingers worming in through the cracks in the shutters, tugging at my heavy eyelids. Eros and I may be able to have our days together now, but it's not like we've abandoned the night either.

"Good morning, Love." His voice curls through the fog of sleep, rousing me with the delight of knowing it'll be his face I see when my eyes open.

His face I *see*. I love this moment in the morning. Drinking in his features, quietly, without pressure or time constraints, and when no one in the world save for him sees my thirsty eyes.

"You scare me with that look," he says.

A scowl cracks my contentment. *He's scared of me?*

"Not like that," he says, kissing my nose as he props himself on an elbow. "The love in your eyes burns so bright. I'm afraid someday it'll burn out. That you'll wake up and realize eternity with me isn't all it's cracked up to me."

Chuckling at him, I close my eyes and sigh. "Funny, isn't it?" I say, snuggling in close to his chest.

"What?" He sounds confused, but his voice is still gentle, loving.

"I always believed my mother when she said, '*you cannot escape what is destined*.' But here I am." I give him a squeeze. "I guess she was wrong."

"Psyche," he says, and the intensity of his voice makes my eyes flutter open again. "Your mother wasn't wrong. You are my destiny."

ACKNOWLEDGEMENTS

Where to begin? There are so many people who helped my dream for *Destined* become a reality.

My loving husband, Holt, who never once complained when I used my evenings to write instead of hangout with him, and who has helped me make my guy voices more authentic. Holt, your quiet yet unwavering support has meant everything to me.

My daughters, who "graciously" went to sleep every night at 8 pm so I could have at least 2 hours of writing time in the evenings.

The crit partners who loved Psyche (originally Sadie) and encouraged me to tell her story – even when the early versions were less-than-stellar. Nikki Katz , Lynne Matson, Georgia McBride (also my awesome editor), Kimberly Sabatini, Professor Hinkley, and Heather Howland – you have all been instrumental in making me a better writer. I thank you for each and every read through and revision you've taken the time to give me.

The support I received from #yalitchat has been unmatched. I never would have had the knowledge or the guts to attempt self-publishing without the team over there. For all of you on the MOD squad – LM Preston and Lauren Hamilton, in particular – you have my unending thanks.

My young beta readers were also an early source of encouragement. The Richburg girls – Abby, Morgan and Caroline – who told their dad my story wasn't quite *Harry Potter*, but just as good as *Twilight*, will probably never have any idea how much that meant to me. I thank you for your comments and detailed feedback. And Skye Martin, who liked the book so much she got her teacher to approve a draft of *Destined* for reading credit, you are awesome!

Along the way, so many other people have taken the time to read *Destined* and give me their thoughts and suggestions for making the story even better. While there are too many of you to list, I know who you are, and I thank you.

Readers – this book would be for nothing if you weren't reading it. Thank you for having the interest and trust in my writing to pick up this title.

I couldn't conclude without thanking Josh Longiaru, who lent his talents to the book cover, book tour banner, promo materials and so much more. I feel lucky to have found you. And Damaris Cardinali at Good Choice Reading, a huge outpouring of thanks for organizing my blog tour!

Last but not least – thanks to my mom and dad for never thinking there was anything I couldn't do. Mom, you've listened to me ramble, gush, fret and cycle through every other emotion out there and always been just as excited for me as I am. And Dad, I'll never forget how you read that really early version of *Destined* even though reading, let alone reading literature set in ancient Greece and written for teen girls, couldn't have been your idea of a good time. I love you!

ABOUT THE AUTHOR

www.jhnphoto.com

JESSIE HARRELL
is an appellate lawyer
who lives with her husband and
two daughters in Jacksonville, Florida.
Visit her online at www.jessieharrell.com

18727253R00208

Made in the USA
Middletown, DE
17 March 2015